GOOD DAY
IN HELL

ALSO BY J. D. RHOADES

The Devil's Right Hand

GOOD DAY
IN HELL

J. D. Rhoades

ST. MARTIN'S MINOTAUR
NEW YORK

www.minotaurbooks.com

Library of Congress Cataloging-in-Publication Data

Rhoades, J. D., 1962–
    Good day in hell / J. D. Rhoades.— 1st ed.
        p. cm.
    ISBN 0-312-33421-4
    EAN 978-0-312-33421-5
    1. Fugitives from justice—Fiction. 2. Bounty hunters—Fiction. 3. North
Carolina—Fiction. 4. Serial murders—Fiction. I. Title.

PS3618.H623G66 2006
813.6—dc22

                                                          2005049771

First Edition: March 2006

10 9 8 7 6 5 4 3 2 1

To my parents,
Jerry and Kay Rhoades

ACKNOWLEDGMENTS

As before, thanks to my editor, Ben Sevier, for advice and suggestions that had me tearing my hair out during the revisions—but that made this a better book. Thanks also to my agent, Scott Miller, for his tireless efforts on my behalf.

Sanford J. Walke IV provided valuable information on handguns for a book of mine that never got published, so I used it here. Thanks, Sandy.

For information on the first Gulf War, I am indebted to Anthony Swofford's amazing war memoir, Jarhead, and Rick Atkinson's Crusade: The Untold Story of the Persian Gulf War. Any factual mistakes regarding matters military are, of course, my own.

GOOD DAY
IN HELL

one

The first blow split Stan's lip and knocked him into a stack of re-capped tires at the back of the repair bay. He caught a glimpse of the bright sunlight and the road outside before his step-father's bulk eclipsed the light like an evil moon. The second, third, and fourth blows were softer but more humiliating, delivered as they were by the hand holding the rolled-up magazine.

"This how you pay me back?" his stepfather bellowed, shaking the magazine in Stan's face. Curled up, all Stan could see was part of a bare breast and nipple and a flash of thigh. "All I done for you?" He began punctuating his diatribe with blows across Stan's face from the rolled-up magazine, as if Stan were a puppy who had piddled on the rug. "I (WHACK) put a ROOF (WHACK) over your HEAD (WHACK), put FOOD (WHACK) on your PLATE (WHACK), and all . . ." He shook the magazine in Stan's face. "So you can sit around my business reading PORN?" He threw the magazine aside and grabbed Stan by the collar of his T-shirt.

"I didn't—," Stan blubbered. "It's not—" He hated himself for the tears that sprang to his eyes. Stan was sixteen, almost seventeen, and he was almost as tall as his stepfather. But when the blows came, forehand, backhand, he was as helpless as a five-year-old before the older man's fury. He didn't even dare put his hands up to shield his face. Every time he had tried that, he had been beaten worse, once so badly he had lost a tooth. So he took the punishment, his guts twisting with fear and hate. He tried to make himself go far away, so it would all seem like it was happening to someone else. Sometimes he could make that happen. Those times were easier. It was easier if the loathing he felt was for some other weak, helpless pussy. This time, though, he couldn't do it. It stayed real. It was Stan who felt the collar of the T-shirt rip in his stepfather's hand, Stan who saw the saw the rage double in the man's eyes, Stan who saw the open hand pulled back, closed into a fist, and ready to put the lights out . . .

There was a tinny double ping from out front that signaled a vehicle pulling up. *Saved by the bell,* Stan thought giddily as his stepfather released him and straightened up. "I'll finish with you later," the older man snarled. He turned on his heel and walked out of the repair bay. Stan slid down to the floor and hugged his knees, willing himself not to cry. He leaned over to pick the wadded magazine off the floor. On the cover, a slim blonde girl who looked hardly out of puberty was looking back over her naked shoulder with what was intended to be a sultry look. She really just looked pissed. *Barely Legal,* the magazine title promised. He laid the magazine on the workbench and tried to smooth out the wrinkles where his stepfather had wadded it up. Suddenly, a crimson speck appeared on the girl's pouty face. He stared at it uncomprehending for a moment until the speck deformed and began to run down the arch of the girls' back, across the glossy paper, leaving a watery

2

red trail. Stan put a hand to his nose, felt the wetness there. His hand came away red. "Shit," he said out loud. He looked around for something to stop the bleeding. All he saw was a pair of grease-stained rags draped over the back of the workbench. He stumbled to the front of the repair bay, through the doors to the front office. He glanced at the gas pumps. There was a black Mustang convertible pulled up at the full-service pump. Stan's stepfather was pumping, wearing the obsequious grin he always used with customers. A man stood by the Mustang's front fender, his arms crossed across his chest, nodding and grinning back at whatever was being said. The man was tall, over six feet, and dressed entirely in black: jeans, shirt, even his boots. He wore dark glasses. His black hair was shot with streaks of gray and combed back from his forehead. At one time, he might have been regarded as a handsome man, but the outline of what once had probably been memorably rugged good looks had sagged under the weight of years and hard living.

There was another person in the car on the passenger side, but Stan couldn't see him clearly. He snagged the restroom key off the hook behind the cash register and exited through the side door. The station's single working restroom was halfway down one side, past the door to the other restroom with the OUT OF ORDER sign that had been there for as long as Stan could remember. He fumbled the key into the lock and slipped inside. He glanced into the mirror over the cracked and rust-stained sink. "Oh, *fuck*," he blurted out. The area below his nose was a trail of crimson that led over his puffy and bleeding lip. There were spatters of blood on his light blue uniform shirt as well, the same color as the embroidered "Stan" over the pocket. Stan moaned in fear. The only thing worse than the beatings was the possibility that someone would find out, that the Social Services

3

people would come back, that the whole round of questions and courts and lawyers would start over.

The first time it had happened, Stan had been twelve. He had thought then that they would take him away, put him someplace where he and his mom could be safe. And they had, for a while. But within six months, his mom went back and, eventually, so did Stan. His stepfather had made all the right noises, taken all the right steps. But all that had really happened was that he was more careful to hit Stan where it wouldn't leave marks. For a while. But after a while, caution receded. His stepfather had knocked one of his teeth out for spilling motor oil on the floorboard of the pickup. And the cycle had begun again. Questions, hearings, orders for anger management and parenting classes, and, in the end, Stan was back where he started. Only now that he was older, he realized that everyone knew. Everyone knew how weak he was. He hated that worst of all.

Stan rolled a handful of paper towels off the holder and blotted at his face. He managed to mop most of the blood off, but a steady flow still came from his nose. "Fuck, fuck, *fuck*," Stan muttered. He looked up at the ceiling and pressed the paper towels against his nose. There was a knock on the door.

"Just a minute," Stan gasped, his voice breaking on the last word.

"Come on, hon," a female voice said on the other side of the door. "My back teeth're floatin'."

Stan closed his eyes. "Fuck," he whispered one last time, with feeling. He tipped his head back upright. The bleeding seemed to have stopped but his nose and lip were still visibly swollen. He hurriedly stuffed the paper towels in the wastebasket. He turned to the door, took a deep breath, and opened it.

The girl waiting on the other side looked to be not much older than Stan. She was dressed in a pair of low-rise jeans that looked about ready to slide off of her bony hips and a thin tank top that hugged her upper body. There was an appliqué design of a daisy on the shirt between the slight bulges of her small breasts. She had a large shapeless bag slung over one shoulder. Her face might have been pretty except for her jaw, which looked too big for the rest of her features. It gave her a belligerent look, as if she was daring anyone to disagree with something she had yet to say. Her blonde hair was cut short and moussed into carefully plotted disarray, with a swoop of hair down over her left eye.

"Whoa," she said. "What happened to you?"

"Nothing," Stan said. "I, um, I fell down."

The girl swept the hair away from her face. Her blue eyes narrowed. "Huh," she said. "You fell." She looked back to the front of the station, where Stan could hear his stepfather guffawing over his own joke. Her jaw tightened and she looked back. "I gotta pee," she said.

"Oh. Yeah. Sorry," Stan said. He stepped past her as she stepped into the restroom. As he started to walk away, she said "Hey." Stan looked back at her. She was leaning on the door, looking out.

"What's your name?" she asked.

"Stan," he said.

"That guy out there," she said, jerking her head toward the front. "He your daddy?"

"Stepdad," Stan said. She got a look in her eye that Stan hadn't expected. He had been dreading pity. What he saw looked like . . . determination. She closed the door.

Stan walked around to the front of the station. He reached the front door to the office just as his stepfather came out.

"Make yourself useful," he said, handing Stan a plastic card. "Run this guy's credit card." He stood outside the office door, joking with the older man.

Stan went to the old credit-card machine and got out one of the carbon forms. The credit-card rep had been trying to get Stan's stepfather to lease one of the newer electronic credit-card machines, but so far he hadn't wanted to spend the money. He looked up to see the blonde girl coming around to the front. She was walking quickly, her hand stuffed into the bag over her shoulder. When she reached the spot where the two men were talking, she pulled a large handgun out of the bag and shot Stan's stepfather in the face.

He fell backward, blood gushing between his hands. A horrible bubbling sound came from between the fingers, as if he had tried to scream. Stan stood behind the counter, frozen by shock. He knew his mouth was open, but he couldn't make any sound come out.

The girl looked up at the man in black. "Like we agreed?" she asked.

The man nodded. "Yeah."

The girl handed the gun to the man in black, who stepped over until he was standing with one foot on each side of the body still writhing and flopping on the ground. He looked at the girl, a slight frown on his face. "You're startin' early," he said. He aimed and fired downward. The body beneath him gave one last convulsion and lay still. The man in black stepped over to the counter, where Stan was still rooted to the spot. He pointed the gun at Stan. "Open the register, kid," he said. Stan tried again to speak, but all that came out was a low moan. His hands were apparently smarter than his tongue; they seemed to move of their own accord as he hit the button to open the register. The girl stepped forward and pulled out the cash drawer. She was smiling at Stan. She looked back at the body on the ground. "I used to fall down a lot myself," she said. She poured the contents of the cash drawer into her shoulder bag, her eyes still on Stan, that scary smile still on her face. He felt as if his legs would give way any second. "Roy," the girl said over her shoulder. "Hand me the gun."

He handed the gun over. She placed the barrel almost gently under Stan's chin. The barrel was hot, a circle of pain against his flesh. "Hey, Stan," she whispered. "You want to be famous?"

Stan finally rediscovered words. "Wh . . . wh . . . what?"

"We're gonna be famous," Roy said. He was grinning.

"Yeah," Laurel said. "And you can come along. If you want."

"Hey," Roy said. "That's not—"

"What about it, Stan?" Laurel interrupted him. "You wanna be famous? We can make it happen."

"Laurel," Roy said, "We've gotta get moving."

"Come with us, Stan," the girl said. "What have you got here? Some dipshit gas station out in the country? We're gonna be on TV. In the papers. Books, movies . . . you name it. Or." She looked a little sad. "I can put a bullet in you. Then Roy'll put a bullet in you, 'cause we agreed. Your choice. But you need to tell me now."

Stan swallowed hard. He cut his eyes toward the figure of his stepfather on the ground. It began to dawn on him that he wasn't going to have to get slapped around anymore. He looked back. The girl saw his eyes and her smile got wider. She lowered the gun.

"Okay," he said.

"You sure you want to do this?" Keller said. He pulled the big car up to the curb and put it in PARK.

"*Sí,*" said the brown-skinned man in the passenger seat. He sounded calm, but the way he nervously stroked his thin moustache betrayed him.

"Don't worry, Oscar. This will be easy," Keller said. "This guy Olivera's got no record of violence, he just has a problem with showing up for his court dates. We find him, you explain the situation to him, we bring him back. No problems."

Oscar Sanchez regarded Keller with no expression in his dark eyes. He spoke with the precise diction of someone who had learned his English in a classroom rather than on the street. "Of course. That is why you have brought a gun."

"I always do that," Keller said. "It doesn't mean I think the guy's going to get rowdy. It just helps to be prepared. I have an extra one in the trunk if you want it."

Sanchez smiled thinly. "*Gracias,* but no. I prefer to be just the interpreter."

"You're sure you're okay?"

Sanchez nodded. "I am sure, Jack. I have rested long enough. It is time I made myself useful."

"Okay, let's go then," Keller said as he opened the door. He stood up and tucked a stubby Glock 9MM pistol into the holster at the small of his back. He waited at the curb, looking away uncomfortably as the other man retrieved a dark-colored wooden cane from behind the seat and struggled to his feet. He was in his mid-forties, but the pronounced limp and the cane gave him the look of an older man. Keller slackened his pace to allow Sanchez to keep up. When they reached the door to the small duplex, Sanchez's face was shiny with sweat and he was breathing hard, as if had climbed a flight of stairs. Keller knocked on the door. There was no answer. He knocked again.

After a moment, a teenaged girl opened the door. She was barefoot, dressed in a denim skirt and a brightly colored floral blouse. Her skin was the same shade as Sanchez's, but her eyes were hooded and unfriendly. *"Qué?"* she said.

"Buenos días," Sanchez said. *"Estamos buscando Manuel Olivera. Es él casero?"*

"No sé cualquier persona Manuel nombrado," the girl said.

"She says she doesn't know anyone by that name," Sanchez told Keller.

"Uh-huh," Keller said.

The girl made as if to close the door, but a boy of about seven or eight forced his way around one of her bare legs and blocked the door open. He stared at the two men in the doorway with grave interest. *"Porqué usted desea ver el Manuel?"* he asked. The girl made as if to yank him out of the doorway, but the boy evaded her grip with the ease of long practice and shot past her onto the small concrete stoop. "Who are you?" he demanded in English, looking at Keller.

"Ramon!" the girl hissed. *"Consiga detrás en la casa . . ."*

"My name is Mr. Sanchez," the man with the cane said to the boy. "You can call me Oscar. My friend here is Mr. Keller. Do you know Manuel Olivera?"

"Sure," the boy said. "He's been making out all morning with my ugly sister here." He raised his voice. "HEY MANUEL!" he yelled. The girl shouted something unintelligible at her brother and tried to slam the door, but Keller stiff-armed it the rest of the way open. He shoved his way past the girl and into the apartment.

"You can't do that!" the girl yelled in English. "You got no warrant!" Keller ignored her. The front door opened into a tiny kitchen and an equally miniscule space that the landlord probably optimistically described as a breakfast nook. Keller moved past them and into the living room. The girl turned to Sanchez, her face dark with impotent fury. "He doesn't have a warrant," she said in Spanish.

9

Sanchez shrugged apologetically and replied in the same language. "He isn't a policeman."

Keller found himself in the living room. The only illumination was provided by a color television, which was playing a game show in Spanish. A sagging couch rested against one wall. Beside the couch, a darkened hallway led to the back rooms of the apartment. Keller pulled a pair of handcuffs from the back pocket of his jeans. He drew his gun from the small of his back with his other hand. "Manuel!" he called out. "Come on, man, let's make this easy on everybody." According to Keller's information, Olivera spoke no English, so Keller tried to sound as calm as possible, hoping Olivera would respond to the tone of voice, even if the words meant nothing to him.

It didn't work. Keller heard the slamming of a door at the far end of the hallway. He plunged into the darkness toward the sound.

"What do you mean, he's not a policeman?" the girl said in Spanish. "Why is he in my mother's house, then?"

"He works for Manuel's bail bondsman," Sanchez said. He leaned his shoulder against the doorjamb to take more weight off his knee. "Manuel missed his court date. If Senor Keller doesn't bring him back, the bondsman loses the money." Sanchez took a handkerchief from his back pocket and mopped the sweat from his brow.

"Hey, Mister Oscar," the boy asked. "What's wrong with your leg?"

Sanchez hesitated. "Some bad men shot me in it," he said finally.

The boy eyes widened in amazement. "Cool," he said in English.

There was only one door closed, the one at the end of the hall. Keller stopped short of it. He raised his right knee nearly to his chest, then shot it out parallel to the floor, pivoting on his left leg until his left heel pointed at the door. The heel of his boot smashed the door off its hinges with a shriek of rending wood. The door fell inwards, revealing a narrow bathroom. The window next to the toilet was raised. The room was empty. Keller heard a grunt as a body landed on the ground outside the window. He tried to reach the window, but stumbled on the ruins of the door. Keller cursed as he fell full length on top of the splintered wood. He could hear footsteps outside the window, growing fainter as his quarry got away.

"Did it hurt?" the boy asked. "When the bad men shot you?"

"I hope it did," the girl said spitefully. She sat down on the stoop and crossed her arms on her knees.

"You shouldn't be so hateful," Sanchez told her. "It will put lines on your face." The girl gave him the finger.

Sanchez heard the sound of running footsteps. He turned toward the sound in time to see Manuel Olivera come tearing around the corner of the house. Sanchez could see the whites of his eyes. He raised his hand as if to signal Olivera to a stop. Then he saw the knife in the other man's hand.

Keller heard the girl scream outside as he picked himself up off the ruined door. Then there was a sharp crack, like the report of a small pistol. He felt the blood drain from his face. *Oscar*, he thought. *Oh, fuck. I shouldn't have brought him. I shouldn't have left him alone.* He ran back down the hallway as fast as he could.

When he got back outside, the girl was sobbing, crouched over a prone figure on the sidewalk. Keller saw the glint of a knife in the grass a few feet away. There was blood on the girl's hands. There was blood on the face of the man on the ground. Keller looked him over, mentally comparing the face to the photograph in his file. It was Manuel Olivera.

"I think he needs a doctor," a voice said from behind Keller. He turned. Sanchez was standing there, propping himself against the house. He held up a dark piece of splintered wood. "And I need a new cane."

"You can buy one with your cut of the fee," Keller said.

Sanchez looked surprised. "My . . . cut?"

"Why not?" Keller said. "You did the takedown."

"'Ey!" the man on the ground said as he sat up. He held a hand to his face. Blood flowed from between his fingers. "That son of a bitch," he said in heavily accented English. "He break my fucking nose!"

Keller and Sanchez looked at each other. "You said he didn't speak English," Sanchez said.

"Outdated information, I guess," Keller replied. He opened the handcuffs with one hand. "On your feet, Manuel," he said. "We'll get you a doctor at the police station."

"I sue you, son of a bitch!" Manuel said as he staggered to his feet. "I sue your ass off!"

"We'll make an American out of you yet," Keller said as he put the cuffs on.

∙ ∙ ∙

It was being alone in the car that Marie found hardest to get used to. In the city, the usual practice had been to pair up officers for patrols. There had at least been another presence in the car, another voice besides the ones on the radio, even if some of the conversations with her male colleagues had left her gritting her teeth. But the county sheriff didn't have that kind of manpower, and they had a lot more ground to cover out in the county, so deputies rode alone.

Not that that many people were talking to me by the time I left, she thought bitterly. Not only had she lost her partner, she had had the bad grace to testify to the truth: that Eddie Wesson's death was due to his own bad judgment. After that, conversations stopped when she walked into the room. She was assigned desk work, since no one would agree to ride with her. After two months of that, she had applied for the job with the county. A large number of deputies had signed up for the National Guard to supplement their meager pay. When the Second Gulf War came, the local guard unit was among the first called up and the sheriff suddenly faced the prospect of nearly a dozen deputies being sent to Iraq to guard convoys instead of patrolling the highways and back roads of the county. The department couldn't afford to be picky.

"Thirty-five, County," the radio crackled.

Marie picked up the mike. "Go ahead, County."

"Proceed to the Citgo gas station at 4500 Thurlow Church Road. Possible 10-62."

It took Marie a second to recall the unusual code. Then she got it. "Say again, County?"

The dispatcher's voice remained as flat and unexcited as a computer's. "Possible 10-62, 4500 Thurlow Church Road. Be advised, EMS and detectives en route."

Marie's heart raced. 10-62. Homicide. She kept her voice

13

steady as she replied, "10-4." She hit the switch for the lights and siren and stepped on the gas.

"I ain't sure I like this, Laurel," Roy said. His accent had thickened with his agitation. "We had a plan. We ought to stick to it."

They had driven the few miles through the country to the on-ramp for Interstate 95. They turned south and were quickly caught up in the flow of traffic. Roy turned the radio on low.

"Relax, Roy," Laurel said. "We just got started a little sooner than we planned. But we was about ready anyway. Besides, look at how much more walkin' around money we got this way." She fanned the wad of bills in her hand at him. She looked back at Stan in the backseat. "Thanks, Stan," she grinned.

Stan felt unreal, as if he were dreaming. The adrenaline shock was wearing off, and he was beginning to shake. "Uh, no problem," he said.

"Hey kid," Roy called back to him from the driver's seat of the Mustang. "How come your old man had so much cash lying around?"

"He wasn't my old man," Stan said automatically.

Roy shrugged. "Whatever."

"He has . . . had . . . a system. If you paid cash, he'd give you a big discount on mechanical work. 'Cause he didn't have to claim it for taxes."

Laurel pulled her face into an exaggerated expression of disapproval and clucked her tongue. "People got no respect for the law these days." She and Roy laughed. Then her face turned serious. "And he kept it at the station because he didn't want your mama to know about it?"

Stan nodded.

"You didn't tell your own mama?" Roy said.

Laurel got that scary hard look again. "You know why, Roy," she said. She looked back at Stan. "But you ain't got to be afraid anymore," she said.

Stan didn't know what to say to that. The fact is, he was more afraid than he'd ever been in his life. He felt as if he had just taken a running leap out the door of an airplane without checking to see if he had a parachute.

They drove for a while in silence. After a few miles, they took the off-ramp for U.S. 74. They headed east.

"Umm . . . where are we going?" Stan said.

"Back to my place," Roy answered. "I was just up to Fayetteville to pick up a few, ah, supplies from someone I know. We'll stop by my house and get the rest of what we need, then head out tomorrow night." They took a side road.

"Head out where?" Stan asked.

"Turn this song up, Roy," Laurel interrupted. "I like this one." She didn't wait, but reached over and turned the radio up full, drowning out Stan's repeated question. The crunch of an electric guitar playing a chugging rhythm filled the car.

Move in, Can't you see she wants you
She has you deep in her eyes
You been wond'rin' why she haunts you
Beauty in the devil's disguise . . .

Roy slowed the Mustang down. They were approaching a dirt road that came out of a break in the trees lining the side of the road. Roy pulled in, the car bumping over the rutted track as they passed through the line of trees.

15

She can tell you all about it
She sees it in the stars
She'll burn you if you try to put her down

Oh well, it's been a good day in hell
And tomorrow I'll be glory bound

There was a white van parked back in a clearing a couple of hundred feet off the hard road. Roy pulled the Mustang up beside it. Laurel started singing along with the Eagles:

In that big book of names I wanna go down
In flames
Seein's how I'm goin' down

Oh well, it's been a good day in hell
And tomorrow I'll be glory bound . . .

Roy killed the engine and the song died with it. "Come on, kid," he said as he and Laurel got out. As Stan clambered out of the passenger side, he noticed the ignition lock broken off and dangling by its wires from the steering column. Roy patted the fender longingly. "Too bad," he said. "I kinda like these."

"We been over that, Roy," Laurel said. "Too flashy to keep for long. This one's gonna be on someone's hot sheet by now."

Roy sighed. "I know," he said. "I'm just sayin'." He opened the trunk. Stan looked inside. There were a number of long objects wrapped in blankets inside. Roy pulled one of the blankets aside slightly to reveal the black metal of a rifle beneath. His smile was very white in the gloom. "Military issue," he said. "Can't hardly get 'em, even on the street."

Stan's mouth was dry. "Then how—"

"I know a guy at Fort Bragg," he said. "Funny thing. Once they put the inventory on the computer, it got real easy for a guy who wanted to make some extra dough to make stuff disappear." He pulled a rifle out of one of the blankets, cocked it expertly and raised it to his shoulder. He scanned the trees, looking through the sights, before pulling the trigger. There was the solid click of a dry-fire. "Bang," Roy said softly.

Laurel started singing softly to herself. "Tomorrow I'll be glory booooouund . . ."

two

"He did *what!?*" Angela said. They were in her tiny office at the rear of the storefront that housed H & H Bail Bonds. She looked at Sanchez, who sat in the chair in front of the desk, his leg propped up in the other chair. "Oscar, have you lost your mind?" Sanchez looked away in embarrassment.

"Take it easy," Keller said. He was leaning against the doorjamb, his thumb hooked into the waistband of his jeans. "He did great."

"You can't just go coldcocking people," Angela said. "Even if they are jumpers."

"Well . . . ," Keller said. "He, ah . . . he didn't really have much choice."

Angela sat down. "What aren't you telling me?" She looked from Sanchez's face to Keller's. Neither would meet her eyes. Finally Sanchez sighed. "Manuel Olivera had a knife. He pulled it on me."

"I see." Her face was expressionless. She took a deep breath.

"Oscar," she said after a long moment. "Would you excuse us for a minute?"

Sanchez crossed his arms across his chest. "No," he said. "I am not a child. This is about me. You do not send me out of the room to discuss it."

Angela put her face in her hands. It was warm in the office and she had removed the gloves which she usually wore. The web of burn scars on the backs of her hands shone pale white in the harsh fluorescent lighting of the office.

"Okay then," she said finally as she put her hands down. She looked at Keller. "There wasn't supposed to be any violence." Her face was calm, her voice controlled, but there was no mistaking the accusation.

Keller shrugged, holding his own temper in check. "There was nothing in his priors that said he'd go off like that. There wasn't any way to know."

"He panic," Sanchez said. "Sorry . . . he panicked."

"Okay," Angela said. Her voice cracked slightly on the second syllable. She cleared her throat. "Okay," she said in a firmer voice. "What's done is done. But Oscar, that's the last time. You don't go out on takedowns anymore."

Sanchez stood up slowly. His face was dark with anger. "I decide that, Angela." His accent had gotten thicker with his agitation and the name came out as An-he-la.

Angela stood up and put her hands on the desk. "This is my business, Oscar," she said. "I decide who works for me and how."

Sanchez gestured at Keller. "He puts himself in danger all the time," he said. "And you care for him. I know you do."

"That's different," Angela snapped. "He . . . it's just different."

"Sí, I know," Sanchez said. He hobbled to the door, wincing. Keller moved out of his way. "He is not a cripple," Sanchez said as he walked out. After a few moments, they heard the bell on the front door jingle as he walked out into the street.

Angela sat back down and folded her arms in front of her on the desk. She put her head down on them. Keller sat down in the seat Sanchez had just vacated. He waited silently. Finally, Angela looked up. "I'm fucking this up, aren't I?" she said.

"Yeah," Keller said.

She looked at him. "Keller, you think just once you could lie to make me feel better?"

"I doubt it. It wouldn't work."

"Damn it, Jack, he's a schoolteacher. He's not a bounty hunter."

"He was a schoolteacher back in Colombia," Keller said. "He's been through a lot since then."

Angela laughed sharply. "That's an understatement." Then she sighed. "I just don't want him to get hurt."

"Sounds like you guys are getting pretty close."

"Yeah," she said.

"That's good. He's a good man." Something in his voice made Angela look up.

"What?"

He shook his head. "Nothing." He stood up. "You need me to do anything else?"

She stood up as well. "Come on, Jack," she said. "Don't dodge. This is me you're talking to."

He shrugged. "There's no point. We've both moved on."

"Yeah," she said. "We have. That doesn't mean there's no point in us talking." She smiled sadly. "We've done this conversation, Jack. It never would have worked between the two of us. But you're still my best friend." She walked over and slipped her arm around his waist. He put an arm around her shoulder. He squeezed gently, mindful of the burn scars on her back and shoulders that still pained her. "I know," he said.

She gave him a final squeeze and stepped away. For a moment it left an empty feeling at his side.

"I'll finish the paperwork on Olivera," she said. "You still want to split the fee with Oscar?"

"Yeah."

"What split?"

Keller considered. "Fifty-fifty. I found the guy, he did the takedown. Plus, he needs the money."

She smiled. "You're a pretty good guy yourself, Keller." She picked up a file off the counter and handed it to him. "I've got another one for you, anyway."

He flipped the file open. At the top was a picture of a young blonde woman. It was not a flattering picture; mug shots rarely were. The woman's eyes were puffy and bloodshot under an unruly thatch of short blonde hair. Her prominent jaw was thrust defiantly forward toward the camera. He pulled the picture out and set it aside.

"Laurel Marks," Angela said. "Missed her court date two days ago."

Keller found the release order, written on flimsy blue paper. He saw the amount of bail and whistled. "Seventy-five grand? What the hell'd she do?"

"ADW," Angela said. "She was working as a waitress at the Omelet House on Market Street. Went for one of her coworkers with a carving knife one morning."

"Not a morning person, I guess. Still, seventy-five K is a lot. She doesn't have the kind of priors that would lead to that much bond."

"Not as an adult. But I talked to the magistrate. She's got a

21

pretty bad juvie record. The magistrates know her by sight, and so did Judge Banning. The magistrate was trying to get a message across."

"You're playing in the big leagues now, kid," Keller said.

"Right. And when she drew Judge Banning for her arraignment . . ." She grimaced. "I don't think Banning's reduced a bond since he went on the bench."

Keller looked up. "What kind of record?"

"Drugs, mostly. But some assaults. Little girl's got a temper, it seems."

"Kids don't usually learn that kind of anger on their own," Keller said. "Any Social Services involved?"

Angela nodded. "The magistrate said there was. He didn't know any details."

"Well, not likely that Social Services is going to give us anything. Any family in the area?"

"Both parents are local."

"They the ones who put up the cash?"

Angela shook her head. "No. Some guy. Said he was a friend of hers."

Keller arched an eyebrow. "Huh. Must've been some friend to put up ten percent of seventy-five grand." He flipped the file open again and read the name on the bail bond application. "Roy Randle."

"Yeah," Angela said. "Older guy, maybe early forties."

Keller frowned. "You think maybe he's pimping her?"

"I doubt it," Angela said. "Not many pimps would shell out seventy-five hundred to get a girl out of jail."

"Unless he was trying to keep her quiet." Keller's frown deepened. "This one's got a weird vibe to it."

Angela nodded. She looked unhappy. "I know. But I'll be

straight with you, Jack. Things are kind of stretched right now. If I have to give up seventy-five thousand dollars . . ."

"I know," said Keller. "I'll find her."

"But Jack, please be careful," she said. "You're right. This one feels weird."

Keller looked back at the picture. He felt the beginnings of the hunter's rush he always felt when he got a jumper, the steadily rising drumbeat of adrenaline in his veins that grew and grew as he got closer to the takedown. He almost didn't hear Angela when she said, "So, you seeing Marie this weekend?"

He tore his eyes away. "We're trying to get together, yeah. Still trying to iron out the details."

"How's she doing, anyway?"

Keller shook his head, then sighed. "I don't know," he said. "She says she doesn't want to talk about what happened."

"That's not good, Jack. She killed a man." She said the last sentence quietly, in a near-whisper, even though they were alone. "She's got to deal with that."

He shrugged. "She did what she had to do."

"And the fact that it had to be done makes it easier, Jack?" Angela said. "You know better than that."

"I know," he said. His voice was tight with frustration. "But she won't talk. And I don't know what to do."

Angela put her hand on his shoulder. "I'm sorry," she said quietly. "I'm prying."

"No," he said. He sat down. "You're right. I'm not mad at you. I'm just—" He threw his hands up.

She stood behind the chair, rested her chin on top of his head, and hugged him from behind. "Poor Jack," she said. "Still trying to save everybody." They stayed like that for a moment before Angela sighed and pulled away. "Stay with it, Jack," she said softly.

"You two—" Her voice caught, then she steadied it. "You two are good for each other." She looked out the front window toward the street.

"No regrets?" Keller said after a moment.

She laughed sadly. "Oh, plenty of those, Keller," she said. "But nothing I can't handle."

There was a small crowd gathered at the front doorway of the service station as Marie pulled in. Cars were parked randomly around the concrete slab. Marie picked up the radio. "County, thirty-five is 10-23."

The reply came back immediately. "10-4," the dispatcher acknowledged. "Thirty-five, be advised, EMS is en route." The dispatcher pronounced it "in root."

"10-4, County, I hear them," she replied. She reached into the glove box and pulled out a box of rubber surgical gloves, tucking a pair into her pocket as she got out.

Marie felt her pulse quicken as she jogged over to the small knot of people. There were three men and a woman, clustered in the doorway. "Move aside, please," she said. They looked up at her, faces still blank with shock. No one spoke. No one moved, either. Only when she pushed forward did they give ground, reluctantly, as if they were trying to protect her from what they had already seen. She saw the body of a man, lying on his back on the floor. His hands were over his face. The hands were covered with blood. Flecks of unidentifiable tissue were mixed into the rapidly congealing fluid coating the fingers. Marie knelt by the body. The people pushed back into their earlier positions, looking down at her. She looked up in irritation. "You people need to get back," she said. "This is a crime scene." Nobody moved. "I said, get back!" she snapped. For a brief second she heard the voice she used when she was at the end of her rope with her son, what she called the "Mad Mommy" voice. It seemed to work; the people edged back. Marie fought back the hysterical urge to laugh. *Steady, girl,* she told herself. She bent back to the man on the ground. She took the pair of rubber gloves from her back pocket and pulled them on. Gently, she pulled the hands away from the face.

"Oh, God," she said. She felt her stomach heave. The man's face was a mess of brain, blood, and smashed bone. *I am not going to throw up, I am not going to throw up,* she said to herself as she clenched her teeth. Automatically, her hand slid down to the artery at the base of the man's neck, searching for the pulse she knew she wouldn't find. The sudden howl of the ambulance pulling in made her jump. She stood up as the shrieking spun down to a rumbling purr. Her knees trembled slightly as she turned toward the two paramedics, a man and a woman, who spilled out of the truck and began jogging toward her. They slowed to a walk as they saw Marie's face. She shook her head. They came in anyway and she stepped aside. She felt the trembling in her knees begin to spread to the rest of her body. She closed her eyes. Against the back of her eyelids, like a picture on a movie screen, she saw another body, lying by the side of a road, illuminated by the riot and flash of the lights of her cruiser, her partner's face looking up at her, frozen in a last look that said *what the hell just happened to me . . .*

Stop it. She took a deep shuddering breath and straightened her shoulders. *Do the work,* her own voice came again in her head. *Do the next thing.* For a moment, she fumbled for what the next thing might be. *Secure the scene,* the voice said. *And the witnesses.* She got to work.

By the time the detective pulled up, Marie had the scene lined off with rolls of bright yellow tape from her trunk and the witnesses corralled over to one side of the parking lot. One of the men had complained that he and his buddy had to get to work and had looked like he was going to make an issue of it. He had even muttered something under his breath about "not taking any shit from any girl deputy." Marie had just unclipped the handcuffs from her gunbelt and stared significantly at him. He had backed down and was now sitting on a stack of boxes.

Marie was bent down, drawing a chalk circle around a shell casing near the body when the brown unmarked car pulled in. There was a mini-gumball light pulsing blue on the dash, but no siren. A man got out.

Marie had once had an art class in high school where they had tried to teach her figure drawing. The teacher had told them to start by sketching the basic parts of the body as rounded shapes: an oval for the head, another for the torso, long thin ovals for the limbs. But the man approaching seemed to have been made out of squares and rectangles. His iron-gray hair was cut across the top of his squarish head in a brush cut. His shoulders were broad and blocky and his body seemed to drop straight from them to the ground with no visible waist. His face was pitted with ancient acne scars and his nose had been broken long ago and badly reset, giving him the look of a prizefighter who had had more losses than wins. She was so new, it took her a moment to place the name. *Shelby,* she finally recalled. She didn't know anything about him beyond that. He stopped and looked around at the scene, noting the tape and the witnesses. He looked at Marie for a second, then nodded almost imperceptibly. He walked inside and stood over the body for a moment, looking down. Then he turned slowly, looking things over, before walking back out. He jerked his chin at the paramedics sitting in the open door of the ambulance. "They move anythin'?" he said.

His voice was surprisingly high for such a big man and his accent was pure country.

"No sir," she said.

Shelby cracked a tight grin, showing crooked teeth. Marie decided he was probably one of the ugliest men she had ever met, but there was something about the smile that relaxed her. "Don't call me sir," he said. "I work for my livin'." Marie recognized the non-com joke that must have been old in the time of the Roman legions. Shelby was obviously ex-military.

Marie smiled back, relaxing a little more. "Just checked him over. He was dead when I got here."

Shelby nodded again. "Get any statements?"

"No sir . . . I mean, no," she said. "Waiting for you."

"Awright," he said. He looked around. "Looks like you got ever'thing pretty well squared away," he said. "Good work."

"Thanks," she said.

He looked back at her, then down at her hands. "Y'better wash that blood off, though. Don't want to spread it around. Besides, y'might forget and touch your face or your hair." He grinned mirthlessly. "We don't know where this feller's been."

She looked down. Her gloves were still streaked with gore. "Okay," she said. "Sorry. Let me find a bathroom. I'll be right back."

"I'll be here," he said as he turned toward the people standing by.

Marie located the restroom around the side of the building. She grimaced as she looked around at the grimy tile and cracked fixtures. As she reached for the faucet, she noticed a drop of blood on the edge of the sink. She stopped short, her hand a few inches away from the faucet. She looked around. There was another drop of blood, almost too small to notice unless you were looking for it, on the floor. She looked over at the toilet stall, a feeling of dread twisting her stomach. *Another body in there?* she wondered. Slowly, she pushed the door open. The stall was empty. Marie breathed out. She had not realized till then that she had been holding her breath. Then the paper towels sticking out of the trash can caught her eye. She walked over and looked down. There was blood there, too, ragged stains soaked into the rough flimsy paper.

Marie's head snapped up as a scream came from outside. She slammed the door open with one hand and drew her weapon with the other. She skidded to a stop at the corner of the building as another scream split the air. It sounded like a woman.

She held the 9MM Beretta in a two-handed grip, her elbows slightly bent to take the recoil. The she stepped out, planting her feet shoulder-width apart, her eyes hunting for targets.

Bells hanging on the front door jingled as Keller walked into the small diner. A plump waitress with badly dyed red hair looked up from pouring coffee for a table of men in paint-spattered overalls. "Sit anywhere you want, hon," she called out. "Be with you in just a sec."

This time of day, with breakfast long over and the lunch crowd petering out, the place was mostly empty. A few older men sat on stools at the counter, nursing coffees or glasses of iced tea, newspapers propped up before them or spread on the counter. The rich smells of coffee, eggs, and bacon still hung in the air. Keller slid into a booth. The red-haired waitress came over, the coffeepot still in her hand. The table was already fully set, and Keller turned the inverted coffee cup upright. The waitress filled it and handed him a laminated plastic menu. "Thanks," he said, "but I'll just have the coffee."

"Okay, shug, take your time," she said, patting him on the shoulder. As she started to turn away, Keller said "You got a minute?"

She turned back, a look of mild surprise on her ruddy, kind face. "Can I hep you?" she asked.

"I'm trying to find Laurel Marks. Anyone know—"

The face shut down, all of the friendliness suddenly evaporated. "She don't work here no more."

"I know," Keller said. "I was wondering if—"

"I'll get the manager," the waitress said. She walked off, slowly, as if her feet hurt.

After a few moments, a man in cook's white pants and a sweat-stained T-shirt came out. He was in his late thirties, but hard work and harder partying had already carved deep lines in his face and under his eyes. His scraggly hair poked out at odd angles from beneath his flat round paper cap. A bushy cavalryman's moustache almost, but not quite, hid his badly crooked teeth when he spoke.

"You lookin' for Laurel?" he said. His voice was a raspy croak, his eyes narrow and suspicious.

"Yeah," Keller said. "I work for her bondsman. She skipped bail on us."

The eyes grew less wary. "You tryin' to put her in jail, huh?"

"That's right."

The manager leaned back and smiled. "Well shit, somebody sure's hell ought to. Jesus, that bitch was flat crazy." He extended a hand covered with healed burns and old scars from kitchen mishaps. "I'm Bart," he said. He didn't offer a last name.

Keller shook his hand. "Jack," he said.

Bart leaned back and took off his cap. He ran a hand through his thinning brown hair. He produced a cigarette and lit it. "You got a card, Jack?" he said. "I mean it ain't like I don't trust people, but . . ." He left the sentence hanging.

29

Keller handed him a card. Bart studied it through the haze of his cigarette smoke. "H & H Bonds. Yeah, I used them a time or two." He pocketed the card. "Actually, Alicia's the one you ought to ask about Laurel," he said. He looked around.

"'LICIA!" bellowed suddenly. The men at the counter looked up. The painters at the nearby booth stopped talking. "'LICIA!" Bart yelled again.

A rail-thin blonde girl in the same uniform as the other waitress came out the back, wiping her hands on a rag. "What is it, Bart?" she whined. "I got side work to finish . . ." She stopped as she caught sight of Keller. She smiled at him and walked over to stand beside Bart. "Who's your friend, Bart?" she asked. She tried to make it sound flirtatious, but the nasal quality of her voice spoiled the effect.

"Jack here works for Laurel's bail bondsman. She skipped bail and he's lookin' for her."

"That bitch!" Alicia said. Her voice went up an octave and the word came out as two syllables: *bee-yitch*. "Look what she did to my arm!" She pulled the polyester sleeve of her uniform up almost to one bony shoulder. All Keller could see was the bandage that ran from her shoulder down to her bicep. "She coulda kilt me!" Alicia said dramatically. She looked around to where the men at the counter were still staring. "She coulda kilt me!" she announced again to the room.

Bart slid out of the booth. Alicia took his place. "Don't take too long," he growled at Alicia. "I ain't payin' you to talk." He didn't wait for an answer before walking off.

"Fuck you, Bart," Alicia said, too softly for him to hear. She smiled at Keller again. She twirled a lock of her thin blonde hair around her index finger. "So," she said, "Crazy Laurel skipped out on you." Her voice was light and teasing.

Keller nodded. "Yeah. Thought I'd check and see if anyone

knew where she might hang out. Or where she lived, stuff like that."

Alicia's eyes brightened. "Whatcha gonna do when you catch her? You gonna cuff her?"

"Probably. Most people don't really want to come with me."

She leaned forward. "You bring your cuffs with you? Can I see 'em?"

"They're in the car."

"Maybe you can show 'em to me later," she said.

Keller grinned. "You always ask guys you just met to show you their handcuffs?"

She grinned back. "If they're cute enough," she said.

"You could get in trouble that way," he replied.

"Honey," she said, with all the clueless bravado a twenty-year-old can summon, "I love trouble." She punched him lightly on the forearm, then leaned back. "I'm just playin'," she said.

It was an old game, invitation and withdrawal. Keller played along. *To keep her talking,* he told himself. "I know," he said.

"I don't know all that much about Laurel, tell you the truth," Alicia went on. "She came in, always acted like she was pissed off at somethin'. Most of us just steered clear of her."

"Why'd she cut you?" Keller asked.

She grimaced. "I made some stupid joke about that creepy boyfriend of hers."

"Boyfriend?"

"Yeah," she folded her arms across her chest, as if the memory made her cold. "He was good-looking, I mean for an older guy, but he was old enough to be her father. And he was . . . I don't know, there was somethin' not right about him."

"Was she staying with him?"

Alicia shrugged. "I guess. She always left with him. And he dropped her off in the morning. Anyway, I made some crack

31

about how her daddy was here to pick her up. Next thing I know, she'd cut me."

"Either of them ever say anything about where the boyfriend lived? What he did?"

"Naw. He kept tellin' people he was an actor. Said he knew a lot of people at the movie studio. Talked a lot about movies he'd been in, but they was all older stuff. He never seemed to be workin' these days." She leaned forward and her voice dropped to a confidential whisper. "Dealin' drugs, is what I think."

Keller thought for a moment. He knew a couple of people working at the Screen Gems lot outside of town. Maybe they had a listing of people that had worked there. It would be a long list; the studio was the biggest production facility on the East Coast. This was assuming the boyfriend wasn't just a poser. Still, the boyfriend was all the lead he had right now. "This guy named Roy by any chance?"

"Yeah," Alicia said. "Roy Randle. Sounded fake to me."

"Probably," Keller said. "But I'll check it out. Thanks." He slid out of the booth and stood up.

The flirtatious grin was back. "So when you gonna show me them handcuffs?" She darted a glance at the kitchen, where Bart was haranguing the other waitress about something. She lowered her voice. "I get off in an hour."

"Sorry," Keller said. "My workday's just starting."

"Well," she said, disappointment obvious in her face, "I work every weekday 'til three. Stop by, when you have some time."

"I could be an axe murderer for all you know," Keller said.

She smiled at him. "You don't look crazy," she said.

Shows how much you know, Keller thought. He left a twenty on the table for the coffee and the information and walked out.

Out in the car, he flipped open the file and looked again at the picture of Laurel Marks. He was beginning to get a sense of her, beginning to fill in the spaces behind what he could see in the photo. Now he felt the anger in the set of the jaw, the fury behind the eyes.

He looked back at the restaurant. Alicia was looking out the window at him. When she saw him look up, she waved, then went back to work.

Keller shook his head. Not so long ago, he would have played the game, done the dance of invitation and withdrawal, until the final act, bodies locked together in a momentary coupling in a rumpled bed somewhere. And after that . . . nothing. For the long dead years since the desert, nothing had meant anything to him.

Now, everything had changed. Keller slid the cell phone into the slot of his hands-free system and hit a number on the speed dialer. There was the soft chirring of the ringer on the other end, then a gravelly male voice answered. "Yeah?"

"Mr. Jones," Keller said. "It's Jack Keller."

"Keller," Marie's father growled, "how many times have I gotta tell you to call me Frank?"

"Sorry, Frank," Keller said. "Marie's working, I guess."

"Yeah," he said, "You wanna leave a message?" A loud metallic banging rose in the background, filling the car. "BEN!" Frank Jones shouted. "Cut it OUT! I'm on the PHONE!" The banging stopped.

"Sounds like you're pretty busy," Keller said.

"Thirty years I was a cop," Frank said. "I handled drunks, dopeheads, thieves, about a thousand varieties of asshole . . . and the person that's made me craziest is a freakin' five-year-old."

"You can't shoot him," Keller said. "That's what's making you nuts."

"Yeah," Frank said. "That's gotta be it. Anyway . . ."

33

"Just tell her I called. About this weekend."

"Okay," Frank said. "You comin' up?"

"I don't know yet," Keller said.

Frank's voice turned cooler. "Okay," he said. "Whatever."

Keller was about to say something, but the banging started up again. "BEN!" Frank hollered before coming back on the line. "Gotta go," he said in a harried voice.

"Thanks, Frank," Keller said, but the line was dead.

Shelby was standing over a plump woman in a shapeless flowered dress, on her knees in the parking lot. She had her hands over her face. As Shelby tried to put his hand on her shoulder, she dropped her hands, threw back her head, and screamed again. It was a wordless soul-tearing howl of anguish and despair and it made the hair on the back of Marie's neck go up. Shelby yanked his hand back as if the woman had burned him.

Marie holstered the gun and walked over. The woman's screams had subsided to great convulsive sobs and she had covered her face with her hands again. Marie looked at Shelby.

"Station owner's wife," he said.

"Jesus Christ," Marie said. "She scared the shit out of me."

A strange pained look flickered across Shelby's face for a moment, then was gone. Marie hesitated for a moment, puzzled by the sudden tension between them. She broke it by asking, "The lady make an ID yet?"

He gestured at her. "Looks like she's doin' one right now, doncha think?"

She grimaced. "Yeah, but we've got to . . . ah, shit." Marie knelt beside the woman and wrapped an arm around her shoulders. "Ma'am?" she said softly. "Ma'am, please, I need to ask you something." The woman suddenly turned to Marie and grabbed her shoulders like a drowning person blindly pulling her rescuer under with her. Her pale face was wet with tears and her eyes red and swollen.

"My boy," she croaked. "Oh, God, oh, Jesus, did they kill my boy, too?" Her eyes unfocused and another wail seemed to be building deep inside her. Marie grabbed the woman's shoulders in her own grip. A passerby might have thought they were wrestling. Marie shook the woman slightly. *"Ma'am!"* she barked. The woman came back briefly. "What boy, ma'am? Was your son here?"

The woman nodded vigorously. "How old, ma'am?" Marie persisted. "How old is your son?"

"Suhh . . . suh . . . sixteen," the woman blubbered. Her eyes went away again. She buried her face back in her hands and began sobbing.

Marie got up and looked at Shelby. "I haven't found another body," she said. "But there's some drops of blood in the restroom. And some paper towels in the trash with blood on them. Like someone was trying to clean up."

Shelby gestured toward where the body lay. "No one tried to clean up in there. So maybe the victim got a few licks in on the guy that kilt him."

"Or," Marie said, "Maybe the kid's . . . ." She looked at the woman on the ground. "I'll look around." Shelby nodded. He bent down to the woman on the ground and began trying to raise her to her feet.

Marie checked the back of the station. There was a narrow passageway between the back of the building and a tangle of kudzu vines that had overtaken and strangled a thicket of pine trees behind the station. The narrow path was littered with twelve-ounce plastic soda bottles and discarded food wrappers. Marie slowly made her way down the narrow passage. It was barely wide enough for her to get through. There was no sign of anything or anyone having gone into the woods. She came around the other side of the station where a Dumpster sat, its green paint flaked off to expose the metal beneath, showing cancerous patches of rust. She took a deep breath and held it before looking in. Nothing. She walked back around to the front. Shelby had gotten the woman into the backseat of his car and was crouched down on the pavement next to the car door, nodding at something she was saying. Marie walked into the repair bay.

The lights were off and there were no cars in the bay for repairs. There was a door at the far end on which the word PARTS had been written with a marker on the bare wood. She opened the door and looked inside. She saw handmade wooden shelves filled with haphazardly stacked boxes of hoses, gaskets, fuses, and the like, but no body.

She was closing the door when she noticed the safe. It was tucked away in a corner of the tiny storeroom. The door stood wide open. Marie walked over, crouched down, and looked inside. Empty. She bit her lip and thought for a moment. Then she got up and walked back toward the front of the station. As she passed by the workbench, a flash of pink caught her eye. It was a magazine. She picked it up and grimaced. A girl who looked barely out of high school was on the cover. She was naked. Marie's lip curled in disgust. She moved as if to toss the magazine back onto the workbench. Then she saw the streak of blood on the cover.

She put the magazine gently back down, as close to its original place as she could remember before walking back out into the sunlight. Shelby was coming her way. They met in the middle of the lot.

"Nothing?" Shelby said. Marie shook her head.

"So the boy was took," Shelby said. The kidnapper beat him up, tried to get him cleaned up, and took him."

Marie kept her voice low. "Maybe, but there's a safe in the storeroom. It's open and looks like it's been cleaned out."

"Kidnapping and robbery then."

"There's more," Marie said. "There's a porno magazine on the workbench. There's blood on it, too."

Shelby looked startled for a moment, then looked away. *My God*, Marie thought, *he's blushing*. After a moment, he looked back. "So the killer walked in on the victim readin' a dirty magazine and they din't like it."

"Or the kid was reading the magazine," Marie said. "And that's why he didn't notice the killer coming in. Or killers. We can't rule out more than one."

Shelby shook his head. "We need to call the SBI. Get a crime scene team in here. Meantime, we may have us a child kidnapped."

"Shelby, you need to consider something," Marie said. "Maybe the kid did it."

Shelby looked pained. "Look," Marie said. "I know it may be tough to think about, a child killing a parent . . ."

"Stepparent," Shelby said. "The mother said the victim weren't the natural father." He grimaced. "But yeah, I already thought of that. Don't like to think that way, but it's surely possible." He looked at Marie. "But if that boy is kidnapped and we don't treat it that way . . ."

"Yeah," Marie said. "You're right. We'll get crucified." The uncomfortable look crossed Shelby's face again. *What is eating this guy?* Marie wondered. "So," she said after a moment. "You want to do an Amber Alert?"

Shelby pondered this for a moment. Amber Alert would put a statewide media notification, like that for a tornado or other natural disaster, onto hundreds of participating TV and radio stations. For a child under thirteen when there was a possibility of stranger abduction or imminent harm, Amber Alert was automatic. For disappearances of children older than that, potential abductions were considered on a case-by-case basis.

"No," Shelby said, "not yet. We'll keep lookin' at ever'thing." He looked at Marie, up and down. "Jones," he said.

Marie shifted uncomfortably under his gaze. "Yes, sir . . . I mean, yeah?"

"My reg'lar partner's out. He just had surgery. Prostate cancer."

Marie was startled by the sudden change in subject. "Sorry to hear it."

"He'll be awright," Shelby said. "They got it early. But he'll be laid up for a while an' I'm a little shorthanded right now. Y'want to work this one with me?"

Would I? Marie thought. Work a murder, possible kidnapping? She had been waiting to sit for the sergeant's exam before the death of her partner had derailed her career, and suddenly a whole new path had opened up for her. Her heart leaped for a moment. Then it came back to earth as she looked at the mother weeping in the back of Shelby's car. She felt a momentary flash of shame.

"Yeah," she told Shelby. "Yeah, I'd like that."

He nodded. "I'll talk to the major and set it up."

Marie grimaced. "He's not going to be happy with that. He's a real bear about overtime."

Shelby gave her that snaggletoothed grin again. "He'll get over it. He owes me."

"Okay," she said. She took a business card out of her pocket and scribbled a number on it. "Here's my cell number," she said.

"Good," he said. His face turned serious. "But Jones, I want to ask you something."

"Okay," Marie said, her eyes wary. Now the catch, she thought.

"Could you not take the Lord's name in vain in front of me?" Shelby asked.

Marie was struck dumb for a moment. Shelby went on resolutely.

"I know you get used to rough language in law enforcement," he said. "Before I got saved, I was guilty of it myself. But I'd really appreciate it."

Marie finally found her voice. "Yeah. Okay. Sorry, I didn't know—"

Shelby waved it off. "I know. I don't blame you for it, it'd just make it easier for us to work together, y'understand."

"Sure," Marie said. "No problem. I mean, I'll try . . ."

He nodded, looking satisfied. "That's all any of us can do, Marie," he said. His face lit up with a sudden idea. "Hey," he said. "Whyn't you come over for dinner tomorrow night? Barbara can make up some of her fried chicken. There's plenty."

"Ahh . . . I was going to see my, ah, boyfriend tomorrow night." Boyfriend. The word still felt strange to Marie.

"Heck, bring him, too," Shelby said. "Barbara always makes enough to feed a platoon."

She smiled. "He's in Wilmington," she said, "but maybe I could persuade him to come up."

"Six-thirty, then," he said. "And come hungry."

three

They loaded the weapons in the back of the cargo van. Laurel and Roy climbed in the front. Stan climbed into the cargo compartment through the sliding side doors. He noticed a pair of sleeping bags and a cooler shoved up against the back. He crawled over and propped his back against them. It was hard to see from there, and he couldn't hear what Roy and Laurel were saying. He was left curled up in the back with his thoughts.

Stan's head throbbed with fear and confusion. He was still scared to death. He didn't know what these people were planning to do with him. But Laurel actually seemed to like him.

He stared, fascinated, at the blanket-covered guns on the floor. He could grab one of them, but he didn't know whether there were any bullets in them. And Laurel still had the gun in her purse. The one that had killed his stepfather. A tremor went through him at that memory. He had hated and feared the man, but the thought of him lying dead on the floor of his service station made him feel sick to his stomach.

He looked up toward the front. Laurel was saying something to Roy in the driver's seat. She made a small gesture toward the back of the van and Stan realized she was talking about him. He felt sick again. Roy obviously regarded him as a possible liability. And Roy didn't seem to have any more scruples about killing than Laurel did. Stan closed his eyes and prayed. He had had his doubts about God, especially when his stepfather had beaten him, but now he prayed for all he was worth.

He heard a rustling sound next to him and opened his eyes. Laurel had climbed over the front seat and was sitting next to him. She was holding a joint in one hand.

"Are you scared, Stan?" she said softly.

Stan nodded, unable to speak.

She put an arm around him. He felt the heat of her body as she shifted herself closer to him. She put the joint between her lips and lit it with her free hand. She took a long drag and held the smoke in before passing it to him. "'Ere," she said, her voice tight with the effort of holding in the smoke.

He took the joint and inhaled deeply. There was an unfamiliar, sharp taste mixed in with the familiar taste of the pot. He grimaced and passed it back to her. She flipped it around and placed the lit end in her mouth, tightening her lips to hold the burning ash away from her tongue. She leaned toward him. He followed suit until their faces were inches apart. She began to exhale, slowly and evenly. He pursed his own lips and took in the steady stream of smoke that she forced out of the loosely twisted end of the joint. He shotgunned the smoke until he thought his lungs would burst, then pulled away. She flipped it out of her mouth and took her own turn. She leaned back over until her face was very close to his. "You don't have to be afraid of us, Stan," she whispered. "We're all in this together now."

"I . . . I don't know what you mean," Stan said. His head was swimming with the buzz from the smoke.

"Roy and I, we talked it over. He has his doubts, I won't bullshit you. But we've got a little time to decide. To figure out if you want to be part of what we're going to do." She slid a hand down to the inside of his thigh. Stan jumped at the contact. He looked up at the front of the van. "Umm . . . aren't you and him . . ."

She glanced up front. Roy was still driving. He didn't look back. "Oh, sure," she said nonchalantly. "But he's not jealous. We don't live like that, Stan." She began moving her hand slowly up and down his thigh. "See," she said, "Roy taught me a secret. Everybody else pretends like there are rules. Don't cheat on your taxes. Don't beat up people smaller than you. Don't . . . ." Her face twisted. "Never mind. But see, Stan, no one ever followed those rules with us. They lie. They cheat. They . . . they mess around with people they ain't supposed to. After a while, Roy realized that they weren't really rules. They was just ways people used to get over on you. After that," she reached for his belt, "the world made sense. For the first time, the world made sense."

Stan shook his head. The pot was hitting him harder than anything he'd ever smoked before. The edges for everything seemed fuzzy, indistinct. The walls of the van seemed to pulse and shimmer. He shook his head again.

Laurel giggled at the look on his face. "Killer stuff, innit?" she said, her voice slurred with the effects of the drug. "We put a lil' something extra in." He felt her hands undoing his belt buckle. Through the haze in his head, it felt like it was happening to someone else. Then as she slid her hand inside his jeans, Stan closed his eyes and it all came slamming back into his head. All the horniness he had felt back at the station, poring over the skin mag, spilled back into him. His own heartbeat was thudding in his ears.

"Come on, Stan," she said. "Let me show you what life can be like."

"I'm home," Marie called out as she closed the door behind her.

"Mommeeeee!" her son Ben cried out as he crashed into her knees.

She picked him up and hugged him, grunting a little with the effort. "Hey, big boy!" she said as she kissed him. "You been good for Grandpa?"

"He's been a handful, that's for damn sure," her father said.

Ben put a hand over his mouth and gave her an exaggerated look of shock. He took his hand away from his mouth long enough to whisper, "Grandpa said a bad word."

Marie put Ben down. A sheepish look crossed her father's round, lined face. "Sorry, kid," he muttered.

"Ben," Marie said, "Grandpas and Mommies can say things that little boys can't."

Ben set his lip defiantly. "That's not fair," he said.

"Maybe, but that's the way it is. Now go play, I need to talk to Grandpa."

"No fair," Ben insisted, but he scurried off to his room. Marie hugged her father and kissed him on the cheek. He hugged her back, hard. Retirement had given him a considerable paunch, but his arms were still strong.

"How was he really, Dad?" she said.

He grinned. "No worse than usual, kid. How was work?"

Marie unbuckled her gun belt and hung it up in the closet. "We caught a bad one today, Dad. Murder, maybe child abduction."

Her father walked back into the kitchen. "Tell me about it while I start these chops." He went to the kitchen and grabbed a pair of beers from the fridge. He handed her one and opened the other.

She told him about it as he tended to the pork chops. Her father was a former cop himself, so he picked up the doubts and questions Marie had before she had even gotten to them.

"You think the kid might've done his stepfather?" He asked bluntly.

Marie grimaced. "I don't know," she said. "It's possible."

He grunted. "Tell me about this Shelby."

"He seems like a good guy. Pretty religious. Asked me not to take the name of the Lord in vain."

He rolled his eyes. "Ah, shit. I rode with one of those one time. Damn near bored my ass off. Hey, get the rice started, willya?"

They worked together to prepare dinner, and gradually Marie started feeling normal again. She liked having her dad around. He had come down after her partner had been killed and kept delaying going back. Finally, he had offered to stay and take care of Ben while Marie was working.

"Oh, damn, I forgot," he said suddenly. "Your friend Keller called."

Marie stopped stirring. "What'd he say?"

"Just wanted to talk about the weekend."

She began stirring again. She felt slightly embarrassed. "Ah," was all she said. "Well, Shelby invited me over to dinner tomorrow night," she said. "He said Jack could come, too." She felt suddenly awkward. If Keller came up for dinner, they'd have the choice of driving back to Wilmington afterwards or having him stay with her. If they did that, it would be the first time for that since her father had moved in.

"Seems like you and this guy Keller are gettin' pretty serious," her father said.

She felt herself reddening. "Yeah," she replied. She looked up. His face was serious.

"Look, kiddo," he said. She looked up. "I know you're a big girl now." He smiled sadly. "I may not like it, but it's not like I can do anything about it. But is this guy . . ." He shook his head.

She tried not to sound defensive. She hated this feeling, the mix of defiance and defensiveness that made her feel sixteen years old again. "I'm fine, Dad," she said.

"Maybe," he said, "but there's more than just you to worry about. You ever thought what kind of a stepfather this guy would make for Ben?"

"Ben likes him," she said.

"I know he does," her father said. "He asks me 'When's Tough Guy coming to see me?'" Marie had to smile, remembering the nickname Ben had hung on Keller the first time they met. The smile vanished as her father went on. "And you know what I have to tell him? 'I don't know.' Do you?"

"Do I what?"

"Know when he's coming to see your son. Do you know when he's going to be around? Or *if* he's going to be around?"

Marie was getting angry. "Do we have to settle my entire life before dinner, Dad?" she snapped. "We're working through a lot of things. And Ben's part of that. He's part of me and part of my life. And if you think I don't realize that—"

"Okay, okay . . . ," her father said, raising his hands. "Sorry. I'm sticking my nose in." His face softened. "I should trust you. You never gave me cause to do anything else. I just don't want you or Ben to get hurt. And I worry that this guy will do it."

"He's a good man, Dad," Marie said. *But he's definitely not*

45

staying here tomorrow night, she thought. All she needed was for her father to start grilling Keller like he was grilling her.

"Okay, then," her father said. "You said it, that's good enough for me." They went back to preparing dinner.

"You sure you don't mind keeping Ben?" she said. "If I go to Wilmington for the rest of the weekend?"

"Naah. We'll make a bachelor weekend of it. I, ahh . . ." He hesitated.

"What?"

"I thought I might take Ben to Wal-Mart and get him an air rifle. It's time he started learning some basic safety."

Marie felt her shoulders tighten. "Yeah," she said. "Okay."

"Bullshit," he said flatly. "It's not okay. You get that look on your face every time I mention it. And I'm not going to do it if it's going to upset you."

"He's awfully young," Marie said softly.

"You were his age when I started teaching you to shoot," he said.

She laughed. "Yeah, well, my Dad was kinda weird."

He didn't laugh back. He walked over to her and grasped her shoulders. "Kid," he said softly, "it's not that big a deal whether or not Ben gets an air rifle. But every time I bring it up, it shakes you up. Bad. Worse than it ought to. And I want to know why."

She looked away from his eyes. "I can't talk about it, Dad," she said.

"That bad, huh?" he said. "Worse than what happened to Eddie? Because you can talk about that."

All she could do was nod. He took her chin in his hand and drew her around to look back at him.

"Marie," he said. "Sometimes a cop crosses the line. Sometimes he does things that only another cop can understand. And it's important to know that someone understands. You know what I'm saying?"

In her mind's eye she saw a man standing, framed in the scope of her deer rifle, a cigarette lighter raised above his head. Had he lit it, he would have incinerated himself and everyone around him. She took the slack up on the trigger just like her dad had taught her, felt herself breathe out slow, squeezed, heard the report of the rifle . . .

She jumped slightly. Her father, startled by the movement, let go of her shoulders. "I'm not ready, Dad," she said. "I'm just not ready." She wrapped her arms around him and buried her head in his broad chest. "I'm sorry."

Her father hugged her tightly. "Okay," he said. "When you're ready, then." He pulled away. "Those chops are gonna burn," he said.

"Thanks, Dad," Marie said softly. "Thanks for everything."

He waved it off. "Least I can do," he said. "Go get Ben washed up."

Roy smiled to himself when he heard Stan's muffled cry of release. The kid was shook up, out of his element. But he was also a horny sixteen-year-old. What Laurel was doing would bind the kid to them. Or at least, it would bind him to Laurel, and Roy could handle her.

He drove the van back down U.S. 74, through the flatlands of Robeson and Columbus Counties, headed for the coast. Laurel stayed in the back with Stan. Roy thought about what was about to go down. He was about to claim what had been denied him for so long, what other people's cowardice and deception had taken from him. He thought back to the days when everything had been opening up for him, when everything had seemed in his grasp. He had worked with the stars, and soon, he had known, he'd be one himself. Until the day when it all came crashing down. Because someone else couldn't admit their own fuckup. Because it was easy to blame Roy. His knuckles turned white on the wheel. *Soon,* he thought to himself. *Soon.*

Just before reaching the Cape Fear River Bridge, he took one of the exits in the snarl of ramps that sorts traffic to the various coast roads. A narrow two-lane blacktop paralleled the river, headed down toward the town of Southport. A few miles down, he turned down a dirt road toward the river. Laurel rejoined him, clambering over the front seat.

"He all right?" Roy said in a voice too low for their passenger to hear.

She nodded. "It'll be okay, Roy, I promise," she said.

"We ain't pickin' up every stray that comes along," he said.

She grinned. "Look who's talkin'." He didn't reply. He turned down a dirt road in the direction of the river. A weathered sign announced COMING SOON. RIVERWOODE. LUXURY HOMESITES FROM THE. The bottom of the sign where the price range was written had rotted and fallen off.

They bumped and jounced over the deeply rutted road until they came to a thick steel cable strung between two trees. Laurel grabbed a key ring from the glove box and hopped out. As she was undoing the padlock holding the cable, Stan appeared behind the passenger seat, peering out the front window.

"Where are we?" he said. He looked dazed.

"Home sweet home," Roy said. "For another day or so at least." Laurel got back in the van. She leaned back to peck Stan on the cheek.

After another quarter mile or so, the road emptied out into a clearing. They were on the bank of the river. Wire grass and stunted bushes struggled up from the sandy soil. A double-wide house trailer sat at one edge of the cleared space. There was a prefabricated metal shed on the other side of the clearing. Roy pulled up next to the trailer. They all got out.

"Wow," Stan said, "you got a great view here." He walked through the tall grass toward the riverbank. The Cape Fear River was broad and deep here. Far out on the channel, a massive container ship piled high with brightly colored rectangular boxes glided soundlessly up the river toward the port of Wilmington. Suddenly, Stan tripped. Then he seemed to become taller by a foot as he hopped up on something concealed in the tall grass.

"Hey," he called back. There's a concrete slab here. Was somebody, like, building a house?"

Rage flared white-hot behind Roy's eyes. He opened the back of the van and reached for one of the rifles wrapped up on the floor.

"Roy," Laurel said. She put her hand on his arm. "Easy, baby. He don't know."

Roy rested his hand on the gun for a moment as he throttled his anger back down.

He had been working stunts, taking the falls that the insurance companies weren't willing to let the more recognizable faces take. The film's rising young star had been chafing to do more of his own stunts; it was a martial arts movie, after all, and he wanted to show off his skills. But in the cold calculus of moviemaking it was the faceless ones who got to take the real risks.

Roy didn't mind; he was still young and strong, and the money was great, especially for a farm boy from Duplin County. And he knew that, once he'd paid his dues and made the right connections, he'd be one of the faces on the movie posters. He'd ascend to the heights where it was Dom Perignon and blow jobs from starlets in the backs of limos every night on the way to the next premiere. And his picture in the magazines, every week. That would be the sweetest part. Everyone would know his face. He had the look. He had the talent. And when the bruises he took from being knocked into set walls left him limping and sore, he had the coke and the whiskey to put the pain someplace far away.

Then it had all come down on him. His career had sputtered and died. He had been robbed. And now someone was going to pay while there was still time to collect.

The kid came running up, out of breath. "Man," he said. "What a great place."

"Come on in," Roy said. "We got some things to do before show time."

They walked to the door of the trailer. Roy turned the key in the lock but only opened the door a couple of inches. He reached inside and loosened the noose of wire wrapped around the doorknob. He slipped it off and over the knob, then opened the door and entered.

The interior of the trailer was dark, all the windows closed, and the blinds pulled down. A straight-backed wooden chair sat across the room facing the door. Bound to the chair with a weave of gray duct tape was a double-barreled shotgun pointing at the door. Roy walked over to the chair, winding the wire around his fist as he went. He unhooked the wire from a hook set in the far wall. The wire led around the hook back in the direction of the door, then was tied to the trigger of the gun. A person who cluelessly pulled the door open without stopping to unhook the wire would yank the wire taut around the hook and trigger, firing the gun and taking the full load of buckshot in the chest.

Roy looked back at Stan standing in the door, his eyes wide as he saw Roy disarming the trap gun. "I don't like trespassers," Roy said.

"I guess not," Stan replied. Roy flipped on a light as Laurel and Stan entered.

The interior of the trailer was cramped and cheaply furnished. A pair of movie posters dominated the space over the ragged sofa. Stan glanced at them. "Hey," he said, pointing, "I think I saw that one on TV one time. And isn't the other one the one where that guy got killed filming it?"

It took an effort of pure will for Roy not to pick up the shotgun and blow the kid's head off to shut his stupid mouth. "Yeah," he said. "Damn shame."

"Roy was in them two movies," Laurel said proudly. "And a bunch of others, too."

"Wow," Stan said. "No shit?"

"Yeah," Roy said. "No shit." He turned to Laurel. "Fix us something to eat," he said. "I got some work to do."

She looked for a moment as if she was going to argue about it, but she saw the look in Roy's eye and closed her mouth. "Okay," she said.

Roy went down the narrow hall to the bedroom he'd turned into an office. The tiny space was crammed full with a bed, a dresser, and a battered rolltop desk shoved into one corner. On one wall was a pair of cheap bookcases filled with books on film-making, texts on acting, and biographies of Hollywood stars. One shelf contained a set of three-ring binders, and it was one of those that Roy took down as he sat at the desk. He called them his "shooting scripts," and they contained the plans for each of his productions. He had scouted locations, mapped out entrances and exits, even drawn a few crude storyboards of the scenes he envisioned. Some of those would have to be changed, he thought, as his eyes danced over the crude cartoonish images of mayhem he had drawn. He felt a sudden sharp pain in his head, like an icepick jammed brutally between his eyes. Roy gritted his teeth and rubbed his eyes, willing the pain to go away. After a few moments, it subsided to a dull throb. The headaches were getting closer together and increasing in severity. Laurel hadn't rushed things by much. It was time to make his move.

As if to reassure himself, he went to the desk and took an envelope out of one of the cubbyholes. He unfolded the paper inside and looked at it again, even though he had the words memorized by now. *Inoperable . . . some experimental procedures . . . some chance of success . . .* The letter tried hard to be optimistic, considering that it was a death warrant.

For years Roy had held on, knowing that someday, somehow, he was going to make it back. The people who had used him, the people who had shoved him aside, would fall, and he would rise. It was an article of faith with him. Sometimes he imagined walking back onto the set, pausing for a moment in the doorway as all heads turned to look at him, a shadow backlit by the sun outside . . . the image faded. It wasn't going to happen now. There wasn't time.

He considered the advantages that having a third player would give. The kid hadn't had the rehearsal time that Roy and Laurel had, but he could do some of the grunt work, like driving. That would free up Laurel to take a bigger part in the production. That would make her happy for a while. Until it didn't matter.

Roy and Laurel had fallen in together because each of them saw their own fury mirrored in the other. Laurel had been Roy's audience, the perfect sounding board for his vision of revenge. She was the closest thing he'd had to a friend in a long time. But in the end, she was expendable. When this was all over there'd only be one name on the headlines. It was tough, but that was show business.

After dinner, Marie called Keller. He answered on the second ring. "Hey," he said.

"Hey yourself," she said. "How're you doing?"

"I'm okay," he said. "You?"

"Fantastic," she said. "I've got a chance to work a murder case." She heard him chuckle at that. She laughed as well. "I know, I know," she said. "Only a cop would call that luck."

"So," he said, "that mean you're working this weekend?"

"Possibly," she said. "Shelby . . . that's the detective I'd be working with . . . says he's going to try to get the overtime authorized. But I kind of have to stay around here. Can you come up?" Before he could answer, she added, "We've been invited to dinner with Shelby and his family."

"We?"

"Yeah," she said. "You and me. Like a couple."

There was a long pause. "You there?" she said finally.

"Yeah," he said. Then he laughed. "Dinner with the boss. It sounds so . . . normal."

"You say that like it's a bad thing," she said.

"No," he said, "not bad. Just new for me. I haven't lived what you'd call a normal life."

She thought back to her father's words. "Maybe that's good," she said. "New things, I mean." She paused for a moment. "I miss you, Jack," she said. "I want to see you."

Another pause. "I miss you, too," he said finally. "So yeah. I'll be there. What time?"

"Dinner's at six-thirty," she said. "Pick me up at six?"

"Okay," he said.

I love you, she wanted to say. Instead, she said, "See you then."

Keller hung up the phone and stared at the wall of his living room for a moment. The walls were blank, the furniture simple, mostly thrown together castoffs. He had been about to tell Marie that he had a jumper to catch, that he had to work the case. But then Angela's words had come back to him. *Stay with it,* she had said, *you two are good for each other.*

He had been alone so long, he had no idea if he was any good for her or anyone else. He had spent the years since the war in a self-imposed limbo, wrapping himself in his own fury until it hardened into a kind of armor, protection against any kind of pain. It had made him pitiless, remorseless. It had given him the kind of fearlessness that comes with not caring whether he or anyone else lived or died. All of which had made him very good at his job.

Then things had begun to change. First with Angela, then Marie. He had begun to feel again. The armor had begun to crack. For a moment, he felt a stab of fear. He marveled at that for a moment, like a fisherman who had hauled up some prehistoric creature from the depths. It seemed like eons since he had felt fear or doubt. He wondered if it would slow him down, cost him a step or a second of reflex. He wondered if it would get him killed.

"What did it mean when you said 'like we agreed?'" Stan asked.

He and Laurel were lying in bed together. They were naked. He was on his back, staring, fascinated, at the darkened ceiling.

It seemed to ripple and blur under his gaze. After the three of them had eaten, Roy had broken out a baggie of crystal meth and cut several lines for each of them. Stan had never done meth before. The stuff burned his nostrils fiercely as he snorted up the fat lines. But the rush when it came was a hundred times more intense than the boost he had gotten from the laced joints before. It was like being shot out of a cannon. Stan's heart felt like a car engine with the pedal jammed to the firewall. His thoughts rushed by him almost faster than he could capture them. In minutes, they were all flying high, Roy and Laurel jabbering about whatever came into their heads. Then Laurel took Stan by the hand and dragged him into the bedroom. He had glanced nervously back at Roy, but the older man had ignored them in favor of cutting out more lines. Once inside, she had giggled like a mischievous child as she yanked his pants down and pushed him back on the bed. The next few minutes had been a blur of images flashing in his head like a strobe as Laurel pulled her own clothes off and straddled him. She rode him hard and fast, gasping and tearing at the front of his shirt with her nails. As he groaned with his oncoming climax, she had leaned down and bit him on his cut lip, hard. He had screamed as he came, the meth rush combining with the pleasure and pain and the taste of blood in his mouth in a mind-shattering explosion.

Afterwards, as they lay together, thoughts continued to zip through Stan's head like fireflies. He hadn't realized that he had spoken aloud until Laurel answered.

"What's that, honey?" she murmured, her hand moving down to stroke him again. He didn't think he could get hard again so soon, but he couldn't bring himself to push her away. She was the first real woman who had ever touched him like that, and he was afraid if he stopped her, she wouldn't do it again.

It took him a moment to remember what he'd asked. "Back at the station," he said. "You handed the gun to Roy and he said, 'like we agreed?' Like a question. What did that mean?"

"Oh," she said. "When Roy an' I were talking about this, we agreed early on. We'd share in everything. All the fame, and all the blame. There wouldn't be no killin' that was just done by one of us."

Stan closed his eyes. Whenever he did that, it was like he was seeing tiny flashbulbs going off behind his eyelids. When he heard the bedroom door open, he opened his eyes. He saw Roy's shadow in the doorway and tried to sit up. Laurel pushed him back down.

"Like I said, honey," she smiled down at him as Roy approached the bed, "we share everything."

Keller walked into the office the next morning. Angela came out of the back at the sound of the bell. "Anything?" she said.

"Yeah," Keller said. "I need you to find me any info you can get on this Randle guy Laurel Marks was hanging out with. She may have been living with him."

"Okay," she said. "I'll put Oscar on it."

Keller had picked up a phone book and was thumbing through the R's. He looked up. "Oscar?" he said.

"Yeah. I've been teaching him records searches. Criminal records checks, Register of Deeds, stuff like that."

"It's something to do," Oscar Sanchez said as he hobbled out of the back office. There was a touch of bitterness in his voice as he said, "Since I can no longer work as a laborer."

"Well, hell," Keller said. "You didn't want to do that, anyway, right? It was just a way to earn a few bucks."

Sanchez nodded, his face still glum. He sat down at the computer.

"Lot more future here in working with your brain, Oscar," Keller said.

He looked up and smiled sadly. "Oh, *si*," he said. "Oscar Sanchez, Private Eye. I can see it now." He turned back to the computer. "You forget, I am illegal. I can only rise so high."

"I'm going to get the mail," Angela said abruptly. She walked out the front door, banging it slightly. Oscar looked at the door and sighed.

Keller took a seat at the desk. "Things aren't going too well, I see. With Angela."

Sanchez was silent for a moment. Finally, he said, "I do not know. Things were well for us at first, but after . . . after I was shot . . ." He trailed off and rubbed his face wearily. "I cannot sleep. I keep seeing what happened in my mind. I feel angry all the time, even when there is no need." He bowed his head. "I am not the same man I was, Jack," he said softly. "I do not know how to be that man again."

Keller crouched down beside Sanchez's chair. "Oscar," he said. "Look at me." Sanchez looked up.

"When I was in the army," Keller said, "I and the men with me got lost in the desert. A helicopter . . . I never saw it, but it had to be one of the ones on our side . . . mistook us for an enemy. They fired a missile at us. Every one of my men was killed."

Sanchez looked at him soberly. "How did you survive?"

Keller grimaced. "Dumb luck," he said. "I had walked off to take a piss. If I hadn't, I'd have died, just like them. I saw them burn, Oscar. I heard them screaming." He stood up and put his hand on Sanchez's shoulder. "For years after that," he said, "I couldn't sleep. I was angry all the time. Then I went through anger, to the point, where there was nothing left. I was a dead man, Oscar, except I was still walking around."

"So what changed?"

Keller looked out the window. "I found someone who cared about me."

"Angela." Sanchez's face was expressionless.

"Yeah," Keller said. "She gave me a job, and I found out I liked it. And she liked me. For someone who'd spent a lot of time not being able to stand himself, that was pretty amazing."

"I have wondered . . . well, I know you have been together for a long time. I have wondered why . . . you and Angela . . ."

Keller shook his head. "It's complicated. I guess we just decided we were good as friends. As lovers we'd be a disaster for each other. Too much baggage." Sanchez looked confused at the idiom. "Too much bad stuff in our lives," Keller explained. "Anyway, don't worry on that account."

Sanchez smiled. "I wasn't worried. Exactly."

"Okay," Keller said. "Look, Oscar, a friend of mine has been helping me out with this stuff. A doctor. You want me to . . ."

Sanchez's face had clouded over. "I have no money for a doctor."

"Well, now you've got a job. I mean maybe—"

"No, Jack," Oscar said, then he smiled again. "I'll be fine. Knowing I have friends . . . that helps."

"Okay," Keller said. "You've got my cell. If you find out anything, let me know."

"You need it today?"

"Soon as you can get it," Keller said. "But I'm going to Fayetteville to see Marie tonight. Let me know if there's some reason to believe they're going to make a run for it. Otherwise." He smiled. "I'm taking the night off."

Sanchez arched an eyebrow at him. *"Es verdad?"* He said. "This is a change for you, no?"

Keller smiled. "Maybe so."

four

Stan awoke dry-mouthed and shivering, even though it was warm in the tiny bedroom. Laurel and Roy were gone. He pulled the thin blanket over himself and curled into a fetal position. The night before was coming back to him. Without the distance imparted by the drugs, he felt filthy, soiled.

The door opened. Laurel came in, holding a glass of orange juice in one hand and a fat joint in the other. "Morning, sleepy-head," she said.

Stan sat up. He didn't speak. Laurel slid onto the bed next to him and handed him the glass. He wanted to move away from her but there was no room on the bed. Besides, he was so thirsty. He drained half the juice in one swallow. Laurel snuggled closer to him. "You were great last night," she whispered. Stan shuddered. He drained the rest of the juice, then slid away from her to sit on the opposite edge of the bed. He dropped the glass to the floor and put his head in his hands. He heard the sound of a cigarette lighter flicking, then the sharp tang of pot smoke filled his nostrils. He looked back at Laurel. She was sitting up in the bed, looking at him calmly. She took a drag on the joint, held the smoke in, and passed it to him. He looked at it for a moment. He didn't want it, but he suddenly desperately wanted that distance, that fuzziness around everything, especially his recent memories. He took the joint and inhaled.

"I know you're a little freaked out right now," she said. "You done things you never thought you'd do. But Stan, that's kind of the point. That's freedom, Stan. That's learning that there ain't no rules anymore."

The familiar buzz was coming back, the surge of energy, the feeling of power. The joint, Stan realized, was laced with the meth. He didn't care anymore. He took another pull. "He hurt me," he said sullenly. "*You* hurt me."

She slid over and put her hands on his shoulders. "I know, baby," she said softly. "But that's part of it, too. It's like you're being born again. Like a butterfly coming out of a cocoon. And that hurts some. But you got to learn to live with the pain, Stan. You got to rise above it. You got to not mind it."

Stan shook his head. He couldn't seem to track what Laurel was saying. It sounded like gibberish to him. Maybe it was gibberish. He was too fucked up to tell.

Laurel slid off the bed on the other side and stood up. "Come on, baby," she said. "He wants to see you."

I don't want to see him, Stan thought, but he stood up anyway. He pulled his pants and shirt on and followed Laurel out of the trailer.

Roy heard the trailer door open and lowered the Army .45 that he had been aiming at a beer can on a post, some thirty feet

60

away. He watched as Laurel came out, followed by Stan. The boy kept his head down as they approached, as if he didn't want to look at Roy. That was fine. Last night, they had broken the kid down. Now they would build him back again, in their own way.

"Mornin', Stan," he said casually. Stan mumbled something back.

"You ready to be famous?" Roy said.

Stan looked up. His eyes were bloodshot and unfocused. "What?" he said.

Roy looked at him for a moment. Then he took the gun and held it by the barrel. He handed it to Stan, butt-first. "This is your ticket, kid," he said. "Your ticket to ride. But you got to know how to use it. You ready to learn?"

Stan looked at the gun. Roy held his breath.

Stan reached out and took the gun from Roy's hand. He let the hand fall limply to his side, the barrel pointed down. His eyes were empty of emotion.

Roy smiled in triumph. He had been right. The kid was weak. Had anyone done to Roy what Roy had done to the kid, that person would be dying on the ground right now. But Roy sensed that Stan had no strength of his own. Maybe it was because of the beatings he had suffered, or maybe he was just a pussy. But he had no power inside him. Any power that came to him now would be given to him by Roy. And what Roy gave him, Roy could take away. To make the point, Roy held out his hand for the gun. Stan looked confused, but handed it back to him. Roy ejected the magazine and slammed a fresh one home before handing it back to Stan. The kid looked confused, but took the now-loaded pistol back. He looked at it.

"It was empty?" he said.

"Yeah," Roy said. "But you didn't know that."

"What would you have done if I . . . ," Stan began, then shut up.

61

Taken the gun away and beat you to death with it, Roy thought, but didn't say. There was no need. Roy gestured toward the can on the post. "Try your luck," he said.

Stan raised his arm, holding the gun out clumsily in front of him. His arm trembled with the weight of it. The flat bang of the gunshot rang out, startling a wading heron into panicky flight before the sound was swallowed by the vast silence of the river. The can didn't move.

"Put just the pad of your finger on the trigger," Roy said. "If you curl your whole finger around it, the shot pulls to the right."

Stan raised the gun again and took aim. "Keep both eyes open," Roy reminded him. "Put the dot of the front sight between the two dots on the back sight. Focus on the front sight and lay it on the target. Squeeze the trigger, don't pull it."

This time, the can seemed to explode as the heavy caliber bullet tore through it.

"Can I try it again?" Stan asked.

"Sure," Roy said. They worked with the gun for another half hour, firing round after round against a succession of bottles and cans. Roy finally held out his hand for the gun.

"We got stuff to do before we leave," he said. "And then we got a ways to go."

"Where are we going?" Stan said.

"You'll find out," Roy said, "when the time's right."

Stan turned as he heard Laurel came out of the trailer. He was startled to see that her short blonde hair was now shoulder length and jet black. As she came closer, Stan saw she was wearing a cheap wig. She grinned at him. "Like it?" she said.

"Come on," Roy said. He headed for the trailer. Stan fell in beside him.

Inside, Roy hunted through a cabinet for a few moments before coming out with a box.

"Wait a minute," Stan said. "You're going to dye my hair?"

"No," Roy said. "Laurel is." She came inside and smiled at Stan. "And cut it, too," Roy told her. "First thing people look at is the hair," Roy said. "Most times, that's all they remember. Hair and height. So we change what we can."

"But why?" Stan said. He felt his voice rising with frustration. "I don't understand what's going on."

"Explain it to him," Roy said. "I'll be getting the van ready." He walked out.

"Sit down here, Stan," Laurel said. He sat. She got a pair of scissors out of the kitchen drawer. She took a tablecloth from a nearby cabinet. His shoulders tensed as she draped it over his shoulders.

"Relax, baby," she said. She began to cut. Stan saw tufts of his dark hair falling onto the whiteness of the tablecloth.

"Have y'ever noticed, Stan," Laurel said as she cut, "that every time you turn on the TV, there's something about a killer?"

"What?" he said.

"Like those sniper guys. Or that fella out in California that killed his wife and baby. They're famous, Stan. Ever'body knows them. People write 'em letters in jail."

"I guess," Stan said.

She bent down and whispered in his ear. "Killers are like movie stars in this country, baby. And we're gonna get us some of that."

Her hot breath on his ear was making him hard. "But I . . . I mean I never . . ." He was having trouble thinking.

"I know, baby," she breathed. "But you've wanted to. You wanted to kill your stepdaddy, didn't you?"

"I . . . I . . ."

"C'mon, you can tell me," she whispered. "I know what it's like, Stan. I do. So tell me. You wanted to kill him yourself."

63

"Yeah," Stan said. "I did."

"And I wanted him dead, too, Stan. I never met him, but I wanted him dead. And now he is," she said. "I made that happen, Stan. I wanted someone dead and now he's rotting on a slab somewhere. Do you have any idea how good that feels?" her hand stroked his neck sensuously. Then she kissed him lightly on the ear and stood up. "So what about it, Stan?" she said in a normal voice. "I guess you can still back out if you want. I can't guarantee that ol' Roy out there will understand. But say it now. Or never."

Stan's whole body was trembling. He felt like his head was going to explode. But then he remembered the feel of the gun in his hand, the look on his stepfather's face as Laurel shot him. Something seemed to give way inside him like a guitar string snapping. He suddenly felt very calm.

"I'm in," he said.

It was growing dark when they left the trailer. Stan drove, with Roy in the passenger seat and Laurel hanging over his shoulder from the back. Stan's black hair was now buzz-cut and dyed an improbable shade of blonde. He periodically ran his fingers over it, feeling the unaccustomed spikiness. Roy had done something with his own salt-and-pepper hair to turn it pure white. He had also placed lifts in his shoes that added at least three inches to his height.

"What I don't understand is why so far?" Stan said. "I mean, this place is, like, two hours away."

"I've done a lot of readin'," Roy said. "Cops have a lot of theories about . . . well, about people like us. They call it pro-filin'."

"Like in the movies," Laurel said.

Roy went on. "At first they'll look around at the people close by, hopin' we'll be workin' in what they call our comfort zone." His grin flashed in the semidarkness of the van. "But we ain't goin' to be like no one they ever seen before. We're gonna keep 'em guessing. Instead of them knowin' how we think . . ."

"We're gonna know how they think we think." Laurel giggled like a little girl laughing at an uncle's often-told joke.

They drove past a series of industrial parks, giant slab-sided metal buildings with cryptic names. Those gave way to roadside businesses, mostly auto-repair places and the occasional small grocery. Then they were in the country. Roy had his notebook on his lap, but he put it on the floor and began giving directions from memory. "Turn here . . . left here . . . straight . . ." They had left the main road by now and were wandering apparently aimlessly past bare harvested fields alternating with stands of trees. It was all the way dark by now, and the only lights this far out were their headlights and an occasional lone streetlight set on a post in a farmhouse driveway. Roy's directions were as sure and terse as if he were a harbor pilot navigating them into port. "Here it is," he said finally.

There were a number of vehicles parked outside the wooden building, mostly older sedans and pickups. Here and there, a newer and flashier pickup gleamed in the reflected light off the building, but most of the vehicles were sober, economical.

The building was a simple structure, a rectangle with a steeply pitched roof. It was painted a gleaming white made even brighter in the darkness by the spotlights pointing up from the ground. There was a plain square steeple perched on the roof. A lighted sign out front named the building as the FIRST CHURCH

OF GOD OF PROPHECY. Below were words spelled out in black plastic letters that slid into runners on the sign. FRIDAY PRAYER MEETING. 7:00 P.M.

Stan braked to a stop in front of the church's broad wooden doors. He killed the engine. He could hear a faint drone of sound in the stillness. After a moment, he recognized the sound of people singing. The sound was quickly drowned out by the metallic rattle of Laurel taking the guns out of the burlap that they had wrapped them in to mask them from people looking in. Stan heard the ratchet and click of the weapons being cocked. He looked at Roy, saw that flash of white teeth in the darkness.

"Show time," Roy said.

five

The Shelby house was a one-story modular home on a one-acre lot. There were a dozen similar modular homes on similar one-acre lots around a long loop of road off the main highway. All of the houses were neatly kept, with perfectly trimmed yards and shrubbery.

Shelby greeted them at the front door. He had swapped his coat and tie for faded jeans and a light blue sport shirt. "Come on in the house," he said as Keller and Marie mounted the steps.

Inside, the house was well lit and comfortable. The furniture was old but looked sturdy. There were sounds of barely controlled chaos coming from the kitchen, the clatter of pots and pans and the murmur of female voices.

"Supper's almost ready," Shelby said. "Y'all want somethin' to drink? Iced tea? Coke?" They both chose the tea and Shelby disappeared into the kitchen. It was Barbara Shelby who came out, bearing the tall iced glasses. Marie was surprised to see that she seemed considerably younger than Shelby, no older than her early thirties, pretty and blonde. "Hey," she said, smiling brightly, "Warren didn't say if y'all wanted lemon, so I left it out."

"That's fine," Marie said, taking the glass from her. "I'm Marie Jones."

"Oh, hon, you don't need to tell me who you are," Barbara said. "Warren's been talking about you practically nonstop. Sounds like you've got quite a future." Marie was wary for a moment; since coming to North Carolina, she had dealt with her share of Southern women who could fill just such friendly words with enough venom to knock over a buffalo, but Barbara Shelby seemed totally open and sincere. "And this," Barbara said as she turned, "must be Mr. Keller."

"Jack," Keller said, taking the tea glass with one hand and shaking hands with the other.

"Nice to meet you, Jack," she said.

Shelby came back into the room. "Honey," he said, "somethin's boilin' up on the stove."

Barbara gave a comically exaggerated eye roll. "And you of course," she said in a teasing tone, "couldn't figure out that the thing to do is turn it down?" She turned to Marie. "I swear, sometimes I think if it wasn't for us women, they'd burn the house down." She gave Shelby an affectionate peck on the cheek.

"Anything I can do to help get things ready?" Marie asked.

"Sure, hon, c'mon," Barbara said. "Whoever said too many cooks spoil the broth never had to feed this crew." Marie followed her into the kitchen. Once they were there, Barbara lowered her voice. "Girl," she said, cutting her eyes back toward the living room. "He is *gorgeous*. Where'd you find him? How'd y'all meet?"

"Actually," Marie said, "I was arresting him."

Barbara's eyebrows shot up and she grinned delightedly. "No," she said, laughter bubbling under the words. "You have *got* to tell me that story."

Marie laughed. "Maybe someday," she said. She found herself beginning to relax.

In the kitchen, two girls were putting out plates and utensils on the round dinner table. One was a teenager, with long red hair braided halfway down her back. The other looked to be about seven or eight. She was blonde and blue-eyed like her mother. "Girls," Barbara said, "this is Miss Jones. She works with your daddy. These are my daughters, Carmen and Jordan."

"I'm Carmen," the redhead spoke up. Marie caught a silver glimpse of braces in her shy smile.

"And I'm Jordan," the younger one said.

"Well, duh," Carmen said, rolling her eyes.

"Shut up!" Jordan said.

"*You* shut up, brat!" Carmen snapped back.

"Hush, both of you!" Barbara scolded. "We have company. Now help get this food on the table."

Within a few moments, the four of them had the table loaded and nearly groaning beneath the weight of platters of fried chicken, mashed potatoes, green beans, corn on the cob, and biscuits. Keller and Shelby came in, drawn by the smell of the food. Shelby introduced Keller to his daughters as they sat down. Jordan regarded him openly. "Are you a rock star?" she said.

Keller looked amused. "Not hardly," he said. "Why do you ask?"

She brushed her hand through her own short blonde hair. "You've got long hair like a rock star."

"Jordan!" Barbara said sternly.

Keller just laughed. "No," he said. "Not a rock star, sorry." Carmen looked like she wanted to sink through the floor.

69

"Since Mister Keller's our guest," Barbara said, "maybe he'd like to say the blessing."

Marie glanced at him. His face had gone blank and impassive. "Maybe one of the girls should do it," he said.

There was a brief uncomfortable silence, broken when Barbara turned to Carmen. "Carmen, honey, would you ask the blessing?" Carmen looked at Keller. Marie was amused to see a slight blush rise to her cheeks. The girl dropped her eyes. The rest of them did the same as Carmen stammered out a quick prayer of thanks. When she was done, the passing around of the food occupied everyone for the next few minutes. Then Shelby turned to Marie.

"I expect to be hearin' pretty soon about that overtime."

"Papa," Barbara Shelby spoke up. Her voice was soft, but there was a hint of steel in it. "I thought we agreed. No shoptalk at the table." Shelby looked abashed. Keller seemed fascinated by his plate. There was another silence, soon broken when Barbara turned to Marie. "Warren tells me you're from Oregon?"

"Yeah," Marie said. "Portland."

"Oh, I hear it's beautiful there." That broke the ice and they made small talk through dinner. Marie noticed that Keller seemed to have retreated back into himself. He was civil enough, but he answered all of Barbara's attempts to engage him with monosyllables. He kept checking his watch when he thought no one was looking. Marie felt a flash of irritation. *What the hell is wrong with him?*

After dinner, Barbara refused Marie's offer to help clean up. "You've been chompin' at the bit to talk to Warren about this case," she said. "Me and the girls'll take care of things. Now shoo."

"Okay," Marie said. She went into the living room. Keller and Shelby were looking at one of the framed pictures on the wall. It was a black-and-white, slightly yellowed around the edges. It showed a much younger Shelby, dressed in fatigues. He was in the middle of a group of a dozen other men dressed the same way. All of the men were smiling, some with their arms draped across one another's shoulders. A scrawled inscription in pen at the bottom read simply "Hué. January 1968."

"You still see any of them?" Keller was asking.

Shelby shook his head. "Lot of 'em didn't make it," he said. "Those that did . . . well, there ain't much to say after a while." Keller just nodded. Shelby glanced at him. "I reckon you know what I'm talkin' about," he said. Keller looked at Marie, his brow furrowed in irritation. "She ain't said nothin' specific," Shelby said hastily. "But she did tell me you were over in Saudi. An' I can tell somethin' in life's left a mark on you." He looked at Keller shrewdly. "Maybe more than one thing." He put his hand on Keller's shoulder. "After I got back," he said, "I spent a lot of my life tryin' to drown out what I saw over there. Drinkin', druggin', tomcattin' around. But I didn't find peace 'til I found Jesus. Or more like He found me." Keller said nothing. "I seen some terrible things, Jack," Shelby said. "An' I'll most likely see some more. But I believe God has a plan that we'll know, in His good time."

Keller turned to face him. "I'm glad you found that, Shelby," he said. "I just don't know that it's going to help me."

"It won't, Jack," Shelby said. "Unless you give Him a chance."

"Thanks, Shelby," Keller said. "I'll keep it in mind." He looked around. "Can I use your restroom?"

"Down the hall," Shelby said. "Second door on the left."

The preacher was the first to die.

He rose as the last notes of the hymn died away amid the rus-

71

tle of the crowd sitting down. The back doors to the tiny church swung open and he glanced toward the sound, the look of mild irritation at the latecomers turning to puzzlement, then consternation as he saw Roy and Laurel enter. Then his face dissolved in a wet mass of red as they opened fire on him at once. They were using the M-14s Roy had bought in Fayetteville. Roy fired from the hip while Laurel held the stock against her shoulder. Both rounds hit the preacher at the same time and tumbled him backwards from the pulpit. The congregation froze, shocked into immobility by the volume of the shots in the narrow space. The only sound that broke the deafening silence was the rumble of the preacher's body as he tumbled backwards off the steps of the high lectern. Then someone screamed. As if on cue, Roy and Laurel stepped to the sides, one behind each row of pews, and began firing into the back rows. Laurel took an elderly man in a black suit with a blue carnation in his lapel, the shot tumbling him brokenly over the pew in front of him. A plump man in overalls turned to face Roy and was blown backwards over the next row, his feet going comically up in the air. Chaos broke loose at that point. People began scrambling for the front of the church, clambering over pews and each other. The two began firing steadily, methodically, picking their targets, putting a single bullet into each before seeking and firing again. Their faces were keen and intent, the faces of two people working together on a complicated and intricate task. A knot of four people stumbled into each other and went down in a heap in the aisle. Roy killed each of them in turn as they struggled to regain their feet. A slender woman in a purple dress and flowered hat made it halfway down the aisle before running up against the obstruction of the fallen bodies. Unable to go further, she fell to her knees and threw up her hands as if pleading with God to spare her. Laurel shot her in the back of the head. A big man with his hair slicked back turned and tried to charge Roy. Roy shot the man through the throat. The man fell to his knees. Roy shot him again, this time between the eyes. The air filled with the smell of blood and cordite and then the acrid stench as the bladders and bowels of the dying let go. A few people made it to the door of the choir loft and escaped. Others made the mistake of seeking sanctuary on the altar. They died there beneath the eyes of the stained-glass rendering of the Good Shepherd. Finally, there was no one left inside the sanctuary but the killers and the slain. They moved forward then, in tandem, reaching down to search the pockets of suit coats and of purses. They ignored wallets and change purses in favor of cell phones. Each collected half a dozen. One man groaned in agony as Laurel turned him over. She pulled his bloody flip phone from a holster on his belt. Then she aimed the rifle at him and pulled the trigger. There was only a dry click as the firing pin snapped onto an empty chamber. "Shit," Laurel said. She pulled her automatic pistol from her waistband and finished the wounded man with a shot to the temple.

When the were done, they stood together for a moment and looked at their handiwork. "Let's go," Roy said finally. "Some of 'em got away. There'll be cops here soon."

"Just a minute," Laurel said. She turned and put a round through the stained glass behind the altar. Shepherd and flock dissolved in a kaleidoscope of colored shards.

Stan was behind the wheel, the engine running. He was tapping his fingers nervously as they walked out. Their legs and sleeves were spotted with gore and there was a streak of blood across the bridge of Laurel's nose like a stripe of war paint. A sudden flash of movement caught her eye and she turned and fired at an indistinct figure in a white shirt or blouse stumbling away through the darkness. There was a cry of agony and despair from the darkness and she smiled for the first time.

"Looks like I'm one up on you, Roy," she said as she slid into the backseat.

He grinned and shrugged as he took the shotgun seat. "That's show biz." He reached back toward her. "Hand me one of them phones."

"Uh . . . shouldn't we wait?" Stan said. "I mean if we call the cops now . . ."

"We ain't calling the cops, pardner," Roy said, still grinning. "We're calling the news." Laurel handed him a phone. "They get their shit together, we may get on the eleven o'clock."

"Wait a minute," Stan said. "Let me see that phone." Roy handed it over. Stan turned the phone over in his hand and looked at it. "I got a better idea," he said.

Keller put the toilet lid down and sat on it. He pulled his cell phone out of his belt holster and looked at the screen. He wondered if Oscar had found anything out. He started to hit the speed dial, then stopped himself. "I'm taking the night off," he said out loud. He stood up and moved to the sink. After washing his face in cold water, he dried himself vigorously with one of the thick towels hanging on the rack. He looked at himself in the mirror. *Something's left a mark on you,* Shelby had said. Keller shook his head. They were nice people. Normal people. Nice normal people having a nice normal dinner with friends. And Keller knew as certainly as he knew anything else that he didn't belong here. For the first time, that thought made him sad. He took a deep breath and went back out to the living room.

The atmosphere had changed. Shelby sat on the end of the couch looking glum. Marie's face was expressionless, but her lips were tight with anger.

"What happened?" Keller said.

No one answered for a moment. Then Shelby spoke up. "I just got a call from the major," he said.

He looked at Marie. Her expression said it all. "They didn't approve the overtime," Keller said. She nodded her head with one short angry jerk of her chin.

"I can talk to him again, Jones," Shelby said.

She shook her head and smiled at him. "Thanks, Shelby," she said softly. "But you know and I know it wouldn't do any good." She stood up. "I appreciate you going to bat for me," she said. "I really do."

Shelby stood up as well. "You're a good officer, Jones," he said. "There'll be other chances."

"Yeah," she said. "Maybe." She looked at Keller. "I guess we should go," she said.

"Yeah, okay," Keller replied.

"Now you don't have to—," Shelby began, but Marie cut him off. "I don't think I'd be real good company right now, sorry," she said. "But thanks again."

They got their coats in silence. Barbara Shelby came out of the kitchen, wiping her hands on a dish towel. "You're leaving?" she asked.

"I guess so," Marie said.

Barbara looked dismayed, but quickly recovered her poise. "Well, it was nice meeting you," she said. "Come back any-time."

"Thanks," Marie said. She walked over and gave Barbara a quick hug. "Sorry," she whispered.

"No problem, hon," Barbara murmured back. She glanced at Keller, who was getting his jacket out of the coat closet. She looked as if she was going to say something else, but just gave Marie's shoulder a quick squeeze before letting her go.

75

They walked in silence to Keller's car. Once they were inside, Marie slumped in the passenger seat. Her voice was tight with fury. "Couldn't spare a patrol officer," she sneered. "Can't justify the overtime. *Damn* it!" she said. She slammed a hand down on the dashboard. "Bet they'd have justified the overtime for a guy."

It was an hour and a half drive back to the coast. A few turns brought them to the main artery, Interstate 95, then down through long stretches of darkened country with no company but their own headlights and the looming silhouettes of trees beside the road. They drove in silence for a while, then Marie spoke up.

"The Shelbys are nice people," she said.

"Yeah," Keller said.

"I think Carmen has a crush on you," she said teasingly.

"Huh," Keller said. He didn't know how else to respond. After a few moments, Marie sighed. "It all seems so far away now."

"What does?"

There was another long silence before Marie spoke. "When I was growing up," she said, "my dad loved detective novels. He really liked this series about a guy named Travis McGee. You ever read those?"

"A couple," Keller said, wondering at the apparent change of subject. "There was this thing where they all had colors in the title, I remember that."

"Right," Marie said. "That's the one. Dad loved those. So I loved them too, because I wanted to be like Dad. I read all of them." Keller was silent. "Anyway, remember how McGee lived on this houseboat? Had all sorts of adventures. He got knocked around, shot at, stabbed, blown up . . . and in the end, he usually managed to kill the bad guy. And then . . . he'd go back to his boat, pour himself a drink, and next book he'd be the same guy. Same philosophical attitude." She chuckled. "Same kind of screwed-up attitude toward women, although I didn't notice that 'til later." The smile left her face. "But he was the same guy, even after he'd killed someone. Even after . . . even after he'd nearly been killed himself. He could go right back to being the guy he always was."

"Yeah," Keller said. "That's how it works in stories. But if someone really went through what those guys go through that many times, they'd be totally batshit crazy."

Marie fell silent. After a few moments, she said softly, "Is that what's going to happen to me?"

He glanced over at her. He could barely make out her face in the dim light from the dashboard. "No," he said. "At least I don't think so."

"You sure?" she said.

He thought of the images that still haunted him, the faces and screams of the dead. Marie had seen her partner die, killed by his own bad judgment. She had shot a killer in the back to protect Keller's life. He didn't want to think of Marie going through the same hell he had been through.

"You've got a lot to anchor you," he said finally. "Your dad. Ben."

He heard her shift in the seat, sensed that she had turned to face him. He kept his eyes on the road. "What about you?" she said. When he didn't answer, she went on. "My dad wonders if you'll be there for me."

He waited a few moments before responding. "I'm not going to lie to you," he said. "It's not something I've got a lot of experience in."

"I know," she said softly.

"All I can tell you is I'll try. I'll do my best."

She reached out and stroked the back of his neck gently. "Okay," she said. "That'll do for now." She paused. "Because I want us to be together, Jack. I want to be there for you, too. I noticed you didn't ask."

"Ask what?"

"If I was going to be there for you, too. Did you just assume it or are you afraid to ask?"

He shrugged. "I'm sort of taking this one day at a time."

"That's not an answer, Jack."

"Like I said, it's not something I have a lot of experience in."

"You mean trusting people," she said. "Is it because of what happened to you in the army?" she asked. "Or because your mom walked out on you?"

"Jacky." His grandmother's voice came from the kitchen. "Come eat something."

"I'm okay," Keller said, even though hunger was gnawing at his gut. "Mom said she was going to take me to McDonald's."

"You ought not eat all that greasy food," his grandmother said. The advice was delivered reflexively, without heat. Keller ignored it. The phone rang. He heard his grandmother pick up the receiver.

Keller looked back toward the kitchen, then back out to the driveway. He heard his grandmother pick up the phone. "Hello?" her voice took on a sharper tone. "Where are you? Well, why not?"

Keller leaned his forehead against the window and closed his eyes. There was a lump in his throat that made it hard for him to swallow.

"We've been waiting for two hours, Sheila," his grandmother said. "I don't care if you . . . I just think you should care more about your son . . . don't you talk to me like that . . ."

There was a silence, then the sound of the receiver being hung up. Keller heard the sound of footsteps as his grandmother came into the room. He didn't open his eyes.

"Come on, Jackson," he heard his grandmother say. He felt her hand, bony and delicate, on his shoulder. "Let's go to Mickey D's. You and me."

Keller choked back the lump in his throat. He knew if he let it go, it would burst out and let loose a flood of tears that would drown him, carry him away. "I'm not hungry," was all he said. His grandmother's hand stayed on his shoulder for a moment. Then she patted him once, twice, weakly, and she walked away.

Keller shook his head to clear it of the memory. "It wasn't the walking out," he said. "It was the walking back in at random intervals."

"I'm not her, Jack," she said. "I want to be with you. I want you to want to be with me. And Ben. I want." She hesitated. "I want us to be a family."

And there it is, Keller thought. The hope he'd given up long ago. And with the hope, the bone-deep fear that it was another illusion, that it would fall through again. A part of him was screaming to back away, to turn his back, to go back to the way he had been for so long. But then he remembered what that had been like. *The walking dead,* a friend had called it. He took a deep breath. "Okay," he said. "I want that, too."

"Really?" she said.

"Yeah. Really."

She leaned over and kissed him on the ear. "Good," she said.

Keller lived a few blocks from the ocean in a low-slung, flat-roofed cinderblock house in Carolina Beach. The house was undistinguished except for the huge live oak tree in the front yard. As Keller pulled up next to it, an SUV roared by on the beach road, rap music pounding from inside. A white teenaged boy leaned half out of the window and whooped drunkenly at them. Keller and Marie looked at each other and smiled, a little sadly. *Young and dumb and full of come,* Keller thought.

Marie spoke up as if completing his thought. "Must be nice," she said.

They were just inside the door when Keller turned and took her in his arms. She responded eagerly, her lips soft and yielding at first, then more demanding. She pulled his shirt out of his waistband, then her hands were everywhere on his back and torso, tracing the muscles with her fingertips, then pulling him harder against her. She broke the kiss and looked into his eyes as she slid one hand down to the front of his blue jeans. He groaned out loud as she began stroking him through the rough fabric. She smiled at that and began pulling his zipper down.

"Make love to me, Jack," she whispered hoarsely as she slid to her knees. He closed his eyes and savored the sensation of her lips moving on him for a few moments, then pulled her to her feet and kissed her. "Bedroom," was all he could say.

They began slowly, their hands exploring each other's bodies, each of them searching for the places that would make the other groan out loud, smiling when they found them. Then, suddenly, their lovemaking took on a desperate urgency. They clung to each other as if they were trying to save each other from drowning. Marie had cried out twice in orgasm before Keller felt his own climax approaching. "Please," Marie gasped. "With me . . . please . . ."

Keller felt as if the edges of himself were blurring, that he was expanding, dissipating, and then he was shouting, she was screaming, and he lost all sense of himself as they exploded together.

Afterwards they lay together for a long time, sweaty limbs tangled. They moved languidly, their hands still exploring each other, but gently, without haste. Finally, Marie raised her head and kissed him.

"Wow," she said, her voice rough.

"Wow," he said.

"It keeps getting better," she said.

"Yeah," he replied.

"Think of how good it's going to be ten years from now." She smiled. "Or twenty." She slapped him lightly on the hip. "Let me up," she said, "I've gotta pee." He rolled away and she slid out of bed. He stared at the ceiling. *Ten years,* he thought, *twenty years . . . Christ, I never expected to live that long.* He sat up and swung his legs over the edge of the bed. He rubbed his face with his hands. He got up, found his jeans, and pulled them on. He found his belt. His cell phone lay nearby where it had fallen from the belt clip. He stared at it for a moment, then flipped it open and hit the speed dial. The phone rang several times before Oscar Sanchez answered. "H & H Bail Bonds," he said.

"Oscar," Keller said. "It's Jack Keller. Have you found out anything on this Randle guy?"

"I found an address for him," Sanchez said. "And the fact that this man Randle has changed his name. He was born Roy Dean Clement, in Warsaw. Not the one in Poland, the one in North Carolina. He filed a legal name change in 1983."

"Anything else on the girl?"

"No," Sanchez said. "There was a juvenile court counselor who remembered the name. Also a Social Service lady at the courthouse . . ."

"But the records are sealed and they couldn't tell you anything."

"Correct."

"Okay, thanks, Oscar."

"When are you going there?"

Keller heard running water in the bathroom. "Maybe to-night."

There was confusion evident in Sanchez's voice. "But you are in Fayetteville . . . with Marie . . ."

"I'll call you," he said.

"I have the night shift," Oscar replied. "I will be here."

Keller closed the phone as Marie came out of the bathroom. She had found one of Keller's T-shirts and pulled it on. It barely covered the tops of her legs. "Oh good," she said. "You're more dressed than I am. Will you get my suitcase out of your trunk?"

"Sure," Keller said. He walked outside and fetched the case from the trunk. The night air was turning cool. It was getting late but the traffic on the beach road was still heavy. He looked out into the night. There was a jumper out there, waiting for the takedown. The knowledge nagged at him like an itch he couldn't scratch. He sighed and took the bag back inside.

Marie was seated on the couch. The TV was on and she was flipping through the channels. "Don't feel like sleeping," she said. Keller dropped the bag by the couch and sat down next to her.

"What's on?" he said.

"Nothing," she replied. She sounded morose.

"What's wrong?"

She looked startled for a minute, then smiled. "Sorry," she said. "I guess I'm still pissed off over this work thing."

Keller thought for a moment. An idea occurred to him. "I've got a jumper I need to go after," Keller said to Marie. "The sooner the better—maybe tonight. You want to come with me?"

Her lips quirked slightly. "It'd be better for me than brooding, is that what you're thinking?"

"Pretty much."

She sighed, then smiled. "You're right. Let's go."

"We'll need to go by the office first. Oscar has the info we need. You bring your weapon?"

"Yeah," she said. "It's in my bag. With my badge."

"It's not your jurisdiction," Keller said.

"Yeah," she said, "but your jumper won't know that."

"I've got a shoulder rig you can use that'll fit the Beretta," Keller said. "And a Kevlar vest. It'll be a little big on you . . . what?" Marie was chuckling.

"I was just thinking," she said. "I could write a magazine article. Dating experiences you'll never read about in *Cosmo*."

He laughed. "I can wait, you know," he said. "You don't have to do this."

"No," she said, "You're right. It's better than stewing over things. It helps to keep busy."

"That's the way I always handled it."

She looked at him with a wry expression. "And that worked, did it?"

"Not always," he said, "but it helps pass the time till you get better."

There was a large steel cabinet shoved back against one wall of the house's spare bedroom. Keller opened it with a key and took a stubby shotgun out. The next item was a leather shoulder holster. Marie walked into the room. She had put on a pair of black jeans and a burgundy T-shirt. He handed the holster to Marie. As she began strapping it on, he took out a black vest. He walked over and handed it to her. The words BAIL ENFORCEMENT were stenciled in yellow lettering across the back.

She handed it back. "You take it. You're going in first. I'm just along for backup."

"I've only got the one," he said. "I usually work alone."

"You used to," she said. "But you're getting better about that."

He slung the vest over one shoulder, the shotgun by its strap over the other. "Let's go."

They drove up the coast road, back into the city. Long rolling stretches of inland dunes gave way to a strip of car lots and cheap restaurants near the Port of Wilmington, then to shabby housing projects, then to tree-lined residential streets overhung with Spanish moss. When they got to the downtown area near the courthouse, the restaurants and clubs were in full swing, the illumination from neon signs glowing though the windows from the dimness inside. Clumps of people roamed the sidewalks.

The storefront that housed H & H Bail Bonds was lit, the sign in the window advertising 24 HOUR SERVICE. Oscar Sanchez sat inside behind the desk. He looked surprised when he saw Marie, but quickly recovered his composure. They embraced warmly. There was a clatter of footsteps on the back stairs as Angela came down from her small apartment above the office. She also looked surprised when she saw Marie.

"She's going with you?" she asked Keller.

"What can I say?" Marie grinned ruefully. "He knows how to show a girl a good time."

"What have you got, Oscar?" Keller asked.

Sanchez took a file and spread it out on a nearby desktop. "The address the Marks girl gave us was false," he said. "She has not lived there in some time."

"Right," Keller said.

"So I searched for property in the name of this man Randle. I searched property and tax records in both New Hanover and Brunswick counties."

"And?" Keller said.

"Randle owns a three-acre lot in a subdivision called River-woody."

Marie looked at the printout on top of the stack of papers. "I think that's just Riverwood, Oscar," she said. "Sometimes these developers stick on that extra 'e' to make it seem, I don't know, more English."

Sanchez looked confused. "But this is in English."

"Skip it," Keller said. "How do we find this place?"

Sanchez pulled out another sheet of paper. "I ran the directions on the Mapquest Web site," he said, "but here is the first strange thing. The address on the deed and the tax records is 100 River Lane. But there is no such street listed."

Keller took the sheet from Sanchez and looked it over. "You said the first strange thing. What else?"

Sanchez took another sheaf of papers from the file. "There are many judgments and lawsuits concerning the property."

"Ah," Keller said. "Probably the developer went belly-up, ran out of money, and they never officially opened the street."

"I see," Sanchez said. "That explains much. Many of the lawsuits are for bills not paid. But one was from the United States government. The Environmental Protection Agency."

"The EPA?" Angela said. "What's that about?"

Sanchez looked apologetic. "I do not know," he admitted. "Much of the language was not familiar to me."

"Don't worry, Oscar," Keller said. "If it's a lawsuit, it's not in any form of English either of us would understand."

"In any case," Angela said. "It looks like this guy Randle is the only one who has any property out there."

"Nice little hideaway," Keller said.

"Isolated," Marie agreed. "Glad you brought backup, huh?"

"Yeah," Keller said. "Let's go."

Grace Tranh pushed herself away from her desk in the newsroom and rubbed her face in her hands. She had been working for three hours and she still didn't have her piece finished for the eleven o'clock newscast. The problem was, there was only so much you could say about a county commissioner accused of misusing county funds to buy himself a bass boat. Her eyes flickered at the clock on her desk. 9:40. Shit. Her producer was going to start screaming for copy soon. She wished she was doing a stand-up report somewhere, anywhere. She knew the promotion to anchor of the Eleven was a huge boost to her career. But it was hard to work up any enthusiasm for composing narration to run behind shots of the errant commissioner waddling from his house to his car, shaking his fist at the cameraman.

She decided she needed a cup of coffee. First, though, she needed to check e-mail. The station had thought it would be a good idea to give each anchor and correspondent a "public" e-mail address which was shown beneath their name on the screen as they appeared on camera. The e-mail address was made purposely easy to remember: the correspondent's name and the station call letters. The idea was that it made them seem more accessible to the public. Besides, the station manager had said, beaming at them during the meeting in which he had announced the new policy, maybe they'd get some anonymous tips to big stories. So far, all Grace had gotten was a steady stream of proposals, some of them obscene; a fair number of poorly spelled racist diatribes directed at her Vietnamese heritage; and at least a dozen ads a day for penis enlargement. She sighed as the number of messages mounted on the screen. Rapidly, she scrolled through the list. Delete. Delete. Delete. Then a message header caught her eye:

From: jesusluvsu01@Imobile.com
To: GraceTranh@WPHJ.COM
RE: BIG STORY

There was a tiny icon of a paper clip next to the message header, indicating that the message contained an attachment, such as a document or picture file. She pulled down a menu on the screen. There were four attachments, all pictures: IMG001.JPG, IMG002.JPG, and so on. Grace sighed. Somebody probably thought their church ice-cream social should make the eleven o'clock. Still, she couldn't just blow them off. Someone might complain. She clicked on the icon.

The picture came up slowly, scanning line by line from the top. It looked grainy, like it had been taken with a cheap camera. She saw the cross, saw the altar, and shook her head. She'd been right. Then the bottom half of the picture came into view.

"Holy shit," Grace said.

six

"Huh," Keller said. The headlights of the Crown Vic shone off the steel cable blocking the road.

"What now?" Marie asked.

"Guess we walk," Keller replied. He turned off the engine and killed the lights. They got out and stood by the car for a few moments. Gradually, the blackness began to resolve into shadows, then to actual shapes as their eyes became accustomed to seeing by starlight. Keller opened the back of the car and took out the shotgun and Kevlar vest.

"That's not going to stop a knife," Marie warned him as he slipped the vest on. Keller had filled her in on Laurel Marks's history of violence as they were driving. While a bulletproof vest would stop a blunt, high-speed entry such as a handgun round, the more focused blow of the sharp tip of a knife had been known to penetrate Kevlar.

"I know," Keller said. "But she or this Randle guy might have a gun. And if she has a knife . . . well, that's where you come in."

"Great," Marie said. Keller took out a long black flashlight and handed it to her.

They walked down the road side by side. Darkness surrounded them. There were no other houses on either side of the dirt track. Cicadas buzzed in the trees around them and every now and then the groaning bellow of a bullfrog announced that they were close to water. The road suddenly widened and they stepped into the clearing. They could see moonlight shimmering on the river. The trailer loomed to one side. There was no light through any of the windows.

"Looks like no one's home," Marie said.

"Maybe," Keller said. "Or they heard us from up the road." He unslung the shotgun and advanced slowly. Marie drew her Beretta and walked behind and slightly to one side. When they reached the door of the trailer, Keller took up a position on one side. Marie crouched on the other. "Hand me the light," he whispered. She did. He reached up and tapped firmly on the door. Nothing. He tapped again. Still no response. "Laurel?" he called out. Nothing. Keller relaxed and Marie straightened up. He put a finger to his lips, then pointed to his eyes, finishing with a circular motion of his index finger pointed skyward. *Look around.* Marie nodded. She stepped away from the door and stole silently off into the darkness.

Keller edged slowly down the side of the trailer to the window. The curtains were drawn and he could see nothing. He stopped for a moment to consider, then walked around back. The windows there were also curtained.

He went back around to the front and stood for a moment, watching the front door and considering the situation. He played the flashlight over the dirt driveway in front of the trailer. He could see the tracks left by a large vehicle, a truck or van.

No lights, no vehicle, he thought. *Fuck it, no one's home.* He

89

glanced over to where Marie was standing in the tall grass. He saw her bend over to pick something up. He glanced back at the door. As a cop, she probably wasn't going to approve of what he was about to do. But one thing he had learned in the army was the old adage "Ask forgiveness, not permission." He slung the shotgun onto his shoulder and set the flashlight down on the trailer's rickety wooden steps. He reached into his back pocket and pulled out a small, flat leather case. He stepped up onto the steps and flipped the case open. He withdrew a pair of slender metal picks and set to work. It only took a few moments for him to pick the cheap lock on the trailer's front door. He slid the case of picks back into his pocket, then unslung the shotgun and turned the knob. There was a slight feeling of resistance as he slowly pulled the door open. Keller frowned and pulled harder, then yanked on the knob.

Marie stalked silently through the grass, looking right and left for signs of anyone hiding out in the overgrown area around the trailer. There was no sound other than the crickets and the bullfrogs. She straightened up and holstered her weapon. If the bugs and the frogs were raising this much hell in the grass, it was unlikely there was a human crouching there.

Ahead of her, she saw a cleared space. As she drew nearer, it resolved itself into a raised concrete slab. Someone had been building out here, then stopped for some reason. A glint in the moonlight caught her eye. She bent over to look. There was a spent shell casing on the slab. Her brow furrowed as she noticed several more scattered about. Someone had been doing some target practice and not policing up their brass. She picked up one of the casings and studied it for a moment. *Forty-five caliber,* she thought. She was going to drop it back onto the slab, but reflex stopped her. From her youth when her father had taught her to shoot, through her time in the military, then as a police officer, picking up her spent brass had become ingrained. She was sticking the shell in her pocket when the roar of a gunshot split the night.

Marie's head snapped around in time to see Keller being propelled backwards from the door of the trailer as if being shoved by a giant hand.

"*Jack!*" she screamed. *Oh dear God, please not again God, not again, not Jack, oh please . . .* She drew the Beretta from the shoulder holster and charged toward the trailer.

Keller was lying on his back, groaning. There was blood on his face and left arm. The door of the trailer yawned like the mouth of Hell, the stench of cordite searing her nostrils. Marie screamed, a banshee howl of rage. She raised the gun and fired blindly into the darkness. She fired again and again, screaming curses at the top of her lungs. She forgot fire discipline, forget anything but destroying whatever it was that lurked in that darkness. Finally, the gun was empty and she fell to her knees beside Keller's prostrate body, gasping for breath. She reached over him and picked up the shotgun. She held it trained on the doorway with one hand while she cradled his head with the other. "Jack," she whispered. "Jack?"

"Fuck, that hurt," Keller groaned.

Marie was weeping as she ran her free hand through his hair over and over. "You're okay, please tell me you're okay."

He tried to sit up, then fell back down with another groan. "I feel like I was kicked by a goddamn mule," he gasped. "I think I cracked a couple of ribs." He raised his head. "You get him?"

"I don't know," she said. "There's no movement."

Keller rolled over to his side. He used his arm to raise himself until he was sitting up. Marie could see the shredded and blackened fabric covering the Kevlar vest where it had absorbed the blast. "Give me the shotgun," he grated. She handed it to him. "Where's the light?" She crawled over to where the flashlight had tumbled off the steps. She flicked it on and turned it on the open doorway.

She saw a dangling scrap of wire hanging from the doorknob. As Marie played the light over the interior of the trailer, she saw the shotgun strapped to the chair inside.

"Trap-gun." Keller grunted, struggling painfully to his feet. "There's no one inside."

Marie stood up as well. She played the light over him. "You're bleeding."

Keller looked down. For the first time, he felt the wetness on his face and arm. "May have caught a couple of stray pellets," he said. He sounded remarkably detached.

"We need to get you to a doctor," Marie insisted.

"Yeah," he said. "In a little bit." He walked up the steps to the doorway.

"What are you doing?" Marie said.

"There may be something inside that tells me if Laurel's here," he said. "Or maybe where they've gone. I won't know till I take a look."

"Jack," she said, "you can't go in there."

He looked at her. "Why not?"

"What do you mean, why not?" she said. "Jesus, Keller, I *am* a cop. Or did you forget? You think I'm going to stand by and watch you break and enter?"

"I already did," he said. "Are you going to arrest me?"

"Damn it, Jack," she snapped. "Don't put me in this position."

He shrugged. "Do what you have to do," he said. His eyes were flat and expressionless, but his voice was hard with rage. "I'm going to catch these people. I'm going to bring Laurel

Marks in, and I'm going to find the fucker that set that trap-gun and I'm going to kick his ass." He turned on his heel and walked toward the trailer without looking back.

Marie stood and watched him go. His sudden brutal coldness had shaken her like the aftermath of an electric shock. All of the time she had spent with Keller had still left her unprepared for the times when the core of fury that burned in him was revealed. *This was mistake,* she realized. *I shouldn't have come.*

She saw a light come on inside the trailer, saw Keller's shadow on the curtains. She knew she should go in and try to stop him. But she honestly didn't know what he would do if she did. It frightened her that she didn't know. So she stood outside and watched.

Keller gave the trailer a quick once-over. There were two bedrooms at opposite ends, with a kitchen/dining room/living room area in the center. Both bedrooms had been recently occupied, the beds rumpled and unmade. Keller noted that there were men's clothes in the closet in one bedroom, women's in the other. A shelf in the closet with the women's clothes held a variety of wigs displayed on plastic head-shaped forms. One of the forms was empty. Keller rummaged briefly in the wastebaskets, turning up an empty box of hair coloring. He looked at it for a moment, sucking air through his teeth as he thought. A wig *and* hair color? He put the box down.

Keller walked back out to the living room. There was still a lingering smell of burned gunpowder from the trap-gun set in one corner. Bullet holes from Marie's gun pocked the wall. He looked at it for a moment, the pain in his ribs becoming more prominent and demanding of his attention as his adrenaline high wore off. He kicked the chair over. He still felt the burn of anger at the person who had set the deadly device, mixed with the familiar undercurrent of excitement he always felt when on the trail of a jumper. Then he thought of Marie.

Jesus, he thought. *What the fuck did I just do?* He had been so focused on his hunt that he had . . . *Oh, shit.*

As he came down the steps of the trailer, he saw Marie looking at him with an expression he couldn't interpret at first. Then he realized it was uncertainty, even fear. The realization almost broke his heart.

"I'm sorry," he said. "I, ah, was kind of an asshole."

"Yeah," she said, "You were. How're the ribs?"

"They'll heal," he said. "Look, Marie . . ."

"We'll talk about that later," she said. "You done here?"

"Yeah," he said. She didn't speak, but turned and began walking toward the car. He followed.

In the car, they sat for a moment without speaking. Then Marie spoke quietly. "I'm not sure I can take this, Jack."

"Look," Keller said, "I know I was out of line . . ."

"That's not what I'm talking about," she said. "At least that's not the main thing." She looked at him and he could see tears in her eyes. "I saw you get shot, Jack. I thought you were dead. And I started realizing, when you were inside there, that it's never going to stop. You're going to keep doing this, and nothing's going to stand in your way. Not me, not anything. Until somebody does kill you." She shook her head. "I love you, Jack. But I don't think I can stick around waiting to bury you."

"How about you?" Keller said. "You're a cop. And you of all people know what can happen to cops."

"Yeah. The difference is, Jack, that I don't take stupid risks. Sometimes I think it's almost like you're trying to die. Like you still feel guilty that all your men got killed and you lived."

"That's bullshit," Keller said.

94

She leaned over and kissed him. "I'm not making any decisions right now, Jack," she said. "But this is just . . . it's really
hard."

"I know," he said. "I don't know what else to say."

"Then don't," she said. "You want me to drive?"

"I'm okay," he said.

"Well, let's get to the ER."

"I, ah, don't think that's a good idea," Keller said. "People
might start asking questions. About what happened, and why
I'm wearing a bulletproof vest."

She threw up her hands. "Of course. So now we go home and
I get to tend your wounds."

"You don't have to . . ."

"Oh, just shut up, Keller." She sighed. "And give me the damn
keys."

They rolled through the darkness along the untraveled back
roads. Stan was still at the wheel. Roy sat in the passenger seat,
giving directions. They had doubled back and taken so many
side roads that Stan had no idea where they were. Roy, however,
seemed to have the route memorized.

"Tell me again what you did back there," Roy said. "With the
phone."

"It was one of those new kind of phones," Stan said. "It's got a
camera in it. And you can send the pictures by e-mail." He had
his eyes on the road, but in his mind's eye he was still seeing the
scenes inside the church: the bodies tumbled in the aisles,
crumpled on the steps of the altar . . . the sight had started him
trembling, turned him weak at the knees, until he had raised the
camera's tiny LCD screen to his eye to frame the shot. Painted
by the glow of electronic pixels, the bodies seemed tiny and far

95

away. It had taken him a few minutes to figure out which buttons to push, but he had kept the screen between him and the human wreckage sprawled on the thick carpet of the sanctuary. He couldn't distance himself from the smell, though; the sharp tang of cordite and blood still hung in his sinuses, leaving a taste in the back of his throat. He shivered.

"So who'd you send them to?" Roy said.

"Channel Ten," Stan answered. "That reporter. Grace Tranh."

Laurel leaned over the seat, her head practically on Stan's shoulder. "So how'd you know her e-mail address?"

"They put it on the screen," Stan said. "Whenever she's on."

Laurel began rubbing her lips against his ear. "A picture's worth a thousand words, hmmmm?" she whispered. "That was pretty smart, Stan." She snaked her arm over the other side of the seat to caress Stan's shoulder. She turned to Roy. "You mind taking the wheel for a while?" she asked. "I think Stan here deserves a reward for being so smart."

Roy's grin was a flash of white in the dim greenish illumination of the dashboard lights. "Sure," he said. "Pull over." Stan slowed, then steered onto the shoulder, the van shuddering to a stop as he braked on the rough surface. He barely had time to put the van in park before Laurel was pulling him out of the seat into the back of the van. There was a pair of sleeping bags spread out on the floor. Laurel dragged Stan down with her onto the bags as Roy started up again and headed into the darkness.

seven

"You sure I can't talk you into going to a doctor?" Marie said. She eyed the mottled flesh of Keller's chest and stomach, angry and dark purple where the shotgun rounds had slammed the Kevlar vest against the vulnerable tissue beneath.

"Nothing they can do but wrap me up," Keller said. "And I can do that for free."

"Or get me to do it," Marie said sourly. They were sitting on the couch in the living room. Marie had checked him over thoroughly and determined that there were no pellets lodged beneath the skin. The cuts and abrasions on Keller's bicep and face were either the grazing wounds of a passing hunk of buckshot or the result of being knocked to the dirt.

"You mind?" Keller said. "I've got Ace bandages and stuff. Bottom drawer in the bedroom."

She sighed. "I don't mind doing it. I mind seeing you hurt."

It reminded him of their earlier conversation. "Marie . . . ," he began.

She put a finger on his lips. "Hush," she said. "I'm not bailing on you."

He felt tightness in his chest that had nothing to do with the bruises. "Thanks," was all he could think to say.

She grimaced. "Don't get cocky, Jack," she said. "I meant what I said. I really have to think about this. But I'm not leaving you while you're hurt." She got up and went into the bedroom. He got up and poured himself a glass of water from the tap. He heard her rummaging in the chest of drawers. "Jesus," she said. "You've got enough stuff in here to stock an ER. Do you have a prescription for this? Wait, don't tell me. I don't think I want to know." He could tell from the timbre of her voice and the way she was rambling that the stress of the evening had her wired. She came back out with a roll of Ace bandages. "Turn around," she said. She was wrapping him gently in a protective cocoon of the flesh-colored gauze when her cell phone went off. "Shit," he heard her mutter from behind him. "Sorry, Jack, I have to take this." He felt the pressure on his chest relax and stopped gritting his teeth long enough to take another sip of water. "Hello?" she said. "Yeah, it's me. What? Right now? What's up? No. No I . . . I've been out." There was a pause. "Okay." She put the phone down for a second. "Jack, where's the TV remote?"

"On the side table," he said. She picked it up and flicked on the TV across the room. She turned it to a local station. The screen showed the last few seconds of a commercial for a used-car dealer before cutting to an Asian woman with an expression of professional concern on her beautiful delicate face. Marie turned the sound up.

"This is Grace Tranh, coming to you from the News Ten newsroom," the woman said in a perfectly modulated voice without a hint of accent. "We have an exclusive update on the massacre in a Duplin County church earlier this evening." She put down the paper she was holding and gazed earnestly into the camera. "We must warn you, what you are about to see is very graphic." The picture cut to a blurry photograph of the interior of a building. The anchorwoman continued in voice-over. "These photographs, believed to be made by the killer or killers, were e-mailed to the News Ten studios this evening." It took Keller a moment to resolve and sort out the jumble of objects on the screen. They were bodies, tumbled and mixed together.

"Oh, my God," Marie said. She sounded far away to Keller, as if she had suddenly receded down a long tunnel.

They had found him at dawn, wandering down the empty desert highway, disoriented and dehydrated. His first warning had been the growling whine of a big turbine engine. He stopped and stared dumbly at the unfamiliar lines of the armored vehicle that roared to a stop a hundred yards from him. It was smaller than his own Bradley, and wheeled instead of tracked, but the long snout of the automatic cannon that tracked toward him looked familiar. Slowly, he raised his hands above his head. There was a long pause. He heard the engine rev once, twice, as if the driver were nervously tapping his feet on the gas pedal. Then a hatch popped open on the turret. A helmeted and goggled head poked out and screamed something unintelligible at him. "I'm an American," Keller tried to yell back, but his throat felt as dry and cracked as old leather, and all that came out was a strangled whisper. The man in the turret crawled out and advanced on him, his sidearm held in front of him. As he got closer, he stopped and holstered it. "Holy shit," he saw rather than heard the man say. Suddenly, the desert was alive with other vehicles like the one in front of Keller, screaming across the desert like a pack of predatory dinosaurs. Keller swayed slightly in the wind and noise of their passing. The helmeted man walked up to him. "Who the hell are you?" he hollered through the noise of the maelstrom.

"Keller, Jackson L.," Keller croaked automatically. "Sergeant, serial number—"

"What the fuck are you doing here?" the man shouted. A Humvee painted like the desert squealed to a stop beside the armored car. Another man leaped out, dressed in desert camo. He wore the bar of a first lieutenant on his shoulder. He immediately began screaming at the helmeted man. "Dawkins," he shouted, "What the fuck is wrong with you? You stop to take a piss or something? God damn it, you get your ass back on that LAV and fucking—" He stopped as he really noticed Keller for the first time.

"Who the fuck are you?" he yelled.

Dawkins answered for him. "He was standin' here in the middle of the road," he said.

"My Bradley took a missile," he said. "We got separated—"

"A missile?" the lieutenant said, instantly alert. "Where?"

Keller gestured vaguely toward the desert. "Out there," he said. "They're all dead." He figured at that point it was okay to put his hands down.

The lieutenant seemed uncertain for a moment. Then he turned to Dawkins. "Get him on one of the five-tons," he hollered. "And get fucking moving!"

"He looks pretty bad off, Ell-tee," Dawkins said. "Maybe we should—"

"We'll find him a corpsman," the lieutenant said. "Later. Right now get him some water. I'm not falling behind!" He turned and stalked back to the Humvee.

Dawkins looked at Keller and shrugged. "Come on," he said.

A line of huge ugly trucks was backing up behind the armored car. At Dawkins's shouted instruction, Keller was pulled up into the back of one. The men along the benches lining the open cargo *bay eyed him suspiciously as a couple of them shoved over to let him sit down. Suspicious looks turned hostile as the already cramped quarters got even fuller with the addition of Keller's bulk. The men were dressed in the tan and brown "chocolate chip" camos, but their uniforms seemed plainer, less ornamented with patches and emblems than the ones he was used to.*

"Who the fuck are you?" a voice said. It was a question Keller realized he was going to have to get used to.

"Keller," he said. "First Cav."

There was a stir of disbelieving laughter. "Damn, Army," a voice beside him said. "You a long way from home."

Keller turned. The man beside him was holding out his canteen. There was a smile on his dark-brown face. "You look like you could use a drink."

Keller took the canteen. "Thanks," he said. He tipped the canteen up. The water hitting the back of his parched throat felt like life flowing back into him. It took everything Keller had in him not to drain the canteen to the bottom. He tried to hand it back, but the black man waved him off. 'Naw, man," he said, "I got plenty. Have a drink on the U.S. Marine Corps."

"Thanks," Keller said as he drank again.

The marine extended a hand. "Cyrus Johnson," he said.

Keller took it. "Jack Keller."

"So what happened to you, homes?" Johnson said. "You look like shit."

"My squad got lost," Keller said. "We got hit."

There was another murmur. "By what?" someone said. The men in the truck looked at him eagerly, hungry for information like any grunt.

"Helicopter," Keller said. "I heard the rotors."

The men looked at each other. With no Iraqi air power left to speak of, that could mean only one thing. They looked at Keller, then looked away. Keller looked at Johnson. He was shaking his head sadly.

"Boy," he said, "you got some bad motherfuckin' luck."

Keller heard another voice. Marie was speaking. "That was work," she said. "I've got to get back. Someone's shot up a church . . . Jack, what's wrong?" He couldn't answer.

No one spoke to him after Johnson's pronouncement of evil fortune. No one met his eyes. It was as if they were afraid Keller's bad luck might rub off on them. One of the marines had brought a boom box which he laid across his lap. He was playing Led Zeppelin. The grinding rhythms of "When the Levee Breaks" echoed through the confines of the truck. The marine with the box was rocking back and forth, his eyes closed, mouthing the words. "Goin' down," the lead singer wailed over a blues guitar that sounded like it came from some dark haunted hillside at the edge of the world. "Goin' down, goin' down now . . ."

"Damn, Franklin," Johnson complained. "Turn that weird-ass white-boy shit off. Play some jams, man."

The guy with the boom box opened his eyes. He gave Johnson a loopy, unfocused grin. "Come on, homeboy," he said in a Jersey accent. "This is some serious battle music." Johnson just shook his head disgustedly.

Eventually, the truck came to a halt with a clashing and grinding of gears. "All right you people," a voice bawled. "Un-ass that thing. Come on, Marines! Move! Move! Move!" Keller dismounted the truck with the rest of them. As they moved off together, Johnson gently took Keller by the shoulder.

"You best stay here, Army," he said. "You ain't even got a weapon."

Keller looked down in embarrassment at his empty hands. His weapon was back in his destroyed vehicle.

"He can use mine," a voice said. Keller looked up to see a tall lanky marine standing a few feet away. He had a strange-looking long-barreled rifle with a scope slung over his shoulder. He was holding out an M-16. "I'll be on the 40," he said, gesturing with his chin at the sniper rifle on his shoulder, "an' frankly, I'm tired of carryin' both these motherfuckers."

"Thanks," Keller said as he took the M-16. The sniper just nodded. They all moved out together.

Their objective was a low earth berm a few hundred yards away. There seemed to be no activity behind it, but they deployed by the book, fanning out and going prone. Keller flopped down beside the sniper and his spotter. They were scanning the berm through their respective scopes.

"I reckon nobody's home," said the sniper, but he kept his scope moving. The spotter grunted in agreement, but he kept searching as well. Squads moved toward the fortification in perfect synchronization, one pausing to cover the one advancing, then switching roles to advance while the other one covered. Nothing came from the berm. Finally, a lone marine crested the ridge. He paused for a moment, then straightened up and waved back to the rest.

"Fuck," the sniper said, standing up and spitting off to one side. "This shit is gettin' tedious."

The marines walked up to the berm in small groups, their former tension gone. Keller walked to the crest of the low earthwork and stopped.

The Iraqis had apparently been marching to their position when they were caught in the open by whatever barrage or bomb had found them. They had barely had time to even try to run.

*They were tossed about in untidy rows, some scattered, some piled
one on top of another. Some had landed faceup, what was left of
their features contorted in a silent scream of terror. Others had no
faces, no heads. Some bodies were without limbs, some limbs
without bodies. The marines and Keller stood silently regarding
the killing field.* "Fuckin' A," *the sniper said with satisfaction.*

"Get some," *the spotter agreed.*

Johnson clambered up on the berm beside them. "Da-yum,"
was all he said.

*Keller felt numb. He looked down inside of himself to try to
find some emotion. He felt like there should be some kind of re-
action to the deaths of so many men, both his own and the men
before him who had died in so much terror. There was nothing,
and it bothered Keller, but only vaguely. Then he did feel something, like a slight faraway throbbing in his head. It quickly got
louder, more insistent. Keller realized that it was coming from
outside and he turned.*

*A pair of slender deadly shapes was slicing through the air
some two hundred feet aboveground. The steady thudding was the
sound of the helicopter's rotors beating the air. It was then that
Keller felt something for the first time.*

Rage.

*A red curtain seemed to drop across his vision. He howled like
an avenging angel and raised the M-16. He began firing blindly
at the helicopters, the report of the rifle pounding in his ears like
the blood that was throbbing behind his temples. The marines
were screaming at him, then he was on the ground. Someone
was on top of him, struggling for the M-16. He felt an arm across
his face and bit down savagely. There was a curse of pain, then his
face seemed to explode in bright light, then darkness . . .*

·   ·   ·

"Jack?" he heard Marie's voice. "Jack, what's the—Oh my God!" He felt a sudden sharp pain in his hand and looked down. He had gripped the water glass so tightly that it had shattered. Blood flowed from a laceration on his palm. He stared uncomprehendingly at it for a moment before Marie was grabbing his hand and pressing a wad of gauze against the flowing wound.

"Jack," she said frantically. "Jack, please talk to me. What's wrong?"

He took the gauze from her and pressed it down to stop the flow of blood. "Sorry," he muttered. "I went away for a second."

"I noticed," she said. "You scared me to death. Your eyes . . . Jack, you had a flashback, didn't you?"

He nodded. "I'm okay," he said.

"That picture," Marie said. "On the TV . . ."

"Yeah," he said. "But I'm fine now. Really. What happened?"

"Some lunatic shot up a church out in the country. A lot of people are dead."

"They think it was terrorists?" he asked.

She shook her head. "No one knows," she said. "But everybody's going nuts. They're calling everybody to duty in case it is."

"Okay," he said. "I understand if you've got to . . ."

"I can't leave you like this, Jack," she said.

"I said I'm fine," he insisted.

"*BULLSHIT*, you're not fine!" she yelled. "This is me, Jack. The one who just made love with you. Remember? Don't keep playing this cowboy shit with me!"

He didn't answer.

"At least let me call somebody," she said in a softer voice. "Let me call Angela. Or Lucas."

He pulled the blood-soaked gauze away from his palm. "It doesn't look like this is going to need stitches."

Marie stood up. "Fine," she said wearily. "Everything's just

105

peachy. I'm okay, you're okay. Jesus." She stalked off into the bedroom. Keller got a fresh wad of gauze and began bandaging his hand. After a few minutes, Marie came out. She was carrying her suitcase. She walked over to him, bent down, and kissed him. She broke the kiss and looked into his eyes. "If you want to talk, I mean really want to talk, call me," she said softly.

"I will," he said. "Be careful."

She straightened up and picked up the suitcase. "Yeah," she said. "You too." She walked to the door. She stopped with her hand on the knob. "I really do love you, Jack," she said. "I wish you really believed that."

"I do," he said. "I do believe it."

She shook her head. "No you don't," she said. "If you did, you'd let me in. You'd let me help you."

"Marie," he said, but she opened the door and walked out. Keller sat there for a long time, watching the flickering images on the TV without seeing them.

eight

"Time for scene two," Roy said.

The bright yellow and green neon lights of the diner outshone all the others in the small cluster of buildings that huddled by the secluded off-ramp. The others were dark, lit only by the cold sickly orange light of halogen street lamps. The diner, though, lit the night with a radiance that could be seen from the highway. Even at this late hour, the place was crowded. Cars and pickups were nosed into the spaces in front, and Stan could see down one side of the building to the back, where the dark shapes of eighteen-wheelers loomed. Several were still idling, their engines huffing and grumbling like slumbering pachyderms so the drivers could catch a nap in the sleeper with the heat on.

"No cops?" Laurel said. "Usually there's cops, a late-night place like this."

"No," Roy said. "The cops go down two exits to the Denny's. They get free food there. This cheap bastard just gives 'em coffee."

"You really scoped this all out," Stan said.

Roy didn't answer. "Ready?" he said to Laurel.

She grinned at him, adjusting her wig so that it sat more evenly on her head. "Rock and roll, baby." She turned to Stan. "You want us to pick you up anything to go?"

Stan realized his stomach was growling. Then he realized she was joking. "Yeah, get me something," he jibed back. "A doughnut. Maybe a Danish."

"Just be ready to roll," Roy growled. He slid out of the passenger seat, cradling the M-14 in his arms. Laurel followed. Stan watched them go inside. There was a brief pause, then Stan saw bright flashes, one coming quickly after the other. He heard the muffled pop-pop-pop of the shots and saw a bright red liquid spray in a fan-shaped pattern across a front window. Another window blew out as a stray sprayed a glittering carpet of shattered glass onto the concrete walk by the door. Through the empty window frame, Stan could more clearly hear the screams and curses from inside. His heart was racing with excitement. He could see Laurel's face in his mind. Her eyes were bright, her lips slightly parted.

The gunfire stopped. There was a brief silence broken only by the muttering of the big trucks. Stan imagined Laurel inside with the little camera phone, recording their handiwork. In a few moments, she and Roy came running out of the building. Roy turned to fire once more as they reached the van. Laurel tumbled into the passenger seat. She tossed something wrapped in a napkin to Stan. "Here," she said. She was panting with exertion and excitement.

Stan started to unwrap it. "God damn it," Roy yelled. "Get going!" Stan stomped on the gas and wheeled out of the parking lot. "Down to the ramp," Roy ordered. "Head south." Stan obeyed.

When they were on the main highway, Laurel threw back her head and whooped out loud. *"Fuck,* that was *great!"* she yelled, laughter bubbling in her voice. "God, Roy, I love this. I fuckin' love it. Stan, baby, you have got to try this. It's such a rush."

Stan swallowed. "I want to," he said. "Next time, I want to . . . I want to do more than drive."

Laurel reached over and squeezed his knee. Roy didn't answer, but Stan could feel the older man's eyes on him from the backseat.

"You think you're up to it?" he said quietly.

"Oh, he can do it, Roy," Laurel bubbled. "I know he . . ."

"Shut up," Roy said. "I'm asking him."

"Yeah," Stan said. "I'm up to it."

"Eat your doughnut," Roy said.

Stan looked down. The napkin-wrapped object was still in his lap. He unwrapped it with one hand, the other on the wheel.

"There's blood on it," he said.

"Yeah," Roy said. The challenge in his voice was unmistakable. Stan looked in the rearview mirror. Roy was looking back into his eyes.

Stan's voice trembled slightly. "I don't wanna . . . I don't wanna get AIDS or something," he said.

"Everybody dies of something, Stan," Roy said.

Stan's eyes flicked back and forth from the road unrolling under their wheels to the minor. Roy's eyes were still there. Laurel was silent, looking uncertainly back and forth between them. A police cruiser careened by going in the opposite direction, light bar flashing.

He took a bite.

. . .

The ring of the telephone startled Keller out of his reverie. He picked it up. "Hello?" he said.

"How's it going, Keller?" a deep bass voice replied.

"Lucas," Keller said. "Marie called you."

"Haven't lost that keen sense of deduction, I see." Keller gritted his teeth and didn't answer. "Don't be mad at her, son," Dr. Lucas Berry said. "She cares about you. And I *am* your doctor."

"I'm okay," Keller said. "I had a flashback."

"All right," Berry said. "I'll ignore the contradiction in those two statements right now. Tell me what you saw."

Keller closed his eyes. "I was back with the marines."

"The ones who picked you up."

"Right. We came on an Iraqi position. They moved in on it, but everyone there was already dead. There were bodies . . . ." He stopped for a moment. It was suddenly hard to breathe. "There were bodies everywhere. They were . . . scattered around. And then the choppers came."

"You remember the helicopters," Berry said. "Interesting."

"Why is that interesting?"

"I'll tell you in a minute," Berry said. "Go on. What happened with the helicopters?"

"I, ah, I started freaking out," Keller said. "I started shooting at them."

"Yeah, you did," Berry said. "It took four Marines to take the weapon away from you. And what happened then?"

"That was it," Keller said. "I was holding a glass in my hand. It broke."

"You cut yourself?" Berry said.

"Yeah," Keller said. "It's not serious. I bandaged it up."

"Mmmm," Berry said. "Now what's interesting to me about that flashback is that it's the first time you've actually remembered what happened at the berm. Even when I first started treating you in the army, you'd blocked that out."

"I know," Keller said. "What does it mean?"

"Damned if I know," Berry said. "It could be a major breakthrough. It could mean you're about to crack up completely."

"Great," Keller said.

"Don't worry, son," Berry said. "If I thought you were in danger, I'd be signing commitment papers right now."

"You're a real pal."

"No," Berry said. "I'm your doctor. So tell me, what was the trigger? What were you doing at the time?"

"I was watching TV," Keller said. "There was a story on the news about the church massacre."

"Ah," Berry said. "The pictures. The ones the killers took."

"Killers?"

"Yeah. I've been watching it, too. They talked with some of the survivors. The cops think there were at least two. A man and a woman. So that was probably the trigger. Anything else you can think of?"

"Well," Keller said. "I got shot tonight."

There was a long pause. "Yes," Berry said in a dry voice. "That might very well have a bearing on things. You want to tell me about it?"

"This is privileged, right? Even though it's not your regular job?" While Berry had been treating Keller off and on for years, both in the army and afterwards, his primary practice since his retirement was running a drug-and-alcohol treatment center.

"Yeah," Berry said.

"Okay," said Keller. "I was checking out a trailer where I thought a jumper might be holed up. I, ah, kind of gained entry."

"You broke in."

"Yeah. Anyway. They'd set a trap-gun. A shotgun wired to the door. But I was wearing a Kevlar vest. I just got some bruised ribs."

"This is why it's so much fun treating you for post-traumatic stress disorder, Keller. Most of my patients try to *avoid* life-threatening situations." He sighed. "Okay. Well, the first thing I can tell you is don't be watching the news anymore right now. They're showing those damn pictures every ten minutes. Second, come see me tomorrow. At the center."

"I'm feeling better," Keller said. "Besides, I'm still after this jumper. I've got some work to do."

Berry sighed. "Then there's no use trying to talk you out of it. I know that much. Well, you've got my number."

There was a flash of headlights through the window. Someone was pulling up in the yard outside. "Somebody's here," Keller said.

"Probably Angela," Berry said. "Marie said she was calling her, too."

"Damn it . . ."

"People care about you, Keller," Berry said. "You might as well get used to that. It has certain advantages."

"Okay," he said. "Okay." He got up to answer the door.

"I'm writing you a prescription, Keller. You don't have to take it, but I'm recommending it."

"I don't—"

"I know, I know. You don't like meds. But if you change your mind, call. I can phone it in. It's there if you want it."

"Yeah, okay," Keller said. "Thanks, Lucas." He opened the door as Berry broke the connection. Angela was standing on the front steps, a plastic bag in her hand. Oscar Sanchez was behind her, leaning on his cane. There was a paper bag in his free hand.

"I figured you wouldn't be getting any sleep," Angela said, holding up the plastic bag. "So I brought videos. No war movies, though."

"And I brought beer. And the makings for *empenadas*," Sanchez said. "If you are hungry."

Keller leaned in the doorway. "You guys don't have to do this," he said.

"I know we don't," Angela said. "Now invite us in."

They sat together in the living room, eating, drinking, and watching movies, Angela or Keller occasionally piping up to explain some Americanism to Sanchez or crack a joke about some particularly absurd plot point. Gradually, as the night wore on into the early morning, the intense jittery feeling that Keller often had after a flashback subsided. He stopped seeing the images behind his eyelids whenever he closed his eyes. He noticed that Oscar was yawning and stretching.

"Oscar," Keller said. "Why don't you crash in the spare bedroom?"

"I am all right," Sanchez insisted. "I want to help."

"You have, buddy," Keller said. "The food was great."

"Go on, Oscar," Angela said. "Grab a couple hours. Somebody has to be awake when we open tomorrow." When he looked doubtful, she said, "I'll be in to join you in a little bit."

He smiled at that. "Okay," he said. "Good night, Jack."

"G'night, Oscar," Keller said. "And thanks again."

As the door closed behind Sanchez, Keller looked over at Angela and cocked an eyebrow.

"Don't start, Keller," she warned.

"What?" he said innocently. "I'm glad you two are, um . . ."

She sighed. "We're not, actually. I mean, we're sleeping together, but we're not, you know, sleeping together."

"Wow," Keller said. "I knew he was a good guy, but . . ."

"He's so sweet," Anglea said. "And I'm so . . . I don't know." She took a pull on her beer. "I haven't been with a man since . . . since my husband." She gave a short, harsh laugh. "I'm not sure I remember how."

"I think it'll come back to you."

"You're a funny man, you are," she said. "Plus, there's . . ." She trailed off.

"The scars."

She nodded. "He says he doesn't mind. He's . . . well, he's seen some of them. And God knows, I'm used to them. But I don't know if a man can ever look at me . . . that way again. I'm afraid."

"Afraid he'll be . . ." He let the words trail off.

She nodded again. Neither of them said anything for a long time. Finally Keller said, "I guess you'll never know till you try." He took a drink. "I've been there, too. I was afraid no one was ever going to care about me because I was so fucked up inside. Sometimes I'm still afraid. But there were people who took their chances on me. You. Then Marie. They took their chances with you, you need to take yours. If that makes any sense."

She smiled. "A little."

He smiled back. "I'm starting to ramble."

She laughed then. "A little. Maybe you're tired enough to sleep."

He stood up. "Maybe. But first I need to make a phone call."

She stood up as well. "Okay," she said. "Sleep well."

"You too."

He went into his room and locked the door. He pulled out his cell phone and hit the speed dial. Marie answered after two rings.

"How's it going?" he said.

"Total cluster-fuck," she said. "There's been another multiple shooting. A diner up on I-95. They've called every officer in. But nobody seems to have thought much beyond that."

"I thought after 9/11 everyone had a plan for stuff like this."

"They do. It's in a big binder and everything. But the binder's locked in a cabinet, and no one can find the guy who has the key." Her voice softened. "How are you?"

"Better," he said.

"I thought you were fine before," she said. There was an edge to her voice.

"Thanks for knowing better than that," he said. "And thanks for calling Lucas. And Angela. She and Oscar are here." He took a deep breath. "I'm sorry I shut you out."

"Just quit doing it, okay?" she said.

"Okay," he said. "Be careful."

"I will. Love you."

"I love you, too," he said and broke the connection. He took off his boots and lay on the bed staring up at the ceiling. After a while he drifted off to sleep.

nine

The sun was rising when they got back to the trailer. "Something's wrong," Roy said as they pulled up.

"What?" Stan said. He was feeling sick and shaky again. He wanted some more of the meth. It took the place of the adrenaline rush. He thought could still taste the blood in his mouth, but maybe it was his imagination.

Laurel poked her head up front. "Shit," she said. "The door's open." She pulled the .45 out and racked the slide before reaching back and handing one of the rifles to Roy. "Stay here, Stan," Roy said as Stan took the other rifle from Laurel's hands. "Cover us," Stan opened the van door and trained the rifle on the half-opened trailer door as Roy and Laurel got out of the van. They approached the trailer slowly, warily. Roy gently nudged the door the rest of the way open with the barrel of the M-14. Stan could see the remains of the silver wire dangling from the doorknob. Roy went inside. Laurel followed. Stan didn't know what to do. It seemed as if there was no one there. But Roy had ordered him to stay. Had they forgotten him? Stan fidgeted for a moment. *Fuck* it, he finally thought. He got out and went inside.

The faint sharp stench of gunpowder greeted Stan as he walked in. He saw the shotgun still strapped to the chair, but the chair was lying on its side. There was no one in the living room. There were holes in the wall that hadn't been there before. Bullet holes, Stan realized. "Roy?" he called out softly. "Laurel?" he raised the rifle and walked down the hall into Roy's bedroom.

Roy was kneeling on the floor, crouched over in almost a fetal position. He had his face hidden in his hands. The knuckles were white with strain. Laurel knelt beside him, her arm around him. There was a panicked expression on her face.

"What's wrong?" Stan asked frantically.

"He has these spells, sometimes," Laurel said. "Headaches, like, but worse than a regular one. It happens more often when he gets real stressed."

"Oh, great," Stan said. "And we were letting him drive?"

"Hey," Laurel said. "Show some fuckin' compassion. The man's in pain here."

Roy looked up. His face was gaunt and lined with pain. He suddenly looked a hundred years old to Stan. "I'll be okay," he croaked in a ghastly voice. "It'll pass in a few minutes." He staggered to his feet.

"Somebody triggered the gun," Stan said. "And there's bullet holes in the wall. But there's no blood."

"No shit," Roy said. He lurched into the bathroom. Stan heard him turn the water on.

"But there's no sign of the cops, either," Laurel said. "So maybe it was just some burglars. They didn't want anybody to know they were here, so they took whoever got shot with them."

"Maybe," Roy said as he came out of the bathroom. He was wiping his face with a towel. "But there's still no blood. No sign

117

anybody got shot." He pulled a suitcase out of the closet. "Go pack up. We're gettin' out of here."

"Where are we supposed to go?" Stan said.

"Come on, Stan," Laurel said, taking his arm. "We got a backup place. We weren't supposed to be goin' there just yet. But I don't like this, either. There's somethin' weird goin' on here."

Marie grabbed a chair in the third row of the briefing room. *Finally,* she thought, *we're getting sorted out.* The sheriff himself had arrived shortly after her phone call to Keller. Asses had been chewed. Supervisors had been informed that their jobs were on the line. Before long, order had been restored to the sheriff's department. The buzz of conversation died as Major Simmonds, the chief deputy, stepped to the podium.

"At approximately 1930 hours last night," he began, "a church in Duplin County was attacked by two armed subjects, a white male and a white female. There were multiple casualties, with fourteen people confirmed killed." The low rumble of conversation began again. "Listen up, people," Simmonds snapped. The rumble quieted. "At approximately 2145 hours, a late-night diner off of Interstate 95 was also attacked by two subjects, again a white male and white female, who appeared to be using the same type of weapons, namely military-style assault rifles. It is believed that there may have been a third subject, race and gender unknown, who was acting as driver in the second incident. The subjects left the scene in what survivors described as a white van, make and year unknown. Due to the similarities in weapons used and the general description of the subjects, the incidents may, I repeat may, be linked. The State Bureau of Investigation is working on the ballistics at this time." He shuffled some papers on the podium. "At this time, authorities do not believe that this is an act of foreign terrorism. However, an FBI team is on its way to both scenes to investigate." After Simmonds's earlier rebuke, no one dared speak, but the looks on their faces as they glanced at each other were eloquent.

Simmonds looked up. "The subjects are still at large. We do not know if they plan to act again. Therefore, you are to use extreme vigilance. Also, I want you people highly visible. You will be kept apprised of developments as they occur." He picked up the sheaf of papers and made as if to exit the podium. Hands shot up all over the room. Simmonds looked annoyed. A former pro-football player, he had been handpicked for the chief deputy position, heir apparent to the sheriff himself, largely because of his presentability on television and at political fund-raisers, where he could deliver a pre-scripted speech with the best of them. Thinking on his feet, however, was not his strong point. "I didn't ask for questions," he said ominously.

"What weapon?" some bold soul called out.

"What?" Simmonds said. His face was beginning to redden.

"Are we facing down people with machine guns out there?" someone else piped up.

"Does it make a difference in how you do your jobs?" Simmonds demanded.

"You damn right it does," a deep voice said. There was a ripple of nervous laughter.

Simmonds looked close to apoplexy. "You'll be kept informed of developments as they occur." He walked out.

"Well, that'd be a first," a stocky deputy in the row ahead of Marie muttered.

A lanky blonde deputy with a hint of moustache on his upper lip spoke up. "I heard they was using weapons stole from Fort Bragg," he offered.

Marie turned to look at him. "Where'd you hear that?"

"I got a cousin works there. They got the whole place locked down and CID guys are crawlin' all over everbody." He was interrupted when another deputy took the podium. In a tense voice, he began reading off assignments. When he was done, he looked up.

"Be careful out there, folks," he said. It was a standard end to a briefing, but this time it was delivered with more than the usual sincerity.

The murmur of conversation was muted as they got up to leave. Marie noticed Shelby leaning against the back wall talking to another detective. She walked over.

"Hey," she said.

"Hey," he replied. He looked slightly embarrassed. The other detective said his good-byes and walked off.

"Don't feel bad, Shelby," she said. "I know you tried."

He seemed to relax slightly. "Yeah, I did. Sorry it din't work out."

She shrugged. "Guess they're going to really be paying some overtime now."

He laughed. "I guess."

She dropped her voice slightly. "So what's this I hear about these people using military weapons?"

He looked around. "Nothin' confirmed, now," he said, "but it does look like some of the guns they was usin' might've come from Fort Bragg."

"Tell me they don't have machine guns, Shelby. I've been shot at with those, and it's not a hell . . . sorry, it's not a lot of fun."

He shook his head. "Naw. No full-auto stuff. An' like I said, these were older—Vietnam-era. Some M-14s and at least one .45-caliber pistol. One of them used the .45 to kill one of the victims in the church, execution style."

"Wait a minute," Marie said. "Wasn't that guy that was shot in the service station killed with a .45?"

He furrowed his brow. "Yeah, but there's a lot of .45s out there."

"Just a thought," she said. "I mean, we're right next to Bragg. Maybe somebody picked themselves up a new toy and wanted to try it out."

He nodded. "I'll have a look. SBI's got all the bullets on the church and diner shootings. But I'll fax 'em the photos we got on the bullet from the gas station shooting. Couldn't hurt."

"Yeah," Marie said. "Well, I've got to get on the road."

He nodded. "Be careful," he said seriously. "I'll keep you in my prayers."

"Thanks," she said. "I'll take whatever edge I can get."

ten

Keller awoke to the sound of clattering dishes in the kitchen and the smell of fresh-brewed coffee. He sat up and stretched, then winced at the pain in his ribs. He took off his shirt and looked at himself in the mirror. His chest was still badly bruised, an archipelago of angry purple marks. He became aware of another sound from the kitchen. He had trouble making it out at first. Then he smiled as he realized what it was. Someone was whistling.

He went out to the kitchen. Sanchez was putting away dishes.

"You didn't have to do that, Oscar," Keller said.

Sanchez smiled, the first genuine smile Keller had seen from him in quite awhile. "It is no trouble. I was up anyway. There is coffee if you want."

Keller poured himself a cup. "Sleep okay?"

"*Sí,* quite good," Sanchez said. Keller smiled as he took a sip of the coffee. The smile left his face as he tasted it.

Sanchez looked dismayed at the look on Keller's face. "It is not good."

"It's fine," Keller choked out. "It's just a little, ah, stronger than I expected."

Sanchez grinned mischievously. It made him look years younger. "You will get used to it," he said. "It will put the hair on your chest."

"And strip the enamel off my teeth," Keller muttered.

"I see you've discovered Oscar's coffee," Angela said as she walked in. She went over to Sanchez and hugged him. "Good morning," she murmured.

Sanchez looked hesitantly at Keller, then hugged her back. "Good morning," he said. She kissed him lightly on the cheek.

"Jeez, get a room," Keller teased.

Angela picked up a dish towel and threw it at him. "Shut up, Jack," she said, but she was smiling, too. Sanchez looked distinctly uncomfortable. "Now look what you've done," Angela said. "You've made Oscar blush." She kissed him again, then gave a final squeeze and stepped away. "I can make breakfast, if you've got anything to fix," she said. She opened the fridge. "Hmm. Guess not."

"Sorry," Keller said, "but this coffee'll probably keep me going through dinner." He took another sip. "Actually, it kind of grows on you."

"Stick to one cup," Angela warned. "Two, and you get so wired you start gnawing down trees like a beaver."

"If you do not like the coffee—," Sanchez began, but was cut off by their laughter. Finally, he smiled. "You Americans are just not used to coffee the way it should be made. You are . . . what is the word . . . wimpy?" They laughed again at that.

"Okay, tough guy," Angela said. "We need to get to work."

"Me, too," said Keller.

"I don't suppose it'd do any good trying to talk you out of going after Laurel Marks again," Angela said. "That boyfriend of hers, the one who set that trap gun, is shaping up to be a class-A nutball. Who the hell sets up something like that?"

"I'll ask him when I find him, if they're still together," Keller said.

Angela sighed. "Okay," she said. "So what's your plan?"

"You said she had parents in the area. Maybe I'll try and talk to them."

"From the way she talked, they're not exactly on good terms."

"Yeah, but she's on the run. If she gets scared enough, she might turn toward home."

Angela nodded. "Maybe."

"Plus," Keller said, "A guy I know works out at the studio. He's been there since the beginning and pretty much knows everybody. He may be able to tell me something about this Randle character."

"Sounds like a plan," Angela said. "Just don't go opening any more strange doors."

"Got it," Keller said.

Laurel and Stan had packed and were waiting in the van. Roy stood in the living room, staring at the posters on the wall over the couch. The face that stared back at him was that of a handsome young man with lank black hair half covering his face. The young man's eyes burned with an intensity that wasn't all from photo retouching. Roy ran his fingers lightly over the paper, remembering.

He had been flying high that day, a half gram of Peruvian flake hoovered up his nose over the course of the afternoon. It was another one of those days on the set when it looked like nothing was going to happen. The shoot had been plagued with accidents and dissension; several cast and crew members were heard to mutter only half-jokingly that the whole project was cursed.

Roy and some of the crew had been languishing for hours while some obscure script point was worked out. Someone had broken out their stash and before long, they were all bright-eyed and jabbering. After a while, the energy level got too high for them to stay inside. They spilled out of the metal door of the soundstage into the bright sunlight, blinking like coal miners come up from the earth. The set design was dark and gloomy, almost Gothic, and the sudden transition made some of them laugh out loud as if they were nervous.

A cry split the air above them. Roy looked up, shading his eyes against the sun. A pair of seagulls wheeled and beat the air above them.

"Fuckin' birds," one of the stagehands muttered. "I hate those goddamn things." The birds always seemed to be drifting in from the nearby beaches, possibly to feast on the dumpsters behind the cafeteria. They were universally despised for their apparently un-erring aim in fouling sets, cars, and the occasional slow-moving human.

Roy had an idea. "Get one of the pistols," he said. "The real ones. Get the .44."

"What for?" the stagehand said, wiping his running nose with the back of his hand.

"Ain't nothin' in 'em but blanks."

Roy grinned. "Just get it."

They were waiting for him in an uncertain group as he walked onto the wide expanse of the back lot. He was carrying the box of bullets he kept in the trunk of his car. He took the gun from the stagehand and flipped the cylinder out. He began loading.

"I don't know, man," one of the lighting techs said. "This doesn't seem like . . ."

"FUCK!" the stagehand screamed as Roy raised the pistol and fired. One of the seagulls exploded in a cloud of blood and feathers. The rest of the birds took off, screeching in panic. Roy fired again. This time, he was firing at them on the wing. He missed.

"Let me try that," one of the lighting techs said, his eyes bright.

"Asshole," Roy said clearly as he took his hand off the poster. "You were all doin' it too. Same as me. Asshole." He took a cigarette lighter out of his back pocket and flicked it on. Roy applied the flame to the poster where one edge curled up slightly. The aged yellowing paper caught quickly, dark smoke and red-orange flame quickly climbing up the young man's face.

He had awakened the next morning to the sound of the phone. He flailed blindly, searching for it. His head was throbbing so badly that he could actually feel the ringing like a jackhammer inside his head. Finally he made contact and picked it up. "Yaaah?" he croaked. His throat was desert-dry.

The PM's voice on the other end was frantic. "Randle," he said. "There's been an accident. On the set."

Roy sat up and rubbed his face. "Huh?" he responded.

"Did you take out one of the guns? The .44?"

"Ahh . . . yeah," Roy said, still too muzzy-headed to lie. "I took it back, though."

"Fuck, Roy," the PM said. "This is bad, man. This is really bad. Look, don't talk to anybody, okay? Just stay home. Don't come to the set." The line went dead.

The room was filling with smoke. Roy applied the lighter flame to the other poster the same way. The fire raced up that one even faster than the first. Roy didn't look back as he walked out the door.

eleven

The house was set well back from the street, landscaped with tall bushes that screened it from sight of passing traffic. It was a single story 1970s-style structure with a flat roof and many tall picture windows that gave the impression that the house was mostly made of glass.

Keller sat in the drive, his cell phone to his ear. He heard the familiar click and tape hiss on the other end, followed by a woman's voice. He sighed. He had the message memorized. At the beep, Keller said, "Mr. or Mrs. Marks, this is Jack Keller again. I'm calling about your daughter Laurel. I need to speak with you." He gave the number and snapped the phone closed. Normally, he would have just shown up at the parent's house, but when he had checked the address, the place was behind the blank walls of a gated community. He was surprised at that. Knowing what he did about Laurel, he wouldn't have expected her to come from money. He was obviously getting nowhere by calling, though. He'd have to figure out some way to pay a visit, after he talked to Burke.

Burke answered the door at Keller's knock. He was tall and stocky, with big arms and a slight paunch that strained at the belly of his black T-shirt. He had a round face and bright blue eyes that peered out from behind his granny glasses. "Hey," he grunted, then turned and walked back inside.

"As you can see, my husband's still the soul of grace and charm," Burke's wife Gala said in a fondly exasperated voice as Keller followed him into the front hallway. She was almost as tall as Burke, but slender, with thick, curly, light-brown hair that tumbled to the middle of her back. She smiled warmly at Keller, then hugged him. Her smile turned to a look of dismay when Keller grunted with pain.

"Jack," she said, releasing him. "You're hurt. And your hand! What happened?"

"Nothing bad," Keller said. "Just some bruised ribs. And I cut my hand when I broke a glass."

She took him by the uninjured hand. "Come in here and let me see."

"I'm fine, Gala—," Keller began, but Burke cut him off.

"Give in, Keller," he said. "You're not going to get a second of peace 'till she's done with her medicine-woman routine."

"Hush, Peter," Gala said. She led Keller toward the living room. "Sit on the couch and let me see your hand first."

"I'll be in the back when you get done," Burke said as he walked off.

"He's working on some medieval epic," Gala said as she un-wrapped the bandage on Keller's hand. "And the idiot director keeps demanding that Peter change things at the last minute. 'More blood, more blades, more gore.'" She shook her head. "Jackass." She studied the cut on Keller's hand, her brow furrowed. "We can put some aloe vera on this. It'll heal faster. Now let's see those ribs."

"You don't have to do this, Gala," Keller said. She made an impatient sound and reached out as if to start unbuttoning his shirt herself. Keller sighed. Burke was right. Gala could be relentless. He unbuttoned his shirt and stripped it off. She clucked disapprovingly at the Ace bandage wrapping him. "That's not good," she said. "Too binding." She unwound the bandage slowly. "Hmmm," she said as she studied the bruises. "And how did this happen?"

"Got kicked by a horse," Keller said.

"You're lying," she said. "That doesn't look anything like the bruising you get from a horse kick. I've spent enough time around horses to know. If it's none of my business, say so, Jack."

"It's none of your business," he said.

"See?" Gala said serenely. "Isn't that better than lying? Much easier on your karma. Now, go on in the back and talk to Peter while I fix you something to put on this." Keller reached for his shirt. "You might as well leave that off," she said.

There was no use arguing. Shirtless, Keller walked to the back of the house where Burke had his studio.

The room was airy and open, with one of the house's many floor-to-ceiling windows providing natural light. One wall was lined with bookshelves. Another was hung with a variety of bladed and pointed weapons: swords, mostly, with an occasional vicious-looking axe or spear. Burke sat at an easel on which was propped a huge sketch pad. There was a table next to the easel. A huge book lay open on the table. Burke was sketching on the pad with a stick of charcoal, his large hands moving with a surprising delicacy. As Keller watched, the lines took shape. Burke drew a long pole, tipped by a wicked-looking spike. Below the spike was a curved axe blade. On the other side of the pole from the blade was a blunt hammer head. Burke paused, looked down at the book, and sighed. He put the charcoal stick down.

"Nasty," Keller said.

"It's called a poleax," Burke muttered. "Slices and dices and cuts three ways. Of course, it's from the wrong century from the one the movie's set in and the lead actor can't even handle a regular sword, so I'm going to spend a few days teaching him to use this and he's still going to look totally ridiculous. But do these assholes care?" He looked at Keller. "Huh," he said, noticing the bruises. "What's the other guy look like?"

"Don't know," Keller said. "He wasn't there at the time."

"Ohhhh . . . kay," Burke said slowly. "I don't suppose you want to explain that."

"Not really."

"Whatever," Burke said. "So what did you want to ask me about?"

"You've been out at the studio pretty much since it opened," Keller said. "So I thought you might have heard of a guy named Roy Randle."

Burke didn't say anything for a moment. He picked up the charcoal stick and turned back to the easel. He studied the picture before speaking.

"Haven't heard that name in a while," he said.

"So you knew him."

Burke shrugged. "Knew of him. Met him once or twice. You're after him?"

"No," Keller said. "But his girlfriend jumped bail. I think they may be living together. I think if I find him, I find her."

"Ah," Burke replied. He continued looking at the picture.

"Pete," Keller said. "What's going on here?"

Burke sighed. He put the stick back down and turned to Keller.

"You find Randle," he said, "and you might be stirring up some shit that a lot of people want to keep buried, Jack."

Keller pointed to his chest. "Pete," he said. "I got this when I went out to Randle's house. He set a trap-gun in the doorway. It shot me in the chest. If I hadn't been wearing a Kevlar vest, he'd have killed me."

Burke looked unhappy. "He always was a little screwy," he said. "Maybe you should just leave him alone."

"He's a means to an end, Pete," Keller said. "But the girl-friend, the one I'm after, is a little screwy, too."

Burke gestured to a nearby chair. "Have a seat," he said. "I'll tell you what I know about Randle."

Roy stood at the side of the van and watched the smoke billow from the trailer.

"Roy?" Laurel said. "Roy, we've got to get goin', baby, that smoke'll bring people runnin' soon."

"Why're you burning the place down, Roy?" Stan said.

Roy turned to him. "Shut up," he said. "I ain't gonna tell you again." Stan opened his mouth, then closed it with an audible snap as he saw the look on Roy's face. "You send those pic-tures?" Roy demanded. "The ones we took last night at the diner?"

"I did, baby," Laurel said. Roy liked the way Stan seemed to flinch slightly whenever Laurel called him that. He had the kid pretty much where he wanted him, but maybe he should take Laurel tonight in front of him, just to remind the little shit who the top dog was. He climbed into the driver's seat and started the van.

• • •

131

"When the studio opened," Burke said, "a lot of people wanted to work there. Everybody thought it was going to be Hollywood East. Non-union, decent weather, a lot of different kinds of scenery nearby . . . it was going to be the next big thing. So the locals flocked to it."

"Like Randle," Keller said.

"He wasn't really local," Burke said. "He was a farm kid from out in the sticks somewhere. But he was good-looking enough, in pretty good physical shape, so he got some work as an extra. Then he started doing stunts on a couple of Van Damme movies."

"Martial arts, sci-fi stuff," Keller said.

Burke nodded. "Right. Van Damme liked Roy. He liked his fight scenes realistic and Randle was willing to take a punch. So Randle got it into his head that he was going to be a lead actor, just like Van Damme."

"Was he any good?"

Burke shook his head. "He was terrible. He could never lose the accent, for one thing."

"Neither could Van Damme."

Burke laughed. "Okay, you got me there. But Randle never really had any screen presence. The camera didn't love him. It didn't even like him very much. Plus, like I said, he was kind of weird."

Keller leaned forward. "Weird how?"

"Well, a lot of people are ambitious. A lot of people in the business suck up. But the ones who succeed at it are at least a little subtle about it. Randle was anything but subtle."

"He made people uncomfortable."

"Yeah. And there was also . . . I don't know, he just seemed to have a screw loose somewhere."

"So how'd he keep getting work?"

Burke rubbed his face wearily with both hands. "Look," he said, "you didn't hear this from me, okay?"

Keller nodded. "Okay."

"Randle, could, ah, get things for people."

"Drugs," Keller said.

Burke nodded. "Yeah. You've gotta remember, Keller, this was before everybody in the business was swapping stories about rehab. It was everywhere, but so long as people showed up for work, it wasn't a big deal."

"So what happened? Somebody OD?"

Burke shook his head. "Look, Keller, I've still got to work here, okay?"

"Anyone asks, I never heard of you. Now, what happened?"

"You remember hearing about the actor that got shot? On the set?"

Keller nodded. "I read something about it, yeah."

"The official verdict was that a fragment of prop bullet got stuck in the chamber somehow and when they switched to blanks for the shooting scene, the fragment got blown into the guy's chest, juuuust perfectly aligned so as to kill him."

"Uh-huh."

"And you believe that shit?"

Keller shrugged. "Can't say that I ever gave much thought to it. I was overseas at the time."

"Oh yeah. Right," Burke said. "Well, that was the studio's story and they were sticking to it."

"But they were lying."

Burke nodded.

"The gun was actually loaded with live ammo?" Keller said.

Burke nodded again. "There weren't supposed to be any live

rounds on the set. That would have meant we'd have had all kinds of permitting problems. But Randle got bored one day during some downtime. He loaded up one of the guns and started potting seagulls."

"Jesus," Keller said.

"Told you he had a screw loose. He got thrown off the set. But the armorer . . . the guy that was supposed to secure all the weapons . . . was gone for the day. They decided to change the shooting schedule around and film one of the scenes where the hero gets shot. They tried to get the armorer back, but they couldn't reach him. They were behind schedule and over-budget, so they decided to do the scene anyway."

"And they picked up the gun Randle had loaded. And a man died."

"Yeah," Burke said.

"And Randle got blamed."

"There was plenty of blame to go around, Jack," Burke said. "But none of it was, you know, official."

"Why not?"

"There was a lot of money to spread around, too. And there were careers on the line. The insurance companies settled with the widow, everybody got their stories straight, they recut the movie and reshot some scenes, and . . ." He spread his hands apart in a what-are-you-gonna-do gesture. "The show must go on. But no one wanted to work with Randle anymore."

"Why didn't he blow the whistle?" Keller asked.

"People made it clear that he was the one that most of the blame was going to fall on. I mean, we're talking possible manslaughter here, not to mention all the trouble he could've gotten into over the drugs. And face it, he was nobody."

"You know, Pete," Keller said, "for someone who only claims

to have met this guy a couple of times, you know an awful lot about him."

Burke picked up the charcoal stick and started sketching again. "Like you said. I've been around for a while."

"And if I check the credits on that movie, will I find your name? Maybe as armorer?"

Burke never had a chance to answer. Gala entered the room, holding something white in her hands. As she brought it over, Keller saw that it was a bandage. There was a brown liquid coating one side.

"What's that?"

"Oil of comfrey poultice," Gala said. "I grow the roots myself. It's an old remedy for bruises and wounds." Keller must have looked dubious; Gala got an impatient look on her face. "This will help, I promise. Now raise your arms." Keller complied and she affixed the soaked bandage across his chest, fastening it back with the Ace bandage. *At least it doesn't smell bad,* Keller thought. Some of Gala's home remedies could be pungent.

"There," she said when she was done. She handed him a brown glass bottle. "Keep replenishing the poultice till this is gone," she said. "Now let me see your hand." She briskly applied a thick white oil to the cut on his hand and bandaged it, too. "There," she said. "That'll help you heal faster."

It might have been his imagination, but the pain in his chest did seem somewhat lessened. He stood up and she handed him his shirt. "Thanks, Gala," he said.

"No problem, Jack," she said. "And don't be such a stranger."

"I won't," Keller replied. He turned to Burke. "Thanks for the info, Pete."

Burke stood up and tore the sketch off the easel. "No prob-

135

lem," he said. "Now I've got to go out to the workshop and build this thing." He turned. "Just remember, Jack . . ."

"I know, I know," Keller said. "We spent the whole time talking basketball."

twelve

"No," the producer said. "No way."

"God damn it, Howard," Grace Tranh said. "What the fuck is your problem?"

Howard Reed ran a hand nervously through his wispy comb-over. Grace knew that it always unnerved him when she cursed. She was half his size, with the delicate beauty of a porcelain doll, but when she was worked up, she could turn the air blue. The legend in the newsroom was that Grace had once cursed a producer for five minutes without repeating herself once.

Howard looked around the newsroom. Some of the people behind the desks were intently looking at something, anything but the sight of Grace, hands on hips, spitting fury at the man who was, technically, her boss. Others were smirking openly.

"Look, Grace," Howard said. "People are really pissed that we used those pictures of the church. The families of the victims are talking lawsuits. The management is crawling up my—"

"That's for show," she sneered, "and you damn well know it.

They're making a big deal about how they 'regret' the broadcast of those pictures, but they're creaming in their Armanis over the ratings. We're it, Howard, we're the only station that has those. And we've got pictures of the second massacre, and you want me to sit on them? Fuck that!"

Howard slumped wearily. "I'm sorry, Grace. It's out of my hands."

She shook her head. "When are you going to grow a set of balls, Howard?"

He reddened. "Now wait a damn minute, Grace . . ."

"Forget it," she said. She threw up her hands theatrically and stalked back to her cubicle, leaving Howard helpless in her wake. She threw herself down in her chair and took a deep breath.

Okay, she thought, *go to Plan B*. She pulled her chair over to the computer and clicked on her e-mail program. She stared at the blinking icon for a moment. What she was about to do could get her in big trouble. It could also make her career. She didn't know if the killers still had the cell phone they had taken the pictures with, but since they had sent her more, she figured it was worth a try. But she didn't know how they'd react to being contacted. She began to type.

FROM:GRACET@WPJHNEWS.COM
TO:jesusluvsu01@Imobile.com
SUBJECT:

She paused. What would be most likely to get a response? What wouldn't scare them away or enrage them? She bit her lip and thought for a moment, then typed in the subject line:

SUBJECT: WHY?

She clicked down onto the empty space for the body of the message and began typing:

I'm the one you e-mailed the pictures to. Obviously you want someone to know what you're doing. You want to tell your story. I'd like to help you do that. I'd like to help you explain so people will know why you're doing it.

She studied the message for a moment, typed in her name, and hit "Send."

The shrill warble of the phone startled Roy so badly he nearly drove off the side of the Interstate. "What the fuck?" he yelled.

"It's the phone!" Laurel said. "The one we took the pictures on!"

Stan pulled it out of his duffel bag. "Chill out," he said. "It's an e-mail. Probably for the person that owns . . . I mean, used to own this."

"They can't trace us on that thing, can they Stan?" Laurel asked.

Roy's head whipped around. It had obviously never occurred to him. "Damn it," he snarled, "If your bright idea leads the fuckin' cops to us . . ."

"Just calm down!" Stan snapped back. The lack of sleep and the drug hangover had him strung tight as a drumhead. "You can't trace a cell phone."

"You sure?" Laurel asked.

"Yeah," Stan said. "I'm sure." *Pretty sure, anyway,* he thought. He glanced at the phone's screen. The phone had stopped ringing, but there was a tiny icon of an envelope flashing and the words "one e-mail waiting." He studied the controls for a moment, then pressed the buttons to open the message.

"It's to us," he said.

"What do you mean, it's to us?" Roy said.

Stan studied it for a moment. "It's from that reporter on TV. That Chinese girl."

"What?" Roy pulled the van over to the breakdown lane of the highway. "Let me see that."

Stan handed the phone to Roy. The older man looked down at it for a moment, then looked up. His eyes were bright with excitement. "So you know how to send messages on this thing, right, boy?" he demanded.

"Yeah," Stan said.

Roy pulled the van back onto the highway. "Okay," he said. "Send this back."

Marie had been on patrol for five hours when the BOLO came in. She had driven more or less randomly through her assigned patrol zone, stopping occasionally to check in on storeowners, drinking stale coffee and trading small talk—"showing a presence," as the sheriff put it. People were anxious, keyed-up; almost everyone asked her if "the church shooters" had been caught. Some asked if they were going to strike again, as if the badge on Marie's uniform blouse was some sort of crystal ball. She put on her best reassuring voice to let them know that everything was under control, that the sheriff's department was on the job. Some were reassured; the rest were silent, their faces still puckered with worry as Marie walked out.

She was driving down a narrow two-lane road between tall stands of pine when the call came in. "All units, Be On Look Out for a white 1979 Chevy Impala, license plate Bravo Victor

Echo One Four Six Three, driver a white male, name of Garrett, Henry J. Driver wanted for questioning, Fort Bragg CID."

Marie pulled up to a stop sign at a deserted crossroads and keyed her mike. "Say again, County, did you say Bragg CID?"

There was a brief pause. "10-4." Another pause. "All units are advised to use caution."

Another voice came through, slightly distorted by distance. "County, twenty-seven."

"Go ahead, twenty-seven."

"County, this subject involved in the church or diner shootings?"

Another long pause. "Twenty-seven, unable to advise at this time."

"Lovely," Marie muttered.

The dispatcher came back on. "If subject is located, hold for further instructions. Authority Federal Bureau of Investigation."

"Whoa, whoa, Janelle," another voice spoke up. "You just said Bragg CID. Now it's the Feebies? What's going on?"

The break in formality seemed to snap the dispatcher out of robotic-speech mode. "Your guess's as good as mine, shug. All I know's what they tell me."

"Okay, y'all," another voice broke through. Marie recognized the voice of an older deputy named Wardell. "Let's stay professional out here." Wardell was a short, chubby, round-faced deputy who had never seemed to advance beyond sergeant despite having been on the department since most of the younger officers were in high school. He served as a sort of unofficial mentor to the newer deputies, a role he seemed to enjoy. In many ways, he reminded Marie of her father. The effect was apparently not limited to her. The chorus of "10-4s" that came back seemed a bit sheepish.

Marie drove in silence for the next half hour. This far out in the county, there was light traffic, but she scanned every car carefully. Then the radio crackled back to life.

"County, All units, twenty-seven. I have a white Chevy Impala, license plate Bravo Victor Echo One Four Six Three, driver a white male. Headed east on Galloway Road between State Road 1243 and Highway 421. Request backup."

Marie tried to map it out in her mind. Unlike some of the other deputies, she hadn't grown up locally, and sometimes had to refer to the county map stashed in her glove compartment to figure out where she was. She glanced over at a signpost at the next intersection as the radio crackled to life again. The voice this time was high-pitched and tight with excitement.

"All units, county, this is twenty-seven. He's, I mean subject, is running. I am in pursuit."

The dispatcher's voice came back. "10-4, twenty-seven. All units, officer needs backup, subject speeding to avoid custody."

Wardell came back on. "Twenty-seven, this is twenty-nine, advise of your 10-20."

Marie could hear the sound of twenty-seven's siren in the background as he came back. "Still eastbound on Galloway, he just crossed Highway 421."

"10-4," Wardell came back. His voice was as calm as if he were doing a routine time check. "Thirty-five, what's your 20?"

Marie keyed her mike. "Headed north on SR 2345, near McDonald Road." she reported. She was glad she had checked the signpost.

"10-4," Wardell said. He sounded almost happy. "Thirty-five, meet me at the crossroads of Johnson Lake Road and Galloway."

Marie hesitated. "Your next left is Johnson Lake," Wardell said patiently. "Take it. I'll be there before you. We'll block the road. Twenty-seven, you run him at us."

The sirens again. "10-4," twenty-seven replied.

Marie accelerated through the left turn, her tires squealing. When she straightened out onto Johnson Lake Road, she hit the lights and siren. In a few moments, she saw the flashing lights of Wardell's car. He had parked across one lane of the deserted road. Wardell was out of the car. He waved to her and pointed at the other lane. She positioned her car across the other lane, nose to nose with Wardell's vehicle.

"Hey," Wardell greeted her as she got out.

Marie tried to match his nonchalance. "Hey," she said. They heard the distant keening of the sirens at the same time. They drew their weapons and took up positions behind their respective vehicles.

"Here they come," Wardell said.

The road was flat and straight, rising gently for almost a quarter mile. The first vehicle they saw was the white Impala, cresting the hill. A sheriff's car was immediately behind, lights flashing, siren wailing. Marie could hear the roar of the Impala's engine over the noise of the siren. There was a slight drop in the pitch of the engine noise as the driver saw the obstruction ahead and let up on the accelerator. Then the engine howled again as the driver gave it the gas.

"That dumbass," Wardell commented. "Aim for the tires." He raised his gun.

Grace sat at the computer, mouse-clicking in a nervous cycle: CNN.com. BBC.com. Washingtonpost.com. Her e-mail program. CNN.com. BBC.com. . . . She knew that it might be hours, or never, before she got an answer. Still, she clicked through, her eyes not seeing the screen, her stomach in knots. Then, she stopped on the e-mail program, watching the little blue bar that indicated an incoming message sweep across the bottom of the screen. She saw the sender: jesusluvsu01@Imo-bile.com. And the subject line:

WHY NOT?

"Yessss," she said under her breath. She clicked on the message.

TO:GRACET@WPJHNEWS.COM
FROM: jesusluvsu01@Imobile.com
SUBJECT: WHY NOT?
DNT CALL US WELL CALL U. GIVE US A #

Grace's hands trembled slightly with excitement as she hit the "Reply" button and typed in her cell-phone number. She had just hit "Send" when a voice behind her made her jump.

"Ms. Tranh?"

She whirled around, startling the young female intern who was standing in the doorway of her cubicle. She resisted the temptation to snarl at the girl, who blinked at her with a look of confusion on her pretty face. "What's up, Tina?" she said, with as much friendliness as she could summon.

"Howard . . . er . . . Mr. Reed, wants to see you. In his office."

Christ, what now? Grace thought. She smiled at the girl. "Thanks, hon," she said. "I'll be right up." She turned and shut down the computer.

She mounted the short flight of steps at the back of the newsroom to Howard's office, a small space with a picture window that looked out over the newsroom. Howard was seated behind his desk. He didn't look at Grace as she came in. She was surprised to see two men there. One was a tall blond, the other was a short man with red hair. Other than the color, their short haircuts were almost identical. Their cheap dark suits also looked as if they had been bought off the same rack. As one of the men—the redhead—extended a hand, Grace caught a glimpse of a shoulder holster beneath the suit coat. *Cop,* she thought.

"Ms. Tranh?" the man said. "I'm Special Agent Clancy, Federal Bureau of Investigation. My partner is Special Agent Gray." The blonde man nodded.

"Ms. Tranh," Clancy said, "I'll get right to the point . . ."

"You're here about the pictures, of course," she said. She looked at Howard, who was looking out his window at the newsroom. She turned her most brilliant smile on Clancy. "I thought you might want copies, so I burned them onto a CD. Let me just go get it . . ."

"Thank you, ma'am," Clancy said. "We'll also need your computer."

That stopped her dead. "What?"

"Your computer. Or at least the hard drive, but it would be easier just to take the whole thing."

Grace's smile felt frozen on her face. "I don't understand what you mean."

"You received an e-mail with those pictures," Gray piped up. "We need to analyze it to see if it provides us with information about these attacks."

"And I'll be glad to provide you with a copy," Grace said. "But my computer . . . I'm sorry, that's impossible." She turned to Howard. "Howard, tell him this is ridiculous. I want to cooperate, but . . ."

Howard still wouldn't look at her. "I told them they could expect our full cooperation, Grace."

Her composure cracked. "Damn it, Howard, all my files are on there! I have names and addresses of confidential sources,

145

stories, e-mails. . . ." *Oh God,* she thought, *e-mails. If they get those . . .*

"Of course," Clancy said, "We'll do everything we can to safeguard your privacy and that of confidential sources. We're only seeking information germane to our investigation."

Germane? Grace thought. *Who the fuck uses words like 'germane'?* "I'm sorry, gentlemen," she said. "I'll have to speak to my personal attorney before . . ."

"It's not your computer, Grace," Howard said. "It belongs to the station. I told them they can have it."

Grace stared at him for a moment. "I knew you were a dickless wonder, Howard," she said evenly. "But I didn't think you were this much of one."

Howard's face turned red with anger. "Far left row, third cubicle," he told the agents. They nodded and walked toward the door. Grace didn't move from in front of the door. They stopped short, looking confused.

"You're not going to be able to get into the computer without my password," she said. "And guess what? The password's not my birthday."

"Yes, ma'am," Clancy said. "We'll need you to give that password to us."

"No," Grace said. "Not without a court order. And maybe not even then."

"Grace . . . ," Howard said.

"Go fuck yourself, Howard," she said.

"We can get a warrant, ma'am," Clancy said. "And once we do, we can crack the password. Eventually. All you're doing is obstructing a federal investigation."

"If you think you can make that charge stick, Clancy, take your best shot," Grace snapped. "I'll see you on the front page."

"You might get less traction from that story than you think, good day in hell

Ms. Tranh," Clancy said. "After 9/11, people might not have a lot of sympathy for a person of, ah, foreign extraction hindering an antiterrorist investigation."

"Foreign *extraction?!*" Grace yelled. "You little shitbird, I'm from *New Jersey!*"

"Calm down, Grace," Howard said.

"Go fuck yourself *twice,* Howard!" she shot back. She turned on her heel and walked out. She took the short flight of stairs two at a time and headed toward her cubicle. She heard the two agents right behind her. Heads turned as she walked by. When she reached the doorway, she whirled on them.

"See if you can get your court order, Clancy," she snarled. "I'll have so many lawyers up your ass, your crap will come out pin-striped." She snatched her purse and suit jacket from off the back of her chair and shoved past the two agents. As she walked out of the newsroom, she surreptitiously checked to confirm she still had her cell phone and that it was turned on.

Marie didn't know what changed the driver's mind at the last moment. He may have caught sight of the pistols pointed at him. He may have lost faith in his vehicle's ability to smash through the roadblock and keep going. But the tortured shriek of tires drowned out the engine roar as he slammed on the brakes and whipped the wheel to one side to try to avoid a colli-sion. The car went sideways in the road, then began to roll. The air filled with the sound of crunching metal as the Impala flipped onto its back, then back onto its tires, then onto its back again. The vehicle's forward momentum carried it up onto its side, where it teetered precariously for a moment before smash-ing back down onto all four tires again with a massive thud, a mere few feet away from Marie's cruiser. The patrol car following had gone onto the shoulder to avoid crashing into its quarry. It slid to a stop in a spray of dirt and gravel.

The door of the Impala popped open and a man stumbled out. He was dressed in jeans and a white T-shirt that stretched tight across his muscular back and chest. His hair was cut short in the "high and tight" military style.

Marie and Wardell started yelling at the man at the same time. "GET DOWN! ON THE GROUND! NOW! ON THE GROUND!" He gave them one panicked glance before bolting toward the woods.

"Aw, for the love of . . . ," Wardell groaned. He pointed his weapon skyward and fired a warning shot. The only effect was to cause the running man to zig, then zag, then he was in the trees. Marie shoved her weapon into its holster and took off after him. She could hear Wardell behind her, yelling at the officer in Unit twenty-seven to call for more backup. Then she heard his heavy footfalls behind her as he followed.

The woods were mostly pine trees struggling to compete with clumps of spindly blackjack oak and underbrush. She could hear rather than see her quarry crashing through the brush, uttering an occasional curse as he stumbled or ran into a low-hanging branch. She caught occasional glimpses of his white T-shirt through the foliage. Suddenly there was a louder crash, followed by the sound of something heavy falling into water. Marie burst through the underbrush to find herself on the banks of a shallow creek. The slow-moving water had meandered back and forth, cutting deep into the sandy soil, leaving a broad, deep gully. The man in the T-shirt was at the bottom of it, struggling to his feet in the muddied water. He began scrabbling up the far side of the gully. "FREEZE, GOD DAMN IT!" Marie yelled as she jumped into the creek. The man turned on her, his eyes wild. He swung a wild haymaker at her head. Marie ducked and swung her arm up at the same time, deflecting the blow. She reached down with her other hand and yanked the canister of pepper spray off her belt. As the man reared back for another punch, Marie let him have it full in the face. He screamed and grabbed at his eyes as the fiery chemical blasted every nerve ending with pain. He fell to his knees, still screaming. Marie heard a huge splash next to her, then Wardell was there. He was panting with exertion, his uniform shirt soaked with sweat. "Damn, girl, you must've been a track star in school," he gasped as he pulled one of the man's hands away from his face. The man's skin was a violent red. Tears streamed from his bloodshot eyes and snot ran like a river from his nose as every mucous membrane erupted from the irritation of the spray.

"Soccer, actually," Marie choked out as Wardell clipped a cuff on the man's wrist. She had caught a whiff of the spray and it was making her gag.

"Must o' been good at it," Wardell said as he pulled at the man's other wrist. "Come on, boy," he grunted. "Don't make Little Speedy here give you another dose o' that spray."

"My eyes," the man groaned. "Oh, God, my eyes . . ."

"Oughta kick your ass for makin' me run, boy," Wardell grunted as he cuffed the man's other wrist, fastening his arms behind him. "What'n the hell's wrong with you?"

"I didn't know what they were gonna do with the guns," the man blubbered. "I swear to God, I didn't know."

"Who?" Wardell said. "Who're you talkin' about?"

"Hang on a sec, Sergeant," Marie cut in. "Maybe we ought to read him his rights."

Wardell scowled for a moment, then shrugged. "Yeah, okay," he said. "You do the honors."

"First off," Marie said. "Are you Henry Garrett?" The man nodded. "You have the right to remain silent," Marie began.

When she was done Mirandizing the man, she took a handkerchief out of her pocket and gently wiped his still-streaming
nose.

"Thanks," Garrett whispered.

"Don't thank me," she shot back. "All that snot was grossing
me out. Now, what's this about not knowing what they were going to do? Who's they?"

Garrett gave her a look like a whipped dog suddenly shown an
act of kindness: grateful and wary at the same time. "I think
they were the people who shot up that church. And that diner."

Wardell sounded disgusted. "And you sold them guns."

Garrett nodded miserably.

"Boy," Wardell said, "Between the army, the feds, and what
we're about to charge you with . . ." He shook his head. "When
they get done with you, they're gonna store your sorry ass *under*
the damn jail." He grabbed the back of Garrett's T-shirt and began pushing him up the embankment.

thirteen

Keller pulled up to the ornately decorated wrought-iron gate and rolled down the window. The security guard in the gatehouse was young, skinny, with a weak chin and a brush cut that had been let go for too long. He looked over Keller's vehicle, his eyes flickering over the balloons filling the backseat and the "Balloon Tyme" logo on the side. Keller had bought the balloons from a local party store. The logo was stuck onto a magnetic sign he had had made at a sign store a while back.

"Hep you?" the guard said.

Keller leaned out. "Got a delivery. The name is Marks?"

The guard looked suspicious. "Nobody tole me nothin' about that."

Keller shrugged. "Just ordered about a half hour ago. Maybe some guy forgot his old lady's birthday or something."

The guard scratched his chin. "I better call the house and check."

"It's supposed to be a surprise," Keller said. "The guy who

called was real serious about that. But I tell you what, you can call my boss and confirm." Keller pointed down to the magnetic sign. "Number's right there."

The guard nodded and picked up the phone inside the gate-house. Keller had called Angela just before pulling up and given her the heads up. The number on the magnetic sign was one of the phone lines for H & H Bail Bonds. He saw the guard talking, then nodding and reaching down. The iron gate swung open and Keller drove through. He waved as he passed by. The guard waved back.

The roads inside Dune Grove Country Club were a winding labyrinth. The street signs were tiny brown wood pointers with painted lettering that Keller supposed was supposed to look rustic. What they were mostly was hard to read. Keller had visited a local real-estate office that heavily advertised sales of lots in Dune Grove. He had picked up a brochure advertising its golf course, tennis complex, horse stables, and spacious lots. It was the map of the club, however, that had most interested Keller. Even with the map, he took several wrong turns that led him down to the end of cul-de-sacs. Huge homes in a variety of styles, all expensive, sat on perfectly landscaped lots. Occasionally, he caught a glimpse of the emerald-green grass of the golf course through the trees. Finally, he found his way to the Marks home. Like the others, it was a big place, split-level, with a half-circle of gravel drive in front. Keller parked and got out. He stood in the drive for a few moments and looked the place over, trying to reconcile this affluence with what he knew of Laurel Marks's life.

The slow tolling of the doorbell chime reverberated inside the house. There was a sound of footsteps behind the door, then a pause. Keller assumed he was being surveyed through the peep-hole set into the door. He tried to look benign. After a moment, the door opened a crack. Half of a female face peered out at him past the still-fastened security chain.

"Yes?" the woman said.

"Mrs. Marks?"

The one eye that Keller could see looked past him to Keller's car parked near the door. "I didn't order any balloons," the woman said. Her voice was a low contralto with a hint of Southern accent.

"Mrs. Marks, my name's Jack Keller. I need to ask you some questions about Laurel."

The door closed. Keller was reaching for the doorbell again when he heard the rattle of the chain being removed. The door swung open. The woman who stood there appeared to be in her late forties. She was short, slender, dark-haired, and expensively dressed. She had been drinking; Keller could smell bourbon from where he stood. "I don't know where Laurel is," she said.

"Yes, ma'am," Keller said. "But if I could come in and ask some questions . . ."

She arched an eyebrow at him. "Why is a balloon delivery-man looking for my daughter?" she asked.

"I work for Laurel's bail bondsman," Keller said. He reached in his pocket and handed her a card. "We need to know where she is."

'Ahhh . . . ," she said, taking the card. "And the balloons were to get you past the gate. Very clever."

Drunk or sober, Keller realized, it would be a mistake to underestimate this woman.

"So, she's in trouble again," the woman said. She let out a short contemptuous laugh. "Figures." She waved a hand in the air negligently and turned away. "Come on in," she said. "Don't know what I can tell you, but it beats watching Dr. Phil."

Keller followed her into the house, down a hallway, into the

153

living room. The room was bright with sunlight from an enormous picture window that looked out over a water hazard on the golf course. White leather-covered furniture was arranged on the dark hardwood floor facing a wide-screen TV. "Nice house," Keller said.

"Uh-huh," the woman said. She plopped down on the sofa and turned the TV down with the remote. On the coffee table in front of the sofa was a bottle of Maker's Mark, a bucket of ice, and an empty glass. "Would you like a drink, balloon man?" she asked.

"Not now, thanks," said Keller.

"Hah," she said. "It's got to be five o'clock somewhere, doesn't it?" She plopped a couple of ice cubes into the glass and sloshed a few fingers of the dark amber bourbon into the glass. She pulled a cigarette out of a pack on the side table and lit it.

"Mrs. Marks . . . ," Keller began.

"Ellen," she said. "And your name was Jack, right?"

"Still is," Keller said. "Ellen, Laurel didn't make her last court appearance. She's dropped out of sight. Do you know anyone she might go to if she was in trouble?"

"Well, it sure as hell wouldn't be here, Jack," she said. The slight whiskey slur made the word come out "heah." "Laurel walked out of this house on her eighteenth birthday and we haven't seen or heard from her since."

"Why was that, Ellen?"

She didn't answer at first. She took a long drink of bourbon, her eyes regarding Keller over the glass. She put the glass down and closed her eyes as the fiery liquid went down. When she opened them again, her voice was steadier. "My daughter has severe emotional problems. She's violent. She's a thief. She's sexually promiscuous. She's also a pathological liar. We did everything we could to help her, but," she shrugged, "enough was enough."

"Is that why Social Services was involved when she was younger?"

"Well, you've certainly done your homework, haven't you?" She took another drink. "Yes, Jack," she said. "Laurel told a teacher that Ted . . . my husband . . . had sexually abused her. It was a lie, of course. He never touched her."

"How do you know it was a lie?"

She gave him a bitter smile. "Because she admitted it was a lie. She recanted. Of course that was after she and her brother had been out of the home in foster care for several months."

"Her brother?" Keller said.

"Yes. His name is Curt. He's a student at . . ." She stopped. "I don't want you bothering him," she said.

"Do you think she'd go to him for help if she was on the run?"

She laughed. "Not by a long sight, Jack. He was very upset by the whole incident. Curt idolizes his father. It tore him apart to see the family separated like that."

"He blamed Laurel," Keller said.

Ellen looked at him blankly. "Of course," she said. "Laurel was to blame. Fortunately, Curt eventually convinced her to tell the truth."

Keller let that go. "Can you think of any place she'd go, any friend she'd call?"

She looked thoughtful for a moment. She opened her mouth as if to say something, but stopped at the sound of the front door opening and closing. There was a sound of something heavy being set down in the front hallway.

"Ellen?" a male voice called out. There were footsteps in the hall. A man entered.

He was in his late fifties, tall, stocky, with the build and swagger of a man used to intimidating by his size alone. His hair was almost gone on top, with only a few strands combed over his

155

sunburned and freckled scalp. His bright green golf slacks and bright yellow shirt made his already ruddy face look nearly apoplectic. He stopped and regarded Keller with narrowed eyes.

"Hello," he said, without an ounce of welcome in a deep, gravelly voice.

Keller stood up, extended his hand. "Mister Marks?"

The man ignored the hand. "Who are you?"

"Mister Keller is a bail bondsman," Ellen Marks said. She hadn't bothered to get up. "He's here asking about Laurel."

The man's jaw tightened. Keller could see the resemblance to Laurel. "We don't know anything about her," he said.

"I understand she's not here, sir," Keller said, "But I wanted to know if—"

"You need to get your ass out of here, Keller," Marks said. "I don't know how you got in, but—"

"She's jumped bail, Mister Marks," Keller said. "If you know anything about where she might be—"

"God damn it," Marks said, "I said get the hell out!" He moved toward Keller as if to grab him.

"I wouldn't," Keller said. His voice was low, but his tone stopped Marks cold. His hands dropped to his sides.

"Ellen," he said, "Call the cops."

"Call them yourself, Ted," she said lazily. She took another drag from the cigarette. "Or try to throw Jack out. That really would beat watching Dr. Phil." She gave a low throaty laugh.

"Don't worry," Keller said. "I'm leaving." He turned to Ellen Marks. "You've got my card," he told her. "If Laurel contacts you, try to persuade her to come in voluntarily. It'll be easier for everyone. Or if you hear anything about her, call me."

"I'll do that," she said. She hadn't taken her eyes off her husband. They were bright with anticipation. Keller realized she wanted her husband to make a move on him, wanted to see him hurt. He shook his head. Ted Marks moved quickly to get out of Keller's way as he walked out.

As he left, Keller saw a tan Lincoln Navigator looming in the driveway behind his car. There were a pair of bumperstickers on the back. One said, I'D RATHER BE GOLFING. The other said, MY SON AND MY MONEY GO TO NC STATE. He remembered Ellen Marks saying that her son was a student and filed that away for reference.

"This phone's almost out of juice," Stan said. He peered out the van window. "Not like it'll make any difference, out here in the sticks. Where the hell are we, anyway?"

"Almost there," Laurel said.

Stan stole a nervous glance at Roy. He had been grim and scary, even more so than usual, since setting the trailer on fire. He didn't know what to make of it. "The turn's up here on the right," he heard Laurel say.

"I know," Roy said. He slowed the van and turned off the hard road onto a narrow dirt track in an overgrown field. Weeds grew in the center of the road and whispered against the sides of the van as they bumped along. There were fields on either side, fenced in by stands of pine. The fields were grown up in waist-high pale grasses. Here and there a young pine thrust up where crops once grew. They passed an old tobacco barn, its tin roof fallen in.

"What is this place?" Stan asked.

"My grandma's old farm," Laurel said. "No one ever comes here."

"No shit," Stan said.

"Which is why it's a good place to hide out," she snapped. "Get it, genius?" Stan felt his face redden.

157

They passed through another stand of trees and came out at the lip of a broad, bowl-shaped valley. There was a grove of pecan trees on the valley floor, lined up in neat rows in the undergrowth. The dirt drive led between the rows to the top of the opposite slope. There, the ground leveled off into a yard in front of a small white farmhouse. Roy parked in front. He got out without speaking.

"What's eating him?" Stan asked.

"He's just stressin', is all," Laurel said. "Let me handle him." She looked at Stan. "I may need to spend some time with him," she said. "You know, to get him calmed down."

Stan frowned. "I don't like that idea."

Laurel glanced at Roy. He was bending down to retrieve the key that was hidden under a rock by the front door. She leaned over and whispered to Stan, "Now, what did I tell you, sweetie? We're not like other people. We don't live by rules like that."

"It ain't a rule," Stan said. "It's just the way I feel."

Laurel glanced back again. Roy had gone inside. She leaned over and kissed Stan quickly. "I know, honey," she said. "I used to feel the same way. But it's better this way. Trust me, okay?"

"I don't like it," Stan repeated stubbornly.

"Well, Stan," she said, her voice suddenly cold, "you better learn to like it. Because this is the way it is." She opened the van door and got out.

Stan heard the deep cough and sputter of a gasoline motor starting up. Laurel slid the van door open and took hold of a huge red cooler. Stan didn't move. He was still in the back, his knees drawn up to his chest. Misery and confusion were gnawing at his gut.

"You gonna help me get this stuff inside?" Laurel said.

"What's that noise?" Stan asked.

"Gas generator," Laurel said. "We set it up for electricity."

"Won't somebody hear?" Stan asked.

"No," she replied. "Not this far off the road. It's a big place. Now help me with this damn cooler."

Stan took the other handle and helped her wrestle the cooler out of the van. It was stuffed full of food, ice, and beer, and they struggled awkwardly with it as they hauled it to the door.

Inside, they found themselves in a small room, with pale white walls and a dusty heart-pine floor. The room was illuminated by a bare bulb hanging from the ceiling by a frayed wire. The only furniture in the room was an old, torn-up couch that looked like something someone had rescued from the side of the road. Across from the couch was a new-looking color TV. Roy was fussing with a black box on top of the set. He gave a grunt of satisfaction and stepped back.

There was a bit of snow and static in the reception, but the picture was reasonably clear. On the screen, a man in an expensive-looking leather jacket was walking up and down between lines of cars, talking about incredible below-invoice deals in an excited voice. Roy sat on the couch, leaning forward with his elbows resting on his knees. His gaze was riveted to the screen. The commercial ended and the screen filled with the picture of a beautiful blonde woman and a handsome bearded man arguing about someone named Troy. A soap opera.

"Where are we?" Roy muttered. He got up and strode angrily across the room to change the channels. He flipped through channel after channel, stopping on the news stations. CNN, Fox, MSNBC . . .

"Wait a minute," Stan said. "You got cable out here?"

Laurel shook her head. "Bought a satellite dish from Wal-Mart. And we got a bootleg descrambler from this guy I know. Ain't no use bein' famous if you can't see yourself on TV."

"I'll check the local yokels," Roy said. He picked up a small

159

box wired to the back of the TV. There was a slider switch on top of the box. "This here's wired to a regular antenna," he said. "For the local stations." He moved the switch. The clear picture gave way to a snowier screen. It was showing a talk show about parents and troubled teens who dressed too provocatively.

Roy banged on the top of the set in frustration. "We should be wall to wall by now," he snarled. "Every station. CNN. Fox. The works."

"We just got started," Laurel said. "We'll get there."

"Maybe we should call that reporter," Stan said. He took the cell phone out of his pocket. The tiny letters "NS" were blinking on the top of the screen. "But we're too far out to use this," he said. "We'll have to get back to civilization."

Roy nodded. He seemed to have calmed somewhat. "We'll do that," he said. "After the next scene."

"Scene?" Stan asked.

"The church was scene one," Laurel said. "The diner was scene two. Tomorrow it's time for scene three."

Stan's confusion didn't do anything to help his mood. "What's scene three?"

Roy grinned. His mood seemed to be improving. "Oh, scene three is the best yet." He walked over to Laurel and took her by the arm. "C'mon," he said. "We need to get some rest. It's gonna be a long night."

Laurel gave Stan a worried glance as Roy led her toward the back of the house.

"Maybe you'd better get some sleep, too, Stan," she said. Roy led her down the hallway. He heard a door close.

Stan stood in the middle of the living room, his hands clenching and unclenching. He wanted to go back there, grab Laurel, tell Roy he wasn't going to share anymore. And that Roy wasn't going to touch him anymore, either. But he was afraid. Just like always. He was afraid of Roy, sure, but he was also afraid that Laurel might not like it, that she might laugh at him and go with Roy anyway. *I hate being scared,* he thought. *I fuckin' hate it.* His stomach knotted. He felt like he was going to throw up. Instead, he walked over to the cooler, opened it, and took out a beer. He cracked it open and walked outside. The van door was still open and he walked over to close it. He saw the black deadly shapes of the rifles lying inside. Stan stood and looked at them for a long time, taking sips of the beer. Then he pulled the door shut. He went and sat down on the porch, looking at the van, thinking.

"Dad?" Marie said. She held the phone tightly to her ear with one hand while the other hand covered her ear to drown out the noise of the conversations in the squad room.

"Hey, girl," her father said. "They got you working hard?"

"Pretty much," Marie said. "Dad, I need you to do me a favor."

"Sure," he said.

"In the laundry," Marie said, "there's a pair of jeans I was wearing yesterday. I need you to go through the pockets."

"What am I looking for?"

She glanced around at the squad room. She didn't want to attract attention at that point. "You'll know it when you find it, Dad, I'm pretty sure."

"Okay," he said. She heard the rattle as he put the phone down on the counter. She saw Shelby walking through the door on the other end of the squad room. He saw her and waved. He started toward her. She raised her index finger, then pointed at the phone. One minute. He nodded and veered off toward the coffeemaker.

Her father's voice came back on the line. "Looks like an empty cartridge casing," he said. His voice was expressionless. "A .45, I'd say."

"Yeah, I think so, too," Marie said. "I need you to bag it and bring it to me here. Can you do that?"

"Yeah, I can do that," he said. "You mind telling me what's going on, kiddo?"

"Not just yet, Dad," she said. "It could be nothing."

"Or it could be evidence," he said. "Right?"

"I don't know yet, Dad," she said.

"Well, if it is, any half-bright lawyer's gonna jack you up on chain of custody."

"Dad . . ."

She heard him sigh. "Sorry, kid," he said. "Old reflexes. I'll have to bring Ben with me. There's no one else to watch him."

"I know," she said. "It's okay. And thanks."

"No problem," he said. "Love you."

"I love you, too, Dad," she said. She hung up. She walked over to where Shelby was sitting, putting a packet of sugar into his coffee.

"Pull up a chair," he said. She sat. "Got some news back from the SBI lab on that casing from the gas station," he said. "It's a match to one found in the church."

"How about the diner?" she said.

He shook his head. "They didn't use a .45 at the diner. But the .45 ties the gas station and the church together . . ."

"And the rifle ammo ties the diner and the church together," she finished.

"Yep," Shelby said. He took a sip of the coffee. "Good thinkin', by the way," he said.

"Thanks," she said. "The guy we caught give anything else up?"

"Oh, he was singin' like a lil' bird for a while there. Seems he was a supply clerk at Bragg. They got a lot of old stuff there. No one knows why the army doesn't just destroy it or sell it off as surplus. But it never gets used. And all the records are kept on computers."

"By him," Marie said. "So he figured he could gimmick the records and no one would ever miss them."

Shelby nodded.

"So who'd he sell to?"

"Didn't know real names, of course," Shelby said. "Just an older man and a young woman."

Marie felt a chill. "Any idea where they were from?"

Shelby shook his head.

"Was one of the guns a .45?"

Shelby looked at her shrewdly. "Could've been. He said there was a pistol, and the era's about right. He was givin' us a list, but then the FBI come and took him," Shelby said.

Marie's heart sank. "The FBI?"

Shelby nodded. "Coupla suits all the way down from D.C. 'Course, the first time that boy heard the word 'federal' he lawyered hisself right up. Ain't said a word since, except . . ." He hesitated.

"What?" she said.

He took another sip of coffee. "Now, don't get upset, Jones," he said. "You know how these boys'll say anything to get over."

"What?" she insisted.

Shelby looked at her. "Garrett says you tortured a false confession out of him. Held him down and pepper-sprayed him till he told you what you wanted to hear."

"WHAT!?" Marie yelled. All conversation in the squad room stopped. She could feel all the eyes on her, so she dropped her voice to a savage whisper. "For Christ's . . . for crying out loud, Shelby! Held him down? The guy's got, what, three inches and thirty pounds on me? Not to mention he's a God . . . ," she was

practically strangling trying to change her language, "he's a flip-
pin' *paratrooper*?"

Shelby had put the coffee down. He was holding both hands
out parallel to the ground in a calming gesture. "Easy, Jones,
easy," he said softly. "Ain't nobody took this seriously yet. Like I
said, these boys'll say anything, once they get lawyered up. And
they found a couple of pounds of methamphetamine in the
trunk of his car. They figger he swapped the weapons for it. No
one's gonna listen to a drug trafficker."

"Except I already have a reputation as a fuckup," Marie said.

"Well, you ain't got one with me," Shelby said. "Or Tom
Wardell, neither, from what I hear."

"Yeah. Well," Marie said. "There's something about me you
may not know."

"I know your partner got killed," Shelby said. "And sounds to
me like it was his own fault."

"I didn't make any friends by telling people that."

"Long as you tell the truth, Jones, you got a friend in me. And
in Wardell. He's talkin' about you all over the department."
Shelby's ugly face split in a grin. "Lil' Speedy."

Marie rolled her eyes. "Oh, Lord," she moaned.

"Hey," he said, "A nickname's a good thing. Shows you fit in."

She smiled. "I guess. You hear anything from upstairs about
this?"

He shook his head as he picked the coffee back up. "Naw.
Don't sweat it, Jones."

"Thanks, Shelby," she said. "You've been a good friend."

He raised the cup to her. "No problem."

"There's something else, though," she said. "Another cartridge
I want to run through the lab."

He gave her the raised eyebrows as he took a sip of coffee.
She took a deep breath and told him about Keller, about going

out to Randle's trailer looking for Laurel Marks, about finding cartridge casings on the ground. She left out the part about Keller breaking in and getting shot by the trap-gun. "So when I heard Garrett talking about an older man and a younger woman," she said, "I started thinking."

Shelby looked thoughtful, "And where's this .45 casing?"

"I stuck it in my jeans pocket," she confessed. Shelby winced. "I know, I know," Marie said. "I didn't think it was important. I just picked it up. My dad's bringing it to the station. Bagged. He used to be a cop. Plus, there's a lot more casings out there. They were all over the ground. We can send someone out there to pick a clean one up."

"Okay," Shelby said. He stood up. "Bring it right to me," he said. "I'll get to the lab and rush it through. If it's something we can use to put a name to those devils that done those two shootings, they'll jump on it. But you better be ready to talk to the FBI pretty quick, an' your friend, too."

Marie took out her phone. "I better let him know."

Keller was almost to the gate when the patrol car passed him going the other way. He glanced in his rearview mirror to see it turning around. He sighed and pulled over. As he did, his cell phone chirred softly. He pulled it off his belt and checked caller ID. It was Marie. He considered answering, but the patrol car pulled in behind him and hit the blue lights. He'd have to call her back later. He hit the "ignore" button and holstered the cell phone.

Keller recognized the cop who tapped on his window, a patrol sergeant named Merrick. They had always gotten along well enough. Keller hoped that wasn't about to change.

"Keller," Merrick said. There was amusement in his voice and

Keller relaxed a bit. "What you doin' out here, stirrin' up the rich folks?"

"Looking for a jumper," Keller said. "Her parents live here."

"The Marks girl?" Merrick said.

Keller was surprised. "You know her?"

Merrick nodded. "Oh, yeah. I was the one who came out here with Social Services the night they took her and her brother."

"You think her father molested her?"

Merrick shrugged. "First she said yes, then she said no. I'll tell you one thing, the dad's a big enough asshole to have done it." He looked back as another car pulled in behind the patrol car. "Ah, shit. Speak of the devil. Best give me license and registration, Keller. Let's make it look good."

"Got it." Keller pulled out his wallet and handed the license to Merrick. He was reaching into the glove box for his registration when Marks came blustering up. "That's him," he said. "That's the guy who was at my house. I want that son of a bitch arrested."

Merrick stood up as Keller handed him the registration. "Arrested for what, sir?"

"He assaulted me!" Marks shouted.

Merrick cocked an eyebrow, looked Marks up and down.

"Really, sir?" he said. He looked at Keller. "You hit this guy?"

"Never laid a hand on him, Sergeant," Keller said.

Merrick handed the registration back. "I tend to believe him, sir," he told Marks. "See, there ain't a mark on you. I know Mister Keller a little. And when he hits somebody, it's pretty obvious they been hit."

"He threatened me!" Marks snarled. "That's still illegal, isn't it?"

Merrick turned to Keller. "What about that, Mr. Keller?"

Keller shrugged. "His wife invited me in. When Mr. Marks

got home, he told me to leave. He acted like he was going to get physical about it. I, ah, advised him against it."

"Pretty good advice." Merrick nodded. He turned back to Marks. "And he was invited in, so it ain't trespassing."

"God damn it, what do I pay my taxes for?" Marks fumed. "Are you going to do your job, or do I have to—"

Merrick cut him off. "You need to get back in your car, sir," he said, leaning on the last word. "Mister Keller's leaving. You best do the same. And Mister Keller?"

"Yes, Sergeant?"

"Don't come back."

"No problem."

"I want your badge number," Marks said in a low, furious voice. "So help me God, I'm going to—"

"My badge number is 714," Merrick said. "My watch commander is Lieutenant Boggs." Merrick's partner, a hulking black cop with the build of a weightlifter, had come up to join them. "Officer Thomas," Merrick said, "Would you walk Mister Marks back to his vehicle?"

"Glad to," Thomas said. Marks looked like he was about to say something else, but thought better of it. He turned on his heel and stomped back to his car, Thomas following in his wake.

"See what I mean?" Merrick said to Keller in a low voice.

"Plenty of assholes around," Keller observed. "Doesn't mean he raped his own daughter."

"Who knows?" Merrick said. "But you best be movin' on, Keller."

"Okay," Keller said as he started the car, "and thanks." Merrick waved as he drove away. Keller noticed there was a different guy in the guard shack as he drove out.

As he drove, Keller remembered the phone call from Marie. He pulled out the phone and hit the speed-dial.

Marie pulled the cell phone out of her pocket after the second ring. "Hey," Keller said.

"Jack," Marie said. "We got a match on the bullet used in that gas station shooting and one of the bullets in that church massacre."

"Okay," Keller said.

"And they're running a cartridge casing, same caliber, that I picked up out at the trailer last night."

"Wait a minute," Keller said. "You think maybe Laurel Marks and Randle are the church shooters?"

"We got the guy who we think sold them the guns used in the shootings at the church and the diner. He said the buyers were an older man and a younger woman."

"I'll be damned," Keller said.

"Yeah. Jack, I'm going to have to talk to the FBI. There's a couple of agents here at the station."

There was a long pause on the other end. "Okay."

She took a deep breath. "I'm going to have to tell them about the trailer. They'll probably want to talk to you."

Another long pause. "Yeah," Keller said finally. "No way around that."

"No," she said. "There isn't. I wanted to give you a heads up."

"Thanks."

"Jack," she said, "you're not mad at me, are you?"

"I'm pissed at this situation," he said. "Not at you."

"You'd better hold off for a while on Laurel Marks," Marie said. "If she's one of the church and diner shooters, let the FBI handle it."

"She's still got our paper out on her, Marie," Keller said. "As far as I'm concerned, she's fair game."

"That's not what I mean and you know it!" Marie snapped. "If she's involved in this, she's gone totally bugfuck. And she and her buddy are heavily armed."

"Yeah," Keller said. "I may need to ask Angela for a raise."

"Jack," Marie said helplessly.

"Don't worry," Keller said. "How likely is it that I'll find her before the feds do?"

"Knowing you, pretty damn likely," Marie muttered.

"What?" Keller said.

"Nothing," she said. "Jack, please go home."

"I am," he said. "I've got a lead, but I'm not going to get to it tonight. I'll talk to you later."

"Yeah. Okay," she said. "Fine."

"Love you," he said.

If you really loved me you'd go home and stay there, she thought. "Love you, too," she said.

fourteen

Stan was lying on the couch drinking a beer and watching the TV when Laurel came out of the bedroom. She had on a pair of cutoff jeans and a man's shirt tied and knotted under her breasts. She came over to the couch. Stan moved his feet so she could sit down. He didn't look at her.

"Hey," she said.

He took a sip of the beer. "Hey," he said finally.

"Anything good on?"

He shrugged. "Not really."

"You still mad at me?" she said.

He shrugged again. "I'm not mad."

"Yeah," she said. "You are." She looked nervously toward the bedroom door. She leaned over and whispered to Stan. "Listen, she said. "If I tell you somethin', you can't ever let on to Roy that I told you."

He looked at her for the first time. He pitched his voice low as well. "What?"

She glanced at the door again. "Nothing happened, Stan. We didn't do nothing."

He snorted and looked back at the TV. "Right."

"I mean it, Stan," she said. "He's havin' one of his spells."

Stan sat up. "Just what is it that he's sick with?"

"There was somethin' wrong with the water back at his old place. Some kind of poison in the ground. He thinks it gave him cancer. In his brain. It's why he gets the headaches. It's one reason he's so mad."

"So why did you—" Before Stan could finish, the bedroom door opened and Roy came out.

"You get any rest?" he said to Stan.

"Yeah," Stan said. "A little."

"Good," Roy said. He looked at the TV. "Hey, it's quarter til eleven," he said. "Turn on Channel Ten." Stan looked at him, then tossed him the remote. "Here," he said. "Change it yourself." Roy caught the remote in the air. He gave Stan a hard look, but didn't say anything as he pressed the button.

The anchor on the screen was a young white guy with capped teeth and perfectly coiffed brown hair. "Hey," Roy said. "Where's that Chinese girl? The one who gave us her number?" No one answered. "God damn it," Roy fumed. "Where the hell. . ." Stan held up a hand to silence him. The graphic that seemed to hang in the air over the anchor's shoulder said "Shooting Investigation." Roy shut up and thumbed the volume control.

"Police and federal investigators have confirmed a definite link between the shootings at a rural church and the massacre at a diner this past Friday."

"All right," Roy said with evident satisfaction. "The feds."

The anchor went on. "Ballistics evidence has shown that the same military-style weapons were used in both shootings. Law

171

enforcement officials however, continue to reassure the public that these acts are not the work of foreign terrorists."

"Damn straight," Roy said. "I ain't no fuckin' towelhead." The anchor had moved on to a story about local football, then went to a commercial.

"Not bad," Roy said. "But where's the Chinese chick?"

Stan crossed the room and picked up the cell phone lying on top of the TV. The battery was dead. "Well, we can't call her on this. Unless we pick up a recharger."

"We can stop at a Wal-Mart on our way out," Roy said. "We're leavin' in an hour. You might want to fix yourself somethin' to eat. It's gonna be a long drive."

"Where are we going?" Stan said.

Roy grinned. "Time for scene three." He walked to the door. Stan watched his back for a few moments, his eyes narrowed, appraising. Then he got up and followed.

Marie came out of the interview room rubbing her eyes. The FBI agent that had conducted what he called a "debriefing" had been polite but relentless. He had taken every statement Marie had made and quizzed her about it from every possible angle, poking at every perceived inconsistency, all the while apologizing for doing so. She felt wrung out, like her brain had been squeezed for every scrap of information. *And this is how they treat the people on their side,* she thought wryly. *I could really use a cup of coffee.* She headed toward the squad room, hoping against hope that there was something left besides bitter bottom-of-the-pot dregs.

As she approached the squad-room door, she heard voices. One was raised, agitated. "It ain't right, doggone it," the voice was saying. "It ain't right, an' you know it." Wardell, she thought.

The other voice came back, deeper, tired-sounding. "I know, Tom," he was saying. By then, Marie had reached the door and pushed it open.

Wardell and Shelby were sitting across a flimsy-looking folding table, each of them hunched over a Styrofoam cup. They looked up as Marie came into the room, then quickly looked away. *Oh shit,* Marie thought. *This can't be good.*

"Hey," she said as she walked over to the coffeepot on another nearby table. Both of them mumbled their responses. The pot was full with fresh brew. *Thank God for small favors,* Marie thought. She poured herself a cup and sat down at the table with Wardell and Shelby. Neither had spoken since she came into the room.

"So," she said. "From the look of you two, I'm thinking someone's got some bad news."

Shelby finally looked at her. "Lieutenant says he wants to see you. As soon as you got done with the FBI guy."

Marie took a sip of coffee. She leaned her head back and looked at the ceiling, stretching her neck. "Great," she said. "Looks like our boy Garrett scored some points."

"It's only an administrative suspension," Shelby said. "With pay. Just till the SBI can investigate the, uh . . ."

"The brutality complaint," Marie said.

Shelby gulped his coffee. "Yeah," he said. "And Garrett's filing a lawsuit. Against you and the department."

She shook her head. "This day just gets better and better."

"It ain't right," Wardell muttered. "I was there. I saw ever'thing. I been with this department for years. They oughta believe me."

Marie smiled at him. "I know you went to bat for me, Sarge," she said. "I appreciate it. And they'll believe both of us. Eventually."

173

"Hey, Jones," Shelby said with forced joviality. "It'll be like a vacation. Paid time off, girl. Can't hardly beat that."

She looked at him. "You feel like taking any vacation time right now, Shelby?"

The fake smile left his face. "Naw," he said as he looked away. "Sorry."

She reached out and patted him on the shoulder. "It's okay." The three of them looked into their coffee cups, silently contemplating whatever it was they saw there. Finally, Marie spoke.

"You know, I grew up wanting to be a cop. Like my dad. I thought he was Batman, Superman, Starsky, and Hutch all rolled into one. I couldn't think of anything better than to be like him." She took a sip of her coffee. "And I love it, you know? I really love this job. But somehow, it's like it doesn't love me."

Shelby looked alarmed. "What are you thinking of, Jones?" he said.

She finished off the coffee. "Nothing, Shelby," she said. "I'm just tired." She heard the door of the squad room open behind her. "Deputy Jones?" the lieutenant said. "I need to speak with you a minute."

As she stood up, Shelby spoke. "Don't do anything you can't undo, Jones," he said. "You're a good officer. This'll blow over. Don't throw it all away."

"Thanks, Shelby," she said. "I'll think about it." She squared her shoulders and followed the lieutenant into his office.

The sharp trilling of the cell phone jarred Grace out of sleep. She stuck her hand out from beneath the covers and flailed for a moment until she found the phone. She lost her grip on it for a moment and it clattered to the floor.

"Fuck," she muttered. She flung the covers off, sat up, and picked up the phone. "Hello?" she said.

"Why weren't you on the news tonight?" The voice was male, deep, with a distinct Eastern North Carolina accent.

"Is this who I think it is?" she replied.

"Don't know. Who do you think it is?"

There was a half-empty bottled water on her nightstand. Her hands were shaking with excitement as she picked it up and took a drink. "One pretty angry guy," Grace said.

There was a pause. "You got that right," the voice said finally. "So why weren't you on TV?"

"Had a little disagreement with my producer," she said. "You might say I got a little pissed off myself."

Another long pause. "You won't be no good to me if you're fired."

"I'm not fired. Like I say, it'll pass." *Especially if I get an interview with you,* she thought. "So what are you mad about, Mister . . . what do you want me to call you, anyway?"

Another pause. "What are they calling me?"

"Who?"

"The cops. Other reporters. They give me a name yet?"

"I don't know what you mean."

"You know, like the Green River Killer. The Boston Strangler."

She ran a hand through her hair. "Uh, no. Not that I know of."

A slight chuckle. "Well, it's still early. They'll think of something."

Her mouth was suddenly dry. She took a sip of water. "What do you want to be called?"

This time the silence went on so long that Grace thought she'd lost the connection. "I create scenes. I imagine them in my head, then I make 'em come true."

"So you're like a writer."

There was a derisive snort of laughter. "Hell, no. Who the fuck cares about the writer? I put everything together. They're my productions beginning to end."

"So you're the producer?"

"Good as anything else."

"Look, Mister Producer," Grace said. "You don't have to hurt anybody else. You've got our attention. If you want to tell your story, just tell it to me. I'll get it out."

"I ain't got nearly enough attention yet. That's about to change though. Right about now."

"What do you mean?"

That chuckle again. This time it made Grace shiver. "It's show time, folks."

"Wait," Grace yelled, but the line was dead. She looked at the clock. It was 5:30 A.M.

Roy snapped the cell phone shut. "Pull over," he said to Stan, who was behind the wheel.

"What's going on?" Stan said as he steered the car onto the rough shoulder of the road. Fields stretched out on either side, bordered by groves of trees.

"You said you wanted a bigger part," Roy said. His voice was almost jovial, like an uncle giving out a special sweet. "You wanted to do more than drive. Now's your chance." He turned to the back of the van. "Laurel, baby," he said. "You remember what to do?"

"Sure, Roy," Laurel said. "You sure you don't want to—"

"Naw," Roy said. He slid out of the passenger side. "You kids have fun. Leave the driving to me." Stan slid to the back as Roy took the wheel. Laurel handed him one of the M-14s. "Remember like I showed you, sweetie," she whispered as they pulled back onto the road.

Stan could feel his heart racing. "I don't know where we're going," he whispered back.

"Look up ahead," Roy said. "You'll know it when you see it."

Stan looked out the front window. The road had widened to four lanes. Then he saw the building.

It was a massive windowless construction of steel walls and piping, rising and sprawling across acres of the flat land, as big as a mountain and as impersonal. The long line of stopped cars pulled into the far right lane looked like toys in the shadow of that pitiless immensity. It was one of the first cool mornings of late fall, and the steam from the exhausts rose in the air behind the vehicles before evaporating in the sun, leaving only a shimmer of exhaust fumes that made the cars seem distorted, unreal, as if they too were getting ready to vanish into the dawn.

A chain-link fence topped with barbed concertina wire ran along the road next to them. The line of cars reached all the way to a break in the fence several hundred yards ahead, where they turned right through the gate into a huge parking lot. Stan could see cars in the lot, people getting out, lights being turned off. As they approached the last car, Roy pulled into the center lane around it. With practiced ease, Laurel grabbed the door handle and pulled the van's sliding door open. A cold clammy blast of morning air and the throat-closing stench of exhaust fumes filled the cargo compartment along with the mutter and rumble of dozens of idling engines. Roy slowed as they passed the car, a beat-up old Plymouth Volare. They were only three feet away from the driver, a middle-aged woman with white hair and the copper-brown skin of a Lumbee Indian. Stan barely had time to register the look of surprise on the woman's face before Laurel shot her in the head. The woman was slammed to the other side of the car, her brains and blood spraying from the open passenger window. Then they were alongside the next car, a Dodge Charger driven by a young black man in cornrows. He was looking back, craning his neck as he tried to determine the meaning of the loud noise behind him. Laurel shot him, too.

"Any time, Stan," she yelled over the roar of the wind blowing through the open door. Stan raised the rifle. He found himself looking down the barrel at another black man, older than the first, with graying hair. The man's jaw dropped as he found himself facing the muzzle of a rifle. Then his face dissolved in red and white and gray as Stan's shot struck him between the eyes. Laurel whooped with excitement. The next car was filled with young Hispanic men, crowded into the car. "Slow down, Roy," Laurel yelled, then she and Stan began firing. Stan saw one of his shots strike the throat of a fat brown-skinned boy who looked no older than sixteen. The boy screamed and clawed at the gushing fountain of red that had suddenly appeared below his ear. Then they were past and pulling up to the next car. Stan began firing reflexively, almost mechanically, at the occupant of each new car that came into view. Faces contorted in fear became faces contorted in agony as his and Laurel's shots struck home.

"Almost time," Roy yelled. Stan looked forward again. People had begun to figure out what was going on. Cars were trying to pull out of the line, some of them running into each other as the drivers panicked.

"One more!" Laurel yelled. Stan turned back and raised the rifle.

The girl behind the wheel of the VW Rabbit was young and thin. What might have been a pretty face was marred by a spray of acne across her nose and cheeks. As Stan's finger tightened on the trigger, the girl did something odd. Instead of trying to run straight away from him as the other drivers had done, she appeared to be trying to climb over the backseat. It was as if she was looking for something. Then Stan saw the car seat. It was made of gray plastic with a thin white blanket spread over it. Stan lowered the rifle. The girl looked back at him, a pleading look in her eyes. She appeared to be trying to reach into the car seat but she couldn't get back far enough. Then Stan noticed a pair of tiny hands reaching out of the seat toward the girl.

"Shoot!" Laurel yelled. She was working at the action of her own gun as if trying to clear a jam. Stan couldn't speak. He tried to raise the rifle, but was stopped cold by the sight of those small, desperately reaching hands. Then Roy gunned the engine and they were pulling away.

"I don't get out now, the road'll be blocked," he called back. Laurel's rifle clattered to the floor of the van as she pushed the door shut. Just as it closed, Stan could see the guard shack next to the gate. The uniformed guard was frantically shouting into a phone.

"Hold on!" Stan shouted. "Open the door!" Laurel pulled the door back slightly. Roy slowed, then accelerated as if unsure what to do. "The guard!" Stan yelled. He raised the rifle. He could see a crudely stenciled sign hung beneath the window of the shack. 195 DAYS NO ACCIDENTS, the sign read. Another sign hung beneath with the same smeared stenciling read: NO DRUGS NO WEAPONS ALL CARS ARE SUBJECT TO SEARCH. Stan shot the guard in the chest. "Go!" he screamed. Roy gunned the engine. Laurel lost her grip on the door and tumbled backwards, cursing. Stan grabbed the door with one hand and pulled hard. The door rumbled on its tracks and slammed shut. Stan moved to the back of the van and looked out the rear window.

There was a tangle of cars in the road behind. The exhaust fumes had been joined by plumes of steam from broken radiators and water lines of cars that had crashed into one another.

He collapsed to the metal floor of the van. Laurel was pulling herself up to a sitting position. She grabbed Stan and pulled him to her, kissing him roughly, her lips demanding. She pulled away and looked at him, her eyes bright. "How was it, Stan?" she hissed. "Was it good? Didn't I tell you? Wasn't it intense?"

"Y-yeah," Stan said. His heart was pounding and he felt a thrill in his blood that was more intense than the meth had ever been. At the same time, he couldn't get the image of the girl with her baby out of his mind. "I . . . I think I missed one," he stammered.

"I know, hon, I saw," Laurel said. "It'll be okay. It'll be fine."

"She had a baby," Stan said. "What the hell was she doing with a baby?"

"It'll be okay," she said again. Her hand smoothed his hair as if to reassure him, but her touch was rough, brutal. She pulled his lips to hers again. Her tongue invaded his mouth.

"Hey lovebirds," Roy called back. "Save it for later. We got work to do." Stan broke the clinch, gasping. He felt the van bumping over rough road. After a few minutes, they stopped.

"Get the plates," Roy said. Stan reached into one of the canvas bags on the floor of the van and pulled out one of the stolen license plates Roy had showed him. They got out.

They were in a dirt clearing behind a grove of trees. The van's appearance had changed. There was a ladder rack with a pair of aluminum extension ladders on the roof. Working quickly, they changed the plates, took the ladders off and unscrewed the racks. Then they climbed back in the van. Stan's high was wearing off and he felt limp and shaky again. He wanted some more of the meth. As if reading his mind, Laurel pulled out one of the "special" joints. She handed it to Stan with a Bic lighter. "Fire it up, baby," she said. "You've had a busy day."

• • •

Keller was up and drinking a cup of coffee when the knock came on the door. He peered through the peephole. A man and a woman were standing there. They both wore dark suits as nearly identical as a man's and a woman's suit could be made. He opened the door.

"Jackson Keller?" the man said. He was tall and angular, with thinning dark hair and a widow's peak. Keller didn't answer. "I'm Special Agent Sanderson, Federal Bureau of Investigation." He showed Keller a flash of badge. He indicated the woman, a slim attractive blonde with her hair pulled back in a severe bun. She was carrying a slim black briefcase. "This is Special Agent Cassidey."

"Yeah," Keller said. "I'm Jack Keller."

"Mister Keller," Sanderson said, "Would you come with us, please?" He stepped back, leaving a path between himself and Cassidey. A dark blue Ford Taurus was parked under the live oak.

Keller didn't move. "Am I under arrest?" he said.

"No sir," Cassidey answered. "We just want to ask you some questions."

Keller stepped back into the house. "You can ask me those here, then," he said. "C'mon in."

Sanderson and Cassidey looked at each other. They obviously weren't used to people refusing to come with them. Sanderson stepped through the door, tentative, as if he expected someone to jump out at him. When no one did, he asked Keller, "Sir, is there some reason you don't want to come with us?"

"Yeah," Keller said. "My grandma told me never to get in cars with strange men." He sat down on the couch and picked up his coffee. "Or strange women," he said to Cassidey, who was still standing in the doorway, "although I've been known to fudge a little on that rule. You coming in or going out, Agent Cassidey?"

Cassidey's lips drew into a thin line. She came in and shut the door. She didn't sit down, however. She stood by the doorway as if blocking Keller's escape. "You guys want coffee?" Keller asked. They both shook their heads. Keller shrugged and lit a cigarette. He picked up his coffee cup and leaned back on the couch. "You had some questions?" he said.

Sanderson took the easy chair. "You've been tracking a young woman named Laurel Marks."

"Yeah," Keller said. "She didn't show up for her court date. We've got paper on her. I'm supposed to bring her back."

"We want to know everything you know about her and a guy named Roy Randle."

Keller took a sip of coffee. "What do you want to know?"

"What were you doing out at Randle's place on the river?"

"Looking for her," he said. "He's her boyfriend. I thought she might be there."

Cassidey spoke up. "You didn't find her."

"No."

"Is that why you burned the place down, Keller?" Sanderson said.

Keller didn't answer. He took a long drag on his cigarette and studied Sanderson for a moment. Then he said, "What the hell are you talking about?"

Cassidey sat next to him on the couch and snapped open the briefcase. She pulled a manila folder out and flipped it open on the coffee table. There was a sheaf of photographs in the folder. Keller had to lean forward to see. He recognized the dirt lot where the trailer had stood. It was mostly gone, burned out to the frame. A figure stood off to one side. It was impossible to tell if the figure was a man or a woman because of the bulky orange coverall it wore. A square helmet that looked like it belonged on a kid's drawing of a spacesuit hid the person's face.

"What's with the HazMat suit?" Keller asked.

"Turns out the place is rotten with toxic waste," Cassidey said. "The development's been on the EPA's Superfund list for years. Somebody used it as a dumping ground. Plus, it looks like Randle had been running a methamphetamine lab. He was just dumping the waste on the ground."

So that's where he got his money, Keller thought. "What makes you think I'm the one who burned it down?"

"Your girlfriend told us all about it. She said you two went out there looking for Laurel Marks. She told us you went in." He smirked. "She said the door was unlocked, but I think we both know better than that."

Keller shrugged. "He had something better than a lock."

"So we heard," Sanderson said. "And we also heard you got pretty pissed off about Randle's security system."

"Yeah. Getting shot is kind of a pet peeve of mine. I'm funny like that."

"We also know some of your history, Keller," Sanderson said. We know you got bounced out of the army on a medical discharge. Went pretty nutso, I hear. Since then you've been in and out of trouble. Even managed to beat a couple of murder charges. And we know you're under psychiatric care."

Keller looked at him. "So?" he said.

Sanderson started to say something, but Keller interrupted. "Look, quit jerking me around. If Jones told you what happened, she also told you we came straight back here. Right after she left, I was talking on the phone with my doctor. Then some more friends stopped by and we were here all night. If you think you can work that time line to stick in enough time for me to drive all the way out there, torch the place, and come back, be my guest.

Otherwise, stop treating me like I'm stupid." He sat back again and took a sip of coffee. "You get a match on the cartridge Jones found out there?"

"That's on a need-to-know basis," Cassidey said. "You don't have any . . ."

"Okay, we're done." Keller said. He stood up. "I've got to get to work. If I catch up to Laurel Marks, I'll be sure to let you guys know. After I've surrendered her downtown and cleared her paper."

Sanderson stood up. "You're off that case, Keller," he said. "You try to interfere in a federal investigation, and we'll—"

"Good luck, guys," Keller interrupted. Sanderson and Cassidey hesitated, then got up. They walked past Keller and out the door. Sanderson turned as they reached the bottom of the steps. "Don't leave town, Keller," he said. Keller didn't answer. Sanderson seemed nonplussed by that. He turned and walked back to the car. Keller closed the door.

He was washing the coffee cup and putting it into the sink when his cell phone rang. He answered. "Keller."

"That you, balloon man?" Ellen Marks's voice was hoarse.

"Mrs. Marks," Keller said. "Yes ma'am, this is Jack Keller. What can I—"

"The son of a bitch hit me," she said. "He hit *me*."

"Who?" he replied. "Your husband?"

"Twenty-two years we've been married," she said. "He's never raised a hand. Can you believe that? It was what I always told myself . . . the things they say can't be true. He's never raised a hand to me. He's never hit me. So I believed every word he said. That son of a bitch." Her voice broke on the last word.

"Mrs. Marks," Keller said. "You need to call the cops."

Her voice was steadier as she said, "Oh, yes, Mr. Keller," she said. "I will. Believe it."

"Why do you think he hit you?" Keller said. "After all this time . . ."

Her laugh was a horrible sound, like that of crows feasting on a corpse. "He didn't like me talking to you. Oh, no, not one little bit. He thought I might lead you to Laurel, and if Laurel started talking again . . . who knows what might happen?"

"So you know where she is," Keller said.

"I know where she might be," she said.

"I'm listening," Keller said.

"You'll need to come to the house," she said.

"Why?" he said, but she had hung up.

fifteen

The news set was in a state of barely controlled chaos as Grace walked in. The morning-news anchor had been on live since the news of the hog-plant massacre had come over the police scanners, but he had long since run out of new information to report. The station had sent the Live-Cam helicopter to the scene, and the young anchor was rereading the official press release from the local sheriff over the aerial shot of the mess on the ground. The monitors showed a jumble of automobiles strewn across the road like toys tossed out by a small child. Here and there, red and blue lights flashed among the tangle as law enforcement tried to sort out the crime scene. Grace walked quietly in the dimly lighted space behind the cameras. Picking her way over thick black cables that stretched across the floor, she made her way to the control room. Howard was standing behind the technical director. He was calling out directions into his headset microphone in a low tense voice. His forehead was glistening with sweat. "Okay," he was saying. "Wrap up and throw to commercial. In five . . . four . . . three . . . ," he counted down the seconds. As the music swelled up and the news logo rolled, he whipped his headset off.

"Howard," Grace said.

"Not now, Grace," Howard snapped. He turned to the technical director. "When we come back—"

"He called me, Howard," Grace said, a little louder.

Howard turned toward her. "What? Who called you?"

She gestured to the monitor that showed the feed from the chopper. "The guy that did this. Or one of them. The ringleader."

Howard looked skeptical. "How do you know it was him, Grace?" he said. "It could have been some kid—"

"Because he told me. He was on his way to do it. He told me it was 'show time.' Right before that happened."

"Holy Christ," the TD murmured. He glanced at the clock. "Two minutes, Howard," he said.

Grace handed Howard a CD and a floppy disk. "I wrote my copy at home before I came in," she said. "It's on this disk. The pictures they sent me are still on this CD. Put me on, Howard."

Howard took the disc. "I haven't had time to review the copy . . ."

She leaned forward. "This is the biggest fucking story in town right now. Probably in the whole country. You can run it right goddamn now, my way, or I can walk out of here, pick up the phone, and be on any one of a dozen national shows by this evening. Your choice."

"A minute-thirty," the TD said. Howard hesitated for a moment, the grabbed the floppy and the CD. "Load it up," he snapped at a nearby production assistant. He turned to Grace. "Get Grace a mike," he snapped into his headset. "Camera two, get ready for the two-shot. One, you're on Gary, three, medium on Grace."

"One minute," the TD murmured.

Howard pulled his microphone away from his mouth. "I'm trusting you, Grace," he said. "Try not to get us all arrested. Or sued." She barely heard the last word as she bolted down the stairs.

The audio guy was fastening a lapel mike onto Grace's blazer even as she slid into the co-anchor chair. She guy glanced over at Gary, who was listening intently to instructions from the control booth in his earpiece. Grace slid her own earpiece in as she swiveled to face camera two for the shot of her and Gary. The TD's voice came over the earpiece, "Three, two, one, and. . . ." The music came up, the logo rolled, and Grace saw her words come up on the TelePrompTer screen in front of the camera.

"In the latest on the Barnwell Foods Massacre this morning," Gary said smoothly, "Action News anchor Grance Tranh has this exclusive report. Grace?"

She turned slightly to look intently into camera three. "In a startling development," she said, "the man believed to be behind not only the Barnwell Foods massacre this morning, but also behind the church and diner shootings a few nights ago, has contacted this reporter with information about his motives. We warn you, some of the exclusive images in this report are extremely graphic. . . ." *Network, here I come,* she thought.

Marie was seated on the floor with Ben playing a complicated game with trucks and blocks for which only he seemed to fully understand the rules. He'd occasionally give a theatrical sigh, followed by an exasperated "*No,* Mom, not *there,*" and correct her error. He was so serious, his brow furrowed with such concentration, that it was all Marie could do not to laugh.

After her conversation with the lieutenant last night, sleep had eluded her. The lieutenant had tried to be reassuring, saying over and over that it was only temporary, that they'd soon enough break Garrett's story down, that she'd be back on the road before she knew it. But, he had said, policy was policy. After a rash of brutality complaints and a number of lawsuits against departments across the state, all complaints had to be investigated thoroughly to avoid later charges of whitewash or cover-ups. And the officers involved had to be on suspension. No exceptions. Marie had taken the news stoically, trying hard to show nothing on her face. She held on to Shelby's advice not to do anything permanent. But she doubted if she was going to come back. And that upheaval had kept her tossing and turning all night. Her eyes felt gritty and she had to stifle the impulse to yawn.

The ringing of the kitchen phone jarred her out of her reverie. She rose to her feet and bent over to give Ben a kiss on the top of the head. "I've got it, Dad," she called. She walked into the kitchen and picked up the phone. "Hello?"

"How're you doing, Jones?" It was Shelby.

"I'm okay," she said. "Thanks."

"They done it again," he said.

She felt a hollowness in the pit of her stomach. "Where?"

"Hog processing plant down east," he replied. "Bunch of people was in line to get in the parking lot 'fore work. They drove up and shot 'em down."

Marie rubbed her forehead. "Guess they haven't made any progress on finding Randle and the Marks girl?"

"Naw," he said. "You want to come out to the house later? We can talk more there."

"Sure," Marie said. "But why . . ."

"Can't talk anymore here," he said. "I'll see you about six o'clock."

189

She hung up the phone as her father came into the kitchen. "That was Shelby," she said. "They think the church shooters just killed a bunch of people on their way in to work."

He grimaced. "Shit," he said. "Bad news. Good of him to tell you about it, though."

"He wants to talk to me," she said. "In person."

He looked impressed. "Looks like you got yourself a friend in high places. This bullshit may blow over after all."

There was a different guard at the gate when Keller pulled up. "Jack Keller for Mrs. Marks," he said, and the guy waved him through. *Well that was easier,* he thought. This time, he found the house with no trouble. He noticed there was a bright red soft-top Jeep Wrangler parked out front. It looked new.

Ellen Marks answered the door at the first ring. She was dressed in a tailored black pantsuit that showed off her curves without being ostentatious about it. She wore large tinted glasses that hid most of her eyes. "Hello, Jack," she said. "Come in." She turned and walked back into the house.

At least she's sober this time, Keller thought. Or at least she hasn't had enough for me to smell it on her. Yet. He followed her back into the living room. He could see out the window to where a golfer was lining up his shot at the edge of the water hazard. Ellen Marks sat down on the couch and lit a cigarette. She didn't speak. She just looked at him. Finally, he broke the silence.

"You said you knew where Laurel might be," he said.

"Let me ask you something, Jack," she said. "If you find Laurel, you're going to bring her in alive, correct? I mean, if you can."

He nodded. "Right. If . . . something happens to her, the

190

court may remit the bond. That means the bondsman may not have to pay the court. But it's up to the court. Still, I don't get paid if that happens."

"So you've got an interest in keeping her alive until you bring her in. A financial interest."

"Right."

She laughed sharply. "Self-interest. That's something I can trust." She took another drag on the cigarette, then studied it for a moment, as if fascinated by the stream of smoke rising from the tip. Then she abruptly stood up. "Follow me." She walked past Keller and out a side door. Keller followed her down a long hallway. They ended up in what appeared to be an office. A large, heavily varnished oak desk dominated one end of the room, with papers arranged neatly on it. There was a leather couch along one wall. Over the couch was a small framed photograph. The frame looked as if it was made with old scrap wood, as if from a barn or old house. It looked jarringly out of place among the sleek leather furniture of the rest of the room. Ellen walked over and stared at the photograph.

It was a small black-and-white, an old Polaroid shot, going slightly yellow with age despite being sealed under glass. It showed a family standing and looking solemnly into the camera. The background behind them appeared to be a grove of trees. There was an unfocused white blur in the distance behind the trees that might have been a house.

There was an older man dressed in overalls, standing stiffly beside and slightly behind a younger woman. His face was lined with care and his body seemed slightly stooped, as if he had been broken and not put back together just right. The woman was younger, her face less worn. There was a hint of laughter in her dark eyes, fighting the sadness in the lines around them. She had her hand on the shoulder of a dark-haired girl about eight

191

years old in a frilly white dress. The dark-haired girl stared into the camera with what looked like resentment, as if she wanted to be somewhere, anywhere else. Another, younger girl beside her looked off-camera, her mouth slightly open as if in surprise. Keller looked more closely at the older girl. She looked familiar.

"Tell me, Jack, would you have ever taken me for a farm girl?" Ellen Marks spoke up. Keller didn't answer. "It's a terrible life, you know," she went on. "If there's too much rain, the tobacco gets blue mold and you go broke. If there's not enough rain, the crops dry out and you go broke. If there's perfect weather, there's so much tobacco at market that the price goes down and you go broke." She took another drag on her cigarette. "And when things work just right, you have to go out and pick it. Your back hurts from stooping over to pick the sand lugs. And you feel like you'll never get that sticky juice off your hands."

He recognized the older girl now. It was Ellen Marks.

"Good thing you got out."

"Yes," she said. "Good thing."

"So, is this your family's old farm?" he asked.

She shook her head, as if suddenly coming back. "Still is," she said. "I keep trying to convince my little sister to sell. But she won't do it. My parents are buried out there, you see. And their parents as well. There's a little family graveyard on the hill."

"You think that's where Laurel might be?"

"She always liked it there. Even after Daddy . . . my father died and the place started to fall apart. She loved to go see her granny. When she could."

"You make it sound like it was a pretty rare thing."

Ellen turned to look at him. "My mother couldn't stand my husband, Jack," she said. "And the feeling was mutual. It was . . . one of the things I found attractive about him."

"But when Laurel was at her grandmother's, her father was never there."

She looked away, out the window. "Yes."

"So where is this place?"

"East of Fayetteville," she said. She walked over to the desk and picked up a paper. "I've already written out directions." Keller reached for the paper. She pulled back slightly. "There were some people here earlier," she said. "From the FBI."

"A man and a woman?" Keller said.

She nodded. "They said . . . they said that Laurel might be involved with those shootings that have been happening."

Keller nodded. "Yeah. I've heard the same thing."

"You won't hurt her, will you?" Ellen said.

Keller ducked the question. "Like I said. I don't get paid if she dies."

She took off her tinted glasses and looked at him. Her jaw was swollen and puffy and one of her eyes was blackened. "That's not all there is, though, is there? It's not just the money?"

Keller knew it wasn't. The takedown was the thing, the end of the hunt when he delivered his quarry into the hands of the magistrate. But he didn't feel like explaining that to Ellen Marks. "Yeah," he said, "that's pretty much it."

She put the glasses back on and sighed. "I'll have to trust that, then," she said. She held out the paper and he took it from her hand.

"Mom?" a voice said from the door. Keller turned. A young man who looked to be in his early twenties was standing there. He was barefoot, dressed in jeans and an unbuttoned shirt. His short brown hair was in disarray as if he'd just gotten out of bed. His skin was pasty and his eyes were baggy and bloodshot. He looked badly hungover.

"Curt," Ellen said. "You're up."

"Who's this guy?" Curt said, jerking his chin at Keller.

Ellen Marks's lips tightened at the rudeness. "This is Mister Keller," she said. "We have some business to discuss."

"About your sister," Keller said.

The effect on the boy was remarkable. Anger flashed in his eyes. He stepped forward, his fists clenched and slightly raised.

I seem to be rubbing all the men in this family the wrong way, Keller thought. He raised a hand and the boy stopped.

"Hold on there, kid," Keller said.

The anger remained in the face but the voice was a harsh, fearful whisper. "Go away!" the boy said. "Leave us alone!"

"Curtis!" Ellen snapped. "What's wrong with you?"

He walked over to his mother and put an arm around her protectively. The action seemed to steady him. "My family's been through too much," he said in a stronger voice. "I don't want my mother upset anymore."

"She invited me here, Curt," Keller said. "She thinks she knows where I might be able to find Laurel."

"Why?" he said.

"Mister Keller works for Laurel's bail bondsman," she said.

"She skipped out on us," Keller said. "I need to find her and bring her back."

"And you're helping him?" Curt said to his mother. "Why?"

Keller started to speak, but Ellen cut him off. "It's just better that she turn herself in, Curt," she said. "She won't be in as much trouble that way." She looked significantly at Keller. *He doesn't know about the shootings,* Keller thought.

"That's right, Curt," Keller said. "If I can talk her into coming in on her own, it might go easier on her." There was a huge difference between might and would, but there was no need to tell the kid that. "Any hints on how I might convince her?"

Curt's face crumpled. "What do you mean by that?" he said.

"Nothing," Keller said. He remembered that Curt had talked Laurel into recanting her accusation of abuse. Suddenly the boy's reactions came into focus for Keller. He felt a wave of revulsion flash through him. Too casually, he said, "I hear you can talk your sister into just about anything."

Curt launched himself at Keller, his fists raised. Keller waited until the boy was almost on him, then stepped slightly to one side. Curt's momentum had carried him partway past Keller, and the wild punch he threw did the rest. Keller pivoted and grabbed the back of the boy's shirt, using the leverage and inertia to propel him into the wall. At the last second, he yanked the collar of the shirt to jerk him upright so he hit the wall with his chest rather than his face.

"CURT!" his mother screamed. Keller drove his body into Curt's, forcing the breath out of him. "I'll say this for you," he grated into the boy's ear, "you've got more guts than your old man. He didn't even try. Now, are you going to behave?"

Curt was sobbing. "You son of a bitch," he blubbered. "You son of a bitch."

"Hey," Keller said, "That's a little harsh, don't you think? At least I didn't sell out my sister for a fucking Jeep." He slammed Curt one more time against the wall, then let him drop. Curt slid to the floor, weeping. Keller turned to Ellen Marks. She was standing, her hand over her mouth. Tears ran down her face from beneath the dark glasses. "Thanks for the directions, Ellen," he said. He walked out, tucking the paper into his shirt pocket. He closed the door behind him, blocking out the sounds of Curt's sobs. His footsteps echoed in the silence of the hall as if he were walking out of a tomb.

· · ·

195

"Can you put this thing down in the parking lot?" Grace asked the pilot. The engine noise inside the news helicopter was deafening, so they had to speak over headset microphones.

He glanced at her. "I could," he said. "But I don't know how much the cops are going to like it."

They were circling over the sprawling hog processing plant. Once Grace had been given control of the story, she had moved quickly, summoning the chopper back to pick her up and carry her back to the scene of the killings. Below her, Grace could see the tiny figures of cops and investigators swarming over the scene. The dead had been taken away; at the range from which the killers had fired, there were no wounded. The road had been blocked off for a quarter-mile on either side of the entrance to the hog plant. The only vehicles on the road were police cars, a few nondescript vehicles that were probably FBI, and the vehicles of the victims. The plant had been evacuated, the line shut down. The parking lot was mostly empty.

"Do it," Grace said, "I'll handle the cops." The pilot looked doubtful for a moment, then nodded. The chopper began to descend. Grace turned back to look at her cameraman in the back of the chopper. He wasn't wearing a headset, so she had to yell. "Wayne, put the camera on me as soon as we get out!"

"We're not live!" he yelled back.

"They won't know that!" Wayne grinned and gave a thumbs-up. Grace loved working with Wayne. He would go anywhere, do anything to get the right shot. In his off hours, he enjoyed bungee jumping and skydiving. While he may have lacked Grace's ambition, the man apparently had no sense of self-preservation at all. Grace liked that in a cameraman.

Grace looked back outside the helicopter and immediately wished she hadn't. The ground seemed to be rushing toward them at a sickeningly high rate of speed. She grabbed the sides

196

of her seat and took a deep breath. Just as it seemed they would slam into the ground, the pilot pulled back on the stick and the nose of the big machine pulled up. They settled onto the asphalt of the parking lot with only a slight jar. Grace ripped her headset off and yanked the door open. The roar of the engine became deafening. She leaped out of the helicopter into the fierce downdraft of the rotor, head down. Wayne followed, slinging his camera onto his shoulder as he went. He handed Grace a handheld microphone.

Grace looked up. A pair of men in dark suits was running toward them across the parking lot, waving their arms and yelling. A small group of uniformed cops was jogging after them. As they drew closer, Grace recognized Clancy and his partner Gray. Before either of them could say anything, she thrust the mike out in front of her. The helicopter engine was winding down, but she still had to raise her voice over the sound.

"Grace Tranh, News Ten," she said. "What can you tell me?"

"I don't have to tell you anything, lady," Clancy began, "except get that goddamn thing out of this—" Gray stopped him with a hand on his shoulder. Clancy looked back at his partner as if he was going to throw a punch. Gray just nodded at the camera, which was pointed directly at the two men. The uniformed cops had come up by this time and were looking uncertainly at Wayne and Grace.

"Is that thing on?" Clancy yelled. "Turn it off!" Wayne's only response was to reach out and adjust the lens slightly as if bringing Clancy into better focus. "God damn it," Clancy said, his face growing even redder, "I said—"

"In five," Wayne said, "Four, three, two, one . . ." Clancy looked about ready to reach out and grab the camera, but Grace began talking as Wayne finished the countdown.

"This is Grace Tranh, live from the scene of the senseless

197

shootings this morning at the Barnwell Foods hog plant in Bladen County. With us is Agent Clancy of the Federal Bureau of Investigation. Agent Clancy, what can you tell us?"

Clancy's belligerence evaporated, but his eyes looked daggers at Grace as he said in a dry, official voice, "We are still conducting a thorough field investigation and we have no comment at this time."

"We understand that there was a survivor of the massacre. Someone who saw one of the killers well enough to give a description. Can you comment on that?"

"There was one person who, for some reason, the perpetrator or perpetrators chose not to fire on. That person is giving a statement now."

"Can you tell us—"

"That's all we have for the moment," Gray broke in. "A complete statement will be issued later." He and Clancy turned and walked off. The uniforms followed.

Grace turned to the camera as if she was talking to the audience. "Wayne," she said softly, "whatever you do, keep acting like that camera's live. Those assholes'll have me in handcuffs the minute they think they're not being watched. And they probably won't even buy me dinner first."

"You got it, babe," Wayne said.

"Miss Train?" someone said.

Grace turned. There was a tall deputy who looked to be in his late twenties standing there. Grace instinctively thrust the mike toward him. In her on-air voice, she began, "We're speaking to Deputy—"

"Ma'am," the deputy said politely, "I know we're not on TV." He nodded toward Wayne. "Your camera guy there has your microphone cord stuck in his pocket."

Grace lowered the mike and looked at Wayne.

"Hey," he said. "I was in a hurry."

I'll kill him later, Grace thought. She turned back to the deputy. "Pretty good powers of observation there, Deputy . . . ," she leaned closer to inspect the nameplate over his right shirt pocket, "Wheeler."

He grinned. "Amazin' what you can notice when you're not busy pitchin' a hissy fit like Mister FBI."

"You'll be chief before you know it," she said flirtatiously.

"Yeah. Right," he said. *Shit, he's not buying it,* Grace thought. She relaxed, however, when Wheeler said, "Pretty slick, though. Runnin' that scam on those FBI guys."

She took the opening. "Guess they're not making a lot of friends around here."

He snorted. "You got that right." Then he turned serious. "You said something about a survivor," he said. "The girl who saw the folks that done this."

"You know who it is?"

He nodded. "She's my cousin. Well, sorta. By marriage."

Grace's heart leaped. "Think she'd like to talk to me?"

He looked thoughtful. "Would she get to be on TV?"

"Absolutely," Grace said.

"I'll talk to her," he said. "She's with some guy right now tryin' to do a sketch of the person she saw."

"A police artist?"

"Yeah."

Grace reached into a jacket pocket, pulled out a card. "Have her call me. Please."

He took the card. "Okay," he said. "One more thing?"

"Sure."

He looked bashful. "Can I have your autograph?"

She laughed. "No problem. You got any paper?" He pulled out a notebook and a pen and handed it to her. "Tell your cousin

199

we'll stick around as long as we can," she said as she scribbled her name down. "If she wants we'll even fly her to the studio."

Wheeler grinned and took the notebook back. "Doubt it," he said. "She don't like to fly."

Keller was headed inland, rolling through the flat coastal plain toward Fayetteville. He considered calling Marie and telling her about his lead. He knew she'd insist on telling law enforcement right away, and they'd be all over the place before he could get there. And Laurel Marks was his takedown. Still, he didn't like keeping things from her. He stopped and thought that over for a minute. He picked the phone up. *If you call her,* a voice in his head reminded him, *you'll lose the takedown on the Marks girl.* He shook his head and put the phone down. He considered the odds against him on the takedown. Two against one, both of them known to be armed, and both of them most likely cold-blooded killers. *No way,* he thought. *Can't be done. Stupid to try.* But the hunter's rush that always drew him on when he was af-ter a runner wouldn't go away. *Jesus,* he thought. *Maybe I really am crazy.* He turned the situation over in his head. He decided to wait until he got closer to Fayetteville, then call. He'd let her know, let her call in the backup, but only after he was assured of getting his quarry. She'd get the credit for the collar on Randle, he'd get the Marks girl. *Everybody wins,* he thought. But he'd have to time it just right.

sixteen

"My babysitter didn't show up," the girl said. "An' I knew if I missed work they'd fire me."

"And that's why you had your baby in the car with you," Grace said.

The girl nodded. "I work in the front office, not on the floor. I figgered I could give him his bottle, keep him quiet, an' maybe I could get by with it. I done it before."

"One minute, Grace," Wayne said. Grace nodded. They were set up in the parking lot, the massive blankness of the hog plant forming a backdrop for the live shot. Wheeler had been right. His cousin wasn't going anywhere near the chopper.

The girl's name was Mindy Chadwick. She was twenty-two years old, a single mother. The child's father hadn't been heard from since right after she had found out she was pregnant. She had already expressed her hope to Grace that the plant would be reopening soon. "I mean, it's sad about those people and all," she had said, "but I need that paycheck."

"Thirty seconds," Wayne said.

"Wayne, does the station have the police artist's sketch yet?"

Wayne stopped focusing long enough to give a thumbs-up. "They just got it," he said. "Ready to put on screen when you give the word."

"Okay," Grace said. She turned to Mindy. "Nervous?" she said.

"A little," the girl admitted.

Grace leaned over and told the girl in a just-between-us whisper, "So am I."

Mindy giggled. "Really?"

No, not really, Grace thought, *but that bullshit always loosens people up.* She smiled.

"Innnnn . . . five . . . four . . . three . . . two . . . one . . ."

Grace raised the mike to her lips. "Tom, I'm here with Mindy Chadwick, a survivor of the massacre at Barnwell Foods that claimed the lives of eight of her coworkers. Mindy, I understand that you actually got a close look at one of the killers."

"Uh-huh," Mindy said. She seemed suddenly paralyzed by the camera eye on her.

Uh-oh, Grace thought. *She's freezing up. Damn it.* "And you've been working with a police artist this afternoon to provide us with our first look at one of the people responsible for this heinous act, and possibly for the church and diner shootings of a few nights ago."

"What?" Mindy said.

Shit shit shit. "Bob," she said, "let's put that up on-screen, shall we?" She paused a second, then said, "Mindy, tell us, why do you think the killer spared your life?"

"I dunno," Mindy said. She was actually looking down at the ground. Grace fought down the temptation to scream at her. "You had your young son in the car with you, isn't that right?"

"Uh-huh."

"Maybe that caused the gunman to show some mercy."

"Uh-huh," Mindy said, then she giggled nervously.

Fuck this, Grace thought. She turned back to the camera, stepping slightly to one side. Wayne smoothly adjusted focus to put her into a one-shot. "A surprising act of mercy in a day of carnage," she said. "In Bladen County, I'm Grace Tranh."

"We're out," Wayne said. Grace looked over at Mindy. She had her hands folded across her chest. She looked miserable. "I din't do too well, did I?"

Grace patted her on the shoulder. "You did fine, hon," she said. *Stupid bitch,* she thought.

Shelby was standing on the porch, waiting as Marie pulled up. "Hey," he said as she got out.

"Hey," she said back. "Thanks for inviting me."

"No problem," he said. "Sorry I couldn't talk earlier, but I was at the station." He opened the door and gestured her inside.

"I understand," she said. "I don't know why you'd take the risk."

"Like I said Jones, you're a good officer. Plus, this sorta concerns you, too."

She felt a stab of fear in her stomach. "What do you mean?"

"The feds went out to that trailer," he said. "But somebody'd burned it down."

"What? Who?" she said.

"They thought at first it might have been that fella of yours," Shelby said. He held up his hands reassuringly as he saw the look on her face. "But his boss gave him a pretty solid alibi. Current theory is that it was Randle hisself. Tryin' to cover up evidence, maybe."

"Or maybe he's just lost it completely," she said.

"They's been a couple o' doctor's sayin' the same thing. De-compensatin' they call it."

"If that's the case . . ." She trailed off.

"Yeah," Shelby finished the thought for her. "He and his friends're gonna kill a lot more people 'fore they take him down." He cleared his throat. "There's one more thing," he said. "One of the survivors got a good look at one of the shooters. Looked him right in the eye. Said it was a young white male. Looked to be in his late teens."

Marie closed her eyes. "Oh, no."

"Ain't seen it yet, but there's s'posed to be a sketch by a police artist comin' down the wires soon. Sounds like our missin' boy from the gas station, though. And this witness can put a rifle in his hand."

"So much for the kidnapping theory."

"He could be under duress. We don't know yet. But since that started out as your case, I thought I'd let you know."

"Thanks for keeping me in the loop, Shelby," she said. "I appreciate it."

"No problem," he said.

She picked the phone back up. "I need to call Jack," she said.

"Now this is more like it," Roy said.

He was kicked back on the couch, drinking a beer. Laurel sat beside him, running a hand idly through his hair. Stan sat on the floor nearby. He had his rifle broken down and was cleaning it the way Roy had taught him. Roy had the remote in his other hand, flipping through the channels. The .45 lay on the arm of the couch.

The cable-news channels were wall to wall with what Roy called "our story." Roy flipped back and forth between the channels. He kept coming back to the one with the graphic that said "Murder in Carolina."

"Stan," he said, "flip the switch so we can catch the local yokels."

Flip it yourself, Stan thought, but he got up and moved the slider switch to get the antenna rather than the dish. The screen filled with static, then Roy punched the remote and Grace Tranh's face filled the screen.

"There she is," Roy said. "There's my girl." Laurel gave him a playful punch on the shoulder. Roy turned up the volume.

Grace was standing beside a thin girl who looked into the camera as if she were terrified. A cold shock ran through Stan's body as he recognized the girl from earlier that day, the girl with the baby. He couldn't hear what Grace was saying from the blood roaring in his ears. Then another shock hit him as his own face filled the screen. He began to tremble. The picture was sketchy, but it was undoubtedly him. He tried to stand, but his knees gave way and he slumped back down to a kneeling position, as if he were praying. He looked at Roy.

Roy was standing, his hands fallen limp at his sides. The beer had slid from his hand and was leaking on the floor, unnoticed. Roy's mouth was opening and shutting like a fish. His face became red, then redder, until it was almost purple. It was only then that he turned to look at Stan.

"You little shit," he said in a low deadly voice.

"Roy," Laurel said. She tried to reach for him. He backhanded her, the movement seeming almost casual, but it was hard enough to knock her backwards onto the couch. That brought Stan to his feet. "Stop that!" he yelled.

"You let one of them live," Roy said in that same tone of voice. "Somebody who could talk to the cops." He took a step toward Stan. "Somebody who could draw them," step, "a fucking," step,

205

"picture!" His fist shot out and hit Stan full in the nose. The punch was enough to knock him backwards into the wall. He felt his nose break, saw the spurt of blood that flowed from him. The pain seemed to fill the whole world, and there was blood covering his hands. Stan looked down at it for a moment. A strange feeling came over him. This was a totally familiar scenario. A man punched him. He took it. But something felt different now. Somehow, everything had changed. He looked up at Roy, who was standing there, glaring at him, breathing hard like a bull ready to charge. But it was Stan who launched himself at the older man, his hands clenched into claws that seemed to slide easily around Roy's neck.

The force of Stan's charge propelled Roy back into the couch. Laurel screamed and barely managed to roll out of the way in time. "No one!" Stan screamed down into Roy's face. He slammed Roy's head back. "Fucking! Hits! Me! Again!" Each word was punctuated by Stan shoving Roy harder back against the couch. Roy's face was even purpler now, his eyes bulging. Stan could see the light in those eyes beginning to fade. He felt it again, the high wild exultation he had first felt upon pulling a trigger. *I'm not afraid anymore,* he thought, *I'm not afraid.* Laurel was clawing at his back, sobbing and begging incoherently. But Stan was laughing with joy. Then he felt a blow to his midsection, like Roy had punched him in the stomach. He ignored it. "That the best you can do, Roy?" he shrieked down into the older man's face. He was strong now. Nothing could stop him. He felt another blow, then another, and suddenly, unbelievingly, his strength was leaving him. *No,* he thought, *No, I'm strong, strong,* but his hands were sliding away from Roy's throat, as if his brain couldn't reach them anymore. His legs were rubbery again, too, and he slid to his knees on the floor in front of the couch. It was then he saw the blood all over his shirtfront. He was soaked in it. It was coming out everywhere. He looked up in disbelief. Roy stood up, holding the gun he had grabbed off the couch where it had fallen. He brought it up to Stan's face. *No,* Stan had time to think one last time before there was a bright flash, a sudden incredible pain, then nothing.

Keller was only a few miles from Fayetteville when his cell phone rang. He checked the number. It was Marie.

"Have you heard the news?" she asked.

"No, I've been working. What happened?"

"They did it again. A hog processing plant in Bladen County."

"Shit," Keller said. "How many dead?"

"Eight. And a survivor got a look at one of the shooters. It might be the kid from the gas-station shooting."

"At least they're keeping you informed," Keller said. "That's a good sign."

"Shelby is, at least," she said. "I'm at his house right now."

Keller thought it over. Now there were three enemies. And night was falling. "Stay there," he said. "I'm only a few miles away."

"What?" she said. "Why?"

"I'll come pick you up," he said. He hung up.

It took him twenty minutes to reach the Shelby house. The door opened as he got out of the car. Marie was standing in the doorway watching him. Shelby stood behind her. Keller waved at him.

"You want to come in, Jack?" Shelby called to him.

"Thanks, but not right now," Keller called back. "I need to see Marie." She looked at Shelby and shrugged. She walked out to the driveway. "Get in the car," he said urgently.

"What?" she said.

"Get in the car. Quick."

She looked baffled. "Okay." She turned and waved at Shelby. "Thanks," she said. "I'll be back to get my car in a little bit." She got in the car. Keller was moving as soon as the door slammed shut. "I think I know where Laurel Marks is," he said. "And Randle."

"What?!" she said.

"Laurel's mother gave me directions to her family's old home place," he said. "Laurel spent a lot of time there. It's abandoned, but it's a logical place for her to hole up. And it's less than ten miles from here."

"And you knew about this while I was standing there talking to Shelby? Damn it, Jack!" She slammed her hand on the dash. She was silent for a moment. "I need to call this in," she said.

"I knew you would," he said.

Her voice was flat. "But you waited to tell me until you were sure you'd get there first."

"We," he said.

"What?"

"I wanted us to get there first. Not just me. You get the collar on Randle, you get back in the department. I get Marks."

"Oh that's great," Marie said. "Nice plan. And you assumed I'd go along with it." She put her head in her hands. After a moment, she said, "This is it, Jack. It's over."

The words seemed to hit him like a physical blow. "What?" he said.

"You heard me." She felt a tear rolling unbidden down her face. "I've tried, Jack," she said. "I've really tried. But you still don't trust me. You still don't let me in."

He was silent for a moment. Finally he said, "You want me to take you home?"

She sighed. "You know better. You know I won't let you go

there alone. And you know that if I'm the one who helps take these people down, I'll be able to write my own ticket in the department. And you know how bad I want that." Her voice was bitter as she said, "You've played me perfectly, Jack. Congratulations." She pulled out her cell phone.

"I didn't mean to—," he began.

"But you did," she said. "You can't help it. Now shut up. I need to make a call."

Shelby stood in the open doorway, watching Keller's car pull away. Something was definitely wrong here.

"Honey," he called back to his wife, "I'm goin' out for a while."

She came back out of the kitchen. "Something wrong?" she asked.

He smiled at her. "No, sugar, I just need some air," he replied.

She clearly didn't believe the reassurance. She crossed the room and hugged him. "Be careful," she whispered.

He hugged her back. "I love you," he said. He had a sudden impulse to go in the kitchen and give a hug to his daughters, but he didn't want to risk losing Keller's vehicle. Keller's taillights shone at the end of the loop road as he started his car. He reached under the seat and pulled out his service revolver.

seventeen

"We got to bury him," Roy said.

"Bury him yourself," Laurel replied. "You're the one that killed him." She was sitting on the floor, her back against the wall and her knees drawn up. Her face was streaked with tears. Stan's body lay on the floor between them.

"The hell was I supposed to do? Let him choke me to death?"

"You didn't have to hit him," Laurel said.

"He's got his picture all over the damn news." Roy said. "He couldn't handle the one thing we gave him to do."

"He was just a kid," she said.

"He's not that much younger than you, Laurel," Roy pointed out.

She looked away from Stan's body and into Roy's eyes. "I ain't been a kid for a long time, Roy. A long, long time."

He stood up. "Okay," he said, "I'll handle the buryin'. But you've gotta help me get him in the van. And while I'm gone, clean all this mess up."

She got slowly to her feet. "Yeah. Okay. Whatever."

They took an old patchwork quilt from the bedroom and spread it on the floor by Stan's body. They wrapped the body in it, rolling him up tightly. When they were done, he was just a long bundle wrapped in bright colors. Laurel took his feet while Roy grabbed the heavier end. The two of them grunted with effort as they hauled him out onto the porch. Roy moved the van closer to the porch and opened the cargo door. As they picked the bundle up, a long groan seemed to come from inside. Laurel jumped back in surprise and dropped her end. Roy lost his grip and the body tumbled to the ground.

"He's still alive," she whispered. "I heard him."

"Naw," Roy said. "That's just air leavin' the body. I heard about it."

"Roy," she said. "We've got to see."

"And what if he is alive, Laurel?" he snapped. "What are we gonna do? Take him to the hospital? How you gonna explain that? If he is alive, only thing that's gonna happen is I put a bullet in his head to finish him off."

"You fucking asshole," she whispered.

"You've killed as many people as me, Laurel," he said. "So get off your damn high horse."

"I didn't know them," she said. "I hadn't . . ."

"Right," he said. "You hadn't fucked them. So goddamn what?" She didn't reply. She just bent down and grasped her end of the bundle. Roy did the same. The body made no further noise as they loaded it in the back of the van. Neither of them spoke until Laurel slid the van door shut.

"Go down the road behind the house," she said. "It goes to the back field. You can bury him there. There's shovels and a pickax in the shed."

Roy nodded. She didn't look at him as she walked back into

211

the house. When she reached the door, Roy called out to her. "Laurel." She stopped, her hand on the knob. "I told you it was a bad idea to bring him along."

She didn't turn around. "You think I don't know that?" she said. She turned. "Just check and see, Roy. Don't bury him alive." She opened the door and went inside. She stood for a moment in the living room door. Stan's blood was a broad irregular stain soaking into the pine floor. The pistol was still on the couch. Stan's rifle was still broken down in the corner. She walked over and picked up the pieces. With practiced ease she reassembled the rifle and slapped a magazine in. She propped it by the window. She picked up the pistol and checked it. She found the box of shells, reloaded the weapon, and set it back on the couch.

She went to the kitchen and got a bucket, a sponge, and soap from under the kitchen counter. She took it back out into the living room and got down on her knees. She looked at the bloodstain soaking its way into her grandmother's floorboards and shook her head. Her granny had always been a stickler for cleanliness. She began to scrub. She looked up from time to time at the rifle and the pistol. Roy would probably be a while getting back, but she'd be ready.

Keller and Marie didn't speak until they were approaching the farm. "Laurel's mother said the road in was about three-quarters of a mile," Keller said. "I'm going to go about halfway in, then kill the lights. From there on in we go in slow. I want to get as close to the house as I can. If we have to drag her, I don't want to have to go too far." Marie just nodded. Her face in the dashboard light was closed.

"Are you not going to talk to me at all?" Keller asked.

212

She didn't look at him. "Let's just do this, Jack," she said.

He took the piece of paper from his left hand and handed it to her. "Now that you know where it is," he said, "you can make the call."

She shook her head, but pulled out her cell phone. "Janelle," she said after a moment. "Hey, it's Marie Jones." A short pause. "I'm fine, thanks. No . . . thanks, I appreciate that. Look, Janelle, I haven't got a lot of time. Who's duty officer tonight? Okay, let me talk to him, please. You too, hon, and thanks." There was another, longer pause. Marie continued to stare straight ahead down the darkened road. Then she began speaking again. "Lieutenant, this is Marie Jones. I've got a tip. I might know where the people from those shootings are holed up." There was a brief burst of chatter from the other end. Marie glanced at Keller and smiled sourly. "Yeah, it's a pretty reliable source."

"Thanks," Keller said. She waved him to silence.

"One of the shooters has a place, an abandoned farm where she likes to go. It's in the county." The chatter became more animated. "Here's the directions." She took the paper and read the directions written there. When she was done, Keller heard the voice on the other end. Marie took a deep breath before answering. "I'm there now." The voice rose. Marie looked at Keller again. "I don't think I can do that, sir," she said. "My source is there, too. And he's going in after Laurel Marks." The voice rose again. "He's her bail bondsman." Keller could hear the tone of command in the reply. "I'll do what I can, sir, but you need to get some units here, ASAP." She shut the phone. She looked at Keller. "He told me to arrest you if you tried to go in."

"Well," Keller said. "You've done it before."

She waved at the road ahead. "Just shut up and drive, Keller."

They advanced slowly up the dirt road. The darkness above

and the underbrush on either side seemed to close in claustro-
phobically until it felt like they were being swallowed down the
gullet of some huge beast. When the road widened out a little,
Keller snapped off the headlights. He sat there for a moment,
letting the motor idle while he let his eyes become accustomed
to the darkness. Then, when he could begin making out shapes
again, he began creeping forward. It seemed to take hours before
the oppressive growth on either side gave way. Keller could see
the dark gnarled shapes of trees on either side of the dirt road.
He caught a glimpse of yellow light ahead and stopped.

"That's the house," he said.

"They still have power out here?" Marie wondered. "I thought
you said the place was abandoned."

Keller lowered the driver's side window and stuck his head
out. Over the low rumble of the Crown Vic's engine, he could
make out the higher rattle of a gasoline motor.

"Somebody set up a generator," he said. "That's good, it'll
mask our noise." He switched off the engine. They eased out of
the car on either side, closing the doors softly. Keller walked
around to the back and carefully opened the trunk.

"You get the vest this time," he said. "And I've got a Beretta
stashed here for you."

"If you would've let me know what you were doing," she said,
"I'd have gotten my own. But you're first through the door. You
take it." He hesitated, then strapped the Kevlar vest on. They
began moving up the road slowly, Keller with his shotgun across
his chest at port arms, Marie holding her Beretta down by her
side. It was a cool night, but there were still a few crickets
singing, the last holdouts against the late-coming winter. As they
got closer, the rattle and drone of the generator got louder and
drowned out all other sound. Marie stopped and put her hand
on Keller's shoulder. She spoke into his ear. "There's no vehi-

cle," she said. "They couldn't get out here without wheels." Keller looked back at her and shrugged. They walked up to the farmhouse. The porch light was on, spreading a fan of golden radiance in front of the house. It looked incongruously homey and welcoming. This time it was Keller who stopped Marie with a hand on her shoulder. He pointed into the darkness a few feet back from where Marie stood, then pointed at the door. *Stay there. Cover the front.* He pointed to his own chest, then to his eyes and gestured toward the side of the house. *I'll look around.* Marie nodded and stepped back out of the light.

There was a light in the window to the left of the door. The rest of the place was dark. Keller stayed out of the pool of light in front of the window and eased around to the side. What appeared to be another window into the same room shone with light as well. Keller crept up to the window and peered in.

Laurel Marks was on her hands and knees on the floor. She appeared to be scrubbing the floorboards. *Kind of late for housework,* Keller thought. Then he saw her pick up the sponge and squeeze it into a bucket. The water that flowed from the contorted sponge was tinged with bright red.

Keller pulled back from the window and leaned against the wall. *What the hell?* He thought. He leaned back around. Laurel had picked up the bucket. It visibly weighed her down, her shoulders slumping as if it weighed a thousand pounds. She was headed for the front door. Keller bolted around the side of the house.

Marie Jones had always prided herself on several things, but one in particular: No matter what she was going through in her personal life, she could always cram that down into the back of her mind and do the job. She had known plenty of officers—most

215

notably her late partner Eddie Wesson—who seemed to bring their bad moods to work with them. But through her divorce, the constant battles with her ex over custody and support, whatever, she could always take them off with her civilian clothes when she put on the uniform. Jack Keller, however, had made that difficult. He was in every corner of her life, and it was hard for her to detach. She still felt the roiling of conflicting emotions toward Keller—anger at him, the ever-present fear for him, and yes, still love, after all. So in the back of her mind, there was a feeling of relief when she saw the door of the farmhouse swing open and she found herself responding instinctively, dropping into a combat crouch, her weapon held out in front of her in a two-handed grip. Marie immediately identified the figure silhouetted in the doorway as Laurel Marks. There was something in her hands, and Marie's finger tightened on the trigger until she saw it was just a galvanized metal bucket. She relaxed that tiniest fraction on the trigger. Laurel stepped out onto the porch, obviously unaware of any other presence until Marie shouted from the darkness, *"POLICE! GET ON THE GROUND!"*

Laurel's face went stupid with shock for a second. Marie seized the moment to yell again, trying to keep the subject shocked and disoriented. *"GET ON THE FUCKING GROUND! NOW!"* she bellowed. Laurel responded by throwing the contents of the bucket at her. Marie saw something coming through the air at her and her finger tightened again. *Water,* she thought, before the trigger broke. *No target. No target.* She was too far away for the splash to reach her and she sidestepped the few drops that made it that far. She was getting ready to shout again when she saw Keller smash into Laurel from the side like a football tackle. She lowered the gun and ran toward the porch.

• • •

Sweat ran down Roy's back as he dug the shovel into the soft ground. The soil here was mostly sand. It was easy to get the shovel in, but once you took a spadeful out, another half a spadeful would sift down into the hole. It made for slow going. Roy glared balefully at the wrapped bundle he had dragged from the van. *Fucking kid*, he thought. He ought to leave him out here to rot. But he kept digging. The night was still. Roy could just make out the sound of the generator distantly over the sounds of his own heavy breathing and the *chuff-swish* of the shovel. Then another sound came to him through the cool air. Someone was yelling. He stopped digging and raised his head to listen. Definitely a voice. He couldn't make out the words or who it was, but the voice sounded angry. Someone was here. Roy dropped the shovel and ran to the van. He took out one of the rifles, checked to see if it was loaded. Then he began jogging toward the house.

Keller knocked Laurel to the rough planking of the porch, his arms wrapped tightly around her waist. She screamed and punched at his head, but he was wrapped too tightly around her and her blows landed harmlessly on his back. He heard Marie's footsteps pounding up onto the porch. She was shouting commands over Laurel's screams. Then the screaming stopped and Laurel was whimpering. "Please," she was saying. "Please don't shoot me."

Keller looked up. Marie was standing over, her Beretta inches from Laurel's face. Laurel was staring at the barrel of the ugly little gun as if hypnotized. Keller released his grip around Laurel's waist and got to his knees. "Roll over," he ordered. "On your stomach. Hands behind you." She complied silently. Keller took the cuffs from his jacket pocket and secured her hands behind her. Marie put her gun away and the two of them helped Laurel

217

stagger to her feet. Laurel got a good look at them for the first time. "Wait a minute," she said. "You aren't cops."

"You're half right," Keller said. "You forget your court date, Laurel?"

Laurel gave him a strange half-smile. "Naw," she said. "I didn't forget. I just been busy."

"Yeah, that's what we hear," Marie said. "Where are the others?"

Laurel looked around. "What others?"

Keller clouted her on the back of the head, hard.

"Jack," Marie said. Keller ignored her. "See, here's the thing, Laurel," he said in a conversational tone. "I'm not a cop. And I don't really give a fuck about Miranda or any of that bullshit. I just need to get you out of here and to a magistrate. If you get banged up a little in the process, the magistrate will understand." His voice gathered intensity. "And I need to know if there's anyone around that'll interfere with that, got it? And if I have to break your fucking jaw to find that out, I'll fucking do it, so why don't you tell me where the fuck Randle is, and that fucking kid that's with you, and we can get this *fucking show on the road*?" He shouted the last words into her face.

Laurel looked down sullenly. "They're dead," she said.

"What do you mean, they're dead?" Marie said.

"They got in a fight. They killed each other. That's their blood in there on the floor."

"Where's the bodies, then?" Keller said. "You better not be lying to me, Laurel."

"I took 'em off in the van," she said. "I buried 'em in the woods."

Keller looked at Marie. "Screw it," he said. He began pushing Laurel ahead of him, down the dirt drive. "We got what we came for."

"I guess y'all did." A voice came from the darkness. Warren Shelby stepped into the light. He was holding his own pistol out in front of him.

"Shelby," Marie said. She lowered her own weapon. "The station called you?"

Keller shook his head. "Too soon," he said. "He followed us."

Shelby nodded. He looked at Marie and his face turned sorrowful. "I'd figured you had better sense than this, Jones," he said.

"She didn't—," Keller began, but Marie cut him off sharply.

"I can handle this, Jack," she said. She jerked her chin at Keller. "He didn't tell me about it until after we left your house," she said.

"Well, at least you didn't lie to me, then," Shelby said. "That's somethin'. But you still should've waited for backup." He looked at Keller. "Where's your weapon, Jack?"

Keller gestured back toward the house. "Propped up by the porch." Shelby looked at him. Keller shrugged. "She wasn't armed, that I could see," he said.

"Awright," Shelby said. "I'm takin' this young lady into custody," he said. "You step away from her, now."

"She's my prisoner, Shelby," Keller said.

Shelby shook his head. "Most likely you can get the judge to remit the bail. I'll swear out an affidavit you were the first to apprehend the subject if you want. But I'm a sworn law officer, and you're not. That does make a difference."

Keller still hesitated. Shelby let out a deep sigh. "Jack, I'd consider it a shame to arrest a man who's broken bread at my table," he said. "But I'll do it if you force me. We all have a particular sin we wrestle with," he went on, "and I reckon yours is pride. But don't let your pride bring you down. Don't let it get in the way of your good sense." There was a long, tense moment, then Keller stepped away from Laurel. Shelby nodded. "All right, then," he said. He turned to Marie. "Officer Jones," he said, "you secure the prisoner. Get her to my car. I'm goin' to go secure Mr. Keller's weapon." Marie stepped over and grasped Laurel by the shoulder as Shelby moved toward the house. He was passing by Keller when there was a flat bang and a flash of light from beside the house. Shelby gave a grunt and sank back against Keller. Keller wrapped his arms around him, trying to hold him up. Shelby sagged, dead weight in Keller's arms. Marie whirled, trying to bring her pistol to bear on the source of the shot, the whites of her eyes showing in the dim light. The second shot took her in the belly and punched her off her feet. She cried out in agony, the gun dropping from her nerveless fingers as she clawed at the pain. Keller screamed as well and let Shelby's limp form slide to the ground. He fell to his knees beside her.

"Oh God," she cried. "Oh, God . . ."

Keller answered with a snarl of rage as he scrambled for Marie's gun on the ground.

"I wouldn't," a voice said. Keller looked up. Randle was standing by the porch, the rifle trained on Keller. "I'm gonna need the key to those handcuffs," he said.

Marie screamed again. The sound tore at Keller like talons in his guts. "Fuck you," he grated at Randle.

Randle put the gun to his shoulder. "I'll make you a deal," he said. "You give me that key, and I won't put another bullet in sweet thing's head. I can't miss from here."

Keller staggered to his feet. There was a red haze before his eyes, pulsing with every beat of his heart. There was a roaring in his ears like surf. *Hello old friend*, he thought. He fumbled in his pocket for the key, pulled it out. He held it in front of him like a talisman. "Come and get it, you cocksucker," he said, his voice an animal growl.

Randle just grinned. "Not hardly," he said. He gestured toward Laurel with the gun barrel. "Unlock her cuffs." He kept the gun trained on Keller as he stepped behind Laurel and fumbled at the lock. Marie's screams had subsided to dull moans. His fingers didn't want to work. Finally, he felt the lock give. Laurel stepped away and faced him. She reached out and ran her hand down his face, gently, caressingly. Then she slapped him, hard. "We oughta make you sit here and watch her die," she hissed. She kicked Marie in the hip, drawing another groan of pain from her.

"It's a nice idea," Randle said. "But with a belly wound like that, it could take a while. And we ain't got time." He raised the gun to his shoulder again. Keller could see the dark circle of the barrel. He heard the crack, waited for the impact, the pain, the oblivion, but it was Randle he saw crumple to the ground. It was then he saw Shelby's arm fall back to the ground, the pistol in his hand.

"*Roy!*" Laurel shrieked as Randle's body thudded to the earth. She moved toward him. But as Keller dove for Marie's gun on the ground, she reversed direction and fled into the darkness as Keller came up with the gun. He fired blindly, knowing it was useless with no target. When the slide popped back and Keller's frantic jerking of the trigger yielded nothing but dry clicks, he tossed the gun aside. He crawled to Marie's limp form on the ground. He rolled her over. Her face was gray with pain and shock. Her eyes were narrow slits of agony. He pulled her head into his lap and brushed her hair away from her face. Her eyes opened a little and she seemed to focus. "Jack?" she said weakly.

"Shhh . . . ," Keller said. His face was wet with tears. "Don't talk."

221

"It hurts, Jack," she said. "It hurts . . . ."

He dimly registered the sound of a car starting. "I know, honey, I know," he said. "Hang on, Marie, help's on the way."

"Where's Ben?" she mumbled. "Is Ben okay?"

"Ben's not here, sweetheart," Keller said. He moved her hands away from where they clasped across her stomach. Her shirt was soaked with blood. He pulled the shirt up. The blood was everywhere. He couldn't find where it was all coming from. He heard another voice, a low murmur. It took him a moment to make out the words, slurred and halting as they were.

"For thou art with me . . . thy . . . thy rod and thy staff they . . . comfort me . . ."

Marie tried to raise her head. "Shelby?" she whispered.

"Shhhh . . . ," Keller said. "He'll be okay."

Shelby's voice subsided to a low mumble for a moment, then became stronger. "God be merciful," he said clearly, "to me, a sinner." Then there was silence, broken only by the rasp of Marie's breathing and the mechanical ratcheting of the crickets. Where the fuck are those people? Keller raged silently. Then he heard it, off in the distance, a gentle thudding that quickly grew to a hammering roar. He looked up as the helicopter swept over the scene, its spotlight-probing the clearing. A godlike voice bellowed over the sound of the rotors. "THIS IS THE POLICE!" the voice boomed. "THROW DOWN YOUR WEAPONS!" Keller looked over. Shelby had rolled over onto his back. The spotlight showed his open eyes looking up into the light. There was a slight smile on his face, as if he were seeing angels. Perhaps he was, but those eyes would never see any earthly sight again. Keller saw the explosions of red and blue light through the trees as what looked like a small army of vehicles came up the road. The chopper continued to circle, filling the world with its sound and glare. Keller stared up into the light like a mystic

222

staring into the sun and hoping it would burn out his eyes. Then there were people next to him, their hands on his shoulders. Keller looked up. Two figures in green coveralls were leaning over. One of them reached down while the other knelt in front of him. Keller felt a tugging. Someone was trying to take Marie. "Come on, buddy," he heard a voice say. "Let me see her."

The car lights flashed, explosions in the darkness, red, blue, white. Keller remembered tracers ripping the desert night, rockets from nowhere filling the world with light and fire and death. And everywhere the sound of the helicopter, the sound that filled the world and drove out all thought. "Go away," he whispered, "Just go away . . ."

"Dude," another voice said, "I can't help her if you won't let go."

"I can't get a pulse," a third voice said. Keller looked down at Marie. Her face was pale and still, the lights flickering chaotically across her skin. He reached up to stroke her hair. His grip relaxed and he felt her being lifted up and away from him.

"I've got a pulse on this one, but it's thready," he heard someone say. He couldn't tell who they meant. He wanted to ask, but all he could do was look up dumbly as figures moved purposefully around him. Finally someone told him to stand. It seemed to take him a long time to comply, as if he had to learn how to walk upright again. But finally, he stood, swaying slightly like a drunk. Then they put the cuffs on him.

Laurel saw the lights and sirens approaching as she turned onto the hard road. She slowed the car down. *Just another car on the road,* she said to herself, *just another car on the road . . .*

Her knuckles were white on the wheel. Had they seen her pull out? Would someone recognize this car? She figured it had belonged to the cop who had come onto the scene, the guy Roy had shot. *If someone recognizes it,* she thought, *I'm fucked.* She didn't even have a weapon. The vehicles passed by at high speed, red and blue flashers pulsing in the darkness. Laurel let out the breath she hadn't realized she was holding. *That was close.*

She drove aimlessly for a long time, her only direction away from the farm. She knew it wouldn't be long before someone called in this vehicle as stolen, but she was paralyzed with indecision. She had gotten used to going along with Roy's plans, but all those were gone now. All the scenes he had planned were back in the farmhouse. Even if she had them, they were written for at least two players. She couldn't carry them out herself.

After a while, she saw the signs for I-95. She pulled onto the highway and slotted herself into the stream of traffic heading south. She could keep driving, maybe go to Florida and hide out there. Then she saw an exit sign and everything clicked into place. She knew there was only one place left to go.

eighteen

The lobby door banged open with a sound like a gunshot. Angela saw the deputy behind the desk jump halfway out of her chair in surprise, then sit back down as she approached. Her leg had been acting up, and she cursed her slowness as she made her way toward the desk with her cane.

"You're holding a Jackson Keller," she said before she had even reached the desk. "I'm here to see him."

"Are you his attorney, ma'am?" the deputy asked. She was a slender black woman who looked too young to be in uniform.

"No," Angela said. "But his attorney is on the way."

"Hang on just a minute," the deputy said. She picked up the phone and pressed a button. She turned away and conducted a murmured conversation, too low for Angela to hear. When she was done, she turned back. "I'm sorry ma'am," she said. "Mr. Keller isn't available."

"What the hell do you mean 'not available'?" Angela said. "Has he been charged with anything?"

"Ma'am," the deputy said, "you need to calm down—"

"I will *not* calm down!" Angela shouted. "Damn it, why is he being held?"

"I don't know, ma'am," the deputy said frostily.

"Well, then, Deputy," a deep voice behind Angela said, "perhaps you'd like to let me talk to someone who does know. Or better yet, let me talk to my client."

Angela turned. A tall white-haired man was standing there. Even though it was four in the morning, he was dressed in an expensive-looking suit. He held an equally expensive-looking briefcase in one hand. He looked as if he'd just stepped out of a courtroom. He walked up to the counter, put down the briefcase, and extended his hand. "I'm Scott McCaskill."

The deputy shook his hand with a sour expression on her face. "I know who you are," she said, hesitating a significant beat before adding, "sir."

"Good," McCaskill said. "Please tell the officer in charge I'm here and I need to see my client."

"Like I said," the deputy replied. "Mr. Keller is—"

"Ma'am," McCaskill interrupted, "In my jacket pocket I have a cell phone. On that cell phone I have speed-dial. On my speed-dial list, near the top, I have the home number of Judge Martin Ballantine. Are you familiar with the name?" The deputy shook her head. "Well," McCaskill went on, "Martin Ballantine is a federal district court judge. Now, I've known Marty Ballantine for a lot of years. He's a good fellow. Heck of a poker player. But he's not what you'd call a morning person." McClellan withdrew the phone from his jacket pocket. "I really would hate to wake him up. But I will if I have to, and I'll be sure to let him know that the reason I'm getting him out of bed to issue a writ of habeas corpus is because a Deputy—" He craned his neck to read the nameplate on the deputy's uniform "—Deputy T. Clevenger refused to let me see my client. Now, how are we going to handle this, Deputy T. Clevenger?"

"Clevenger refused to meet his eyes. "Wait here," she mumbled.

"I will," said McCaskill, "but not long." The deputy fled into the back. McCaskill turned to Angela and smiled. "And how have you been, Angela?" he asked pleasantly.

"Pissed off," she said. "Thanks for coming so fast." She gestured at him. "What do you do, sleep in that suit?"

McCaskill chuckled. "No," he said. "But it's worth taking the time. Makes them"—he jerked his chin at the door—"take you more seriously. So what's this all about?"

"I don't know," Angela admitted. "Jack called me. He said he was being held here. He said . . ." She paused, swallowed. "He said Marie'd been shot."

McCaskill looked puzzled for a second, then comprehension dawned. "Marie Jones? The officer he got involved with?"

"Yeah."

"Dear God," McCaskill said. "Is she dead?"

Angela shook her head. "I don't know," she said. "Oscar went to the hospital to find out. You remember Oscar Sanchez?"

McCaskill nodded. "How could I forget him?" he said. "They don't think Jack had anything to do with Marie's shooting, do they?"

"I don't know," Angela said, her voice cracking. "I don't know anything."

McCaskill put a hand on her shoulder. "Okay," he said, "I'll find out. Just try to stay calm."

Angela took a deep breath, then nodded. "I'm okay," she said.

The front door opened. The man who stepped in was as tall as McCaskill and seemed twice as broad. His close-cropped hair was streaked with gray.

227

"Lucas," Angela said in surprise.

"Hello, Dr. Berry," McCaskill said. There was surprise in his voice as well.

Dr. Lucas Berry walked over and shook hands with Mc-Caskill. "Good morning, Counselor," he said. He turned to Angela. He put his hands on her shoulders and looked into her eyes for a moment without speaking. There was a look of concern on his dark brown face. "How you doing, girl?" he said softly.

She smiled at him. "I'll hold up. How did you know Jack was here?"

"Oscar called me," Berry said. "He said Marie'd been shot. And that Jack was there when it happened." Angela's smile vanished. She nodded.

"Mr. Keller is one of your patients, Dr. Berry?" McCaskill broke in. His face had become bland and expressionless. "I wasn't aware that there were any substance abuse issues . . ."

Berry hesitated. It was Angela who spoke up. "It's not that, Scott," she said. "Dr. Berry treated Jack while he was in the army. Jack still sees him sometimes."

"I see," McCaskill said. He stroked his chin thoughtfully. Angela could almost hear the wheels turning.

"Mr. McCaskill," Berry said, "I assume you're going to try to get Mr. Keller released."

McCaskill spread his hands. "I assume that's what I'm here for, at least in the short-term."

Berry cast a troubled glance at Angela. "I'd like you to consider, Counselor," he said, "that that might not be in Jack Keller's best interest."

"Dr. Berry," McCaskill said. "I've been practicing criminal law for thirty years this past August. I can't think of a situation where leaving a man in jail is in his best interest."

"I appreciate that, sir," Berry said. He looked away for a moment, then sighed. "I'm breaking confidentiality here," he said, "but I don't really see any other way around this." He looked back at McCaskill. "Jack Keller has been in an extremely volatile emotional state. I'm afraid that the trauma of seeing his lover shot in front of him might precipitate some sort of breakdown."

"Then it seems to me the sooner we get him into some sort of treatment, the better," McCaskill said.

"If I thought that was a sure thing, I'd say go for it," Berry said. "But Keller is sometimes a . . . difficult patient. He may resist treatment."

"Let's drop the formality, Doctor," McCaskill said. "It's too early in the morning for it. What are you really afraid of?"

"If Jack Keller saw Marie Jones get shot," Berry said, "he's very likely to go after the person he thinks is responsible."

"And kill them," McCaskill said flatly.

Berry nodded. "And kill them, yes."

McCaskill sighed. "Wonderful," he said. "Nothing I like better than an ethical dilemma before sunrise."

The door behind the counter opened. Deputy Clevenger came in. A man in a dark suit was with her. McCaskill turned to Berry.

"I'm not making any decisions until I talk to Keller. He's my client. He'll be the boss."

"Just remember what I said, Counselor," Berry said.

"Oh, I will," McCaskill said. He sighed again and picked up his briefcase. "I will."

Keller sat with his cuffed hands on the table in front of him, picking absently at a ragged thumbnail. The FBI agent who had introduced himself as Clancy had been talking to him for the last two hours. Clancy, however, had been the only one talking. Keller hadn't said a word since calling Angela. Clancy had spo-

229

ken reasonably at first. All he wanted, he had said, was to know what had happened. How had those people died. When Keller had refused to respond, Clancy had gotten angry. He had yelled. He had threatened. Keller had just sat at the table and looked at his hands, waiting. Finally, another agent had come in and spoken with Clancy in a low, urgent voice. Keller couldn't make out the reply, but he could hear the frustration in Clancy's voice. Clancy stomped out of the room, slamming the door behind him. Keller sat and waited. He was good at waiting.

The door of the interrogation room swung open. Scott Mc-Caskill walked in. Keller spoke for the first time. "Glad you could make it," he said.

McCaskill sat down across from him. "Well, when Angela called," he said. "I didn't know you'd gotten the attention of the FBI. They're a little harder to convince." He opened his brief-case, took out a legal pad and a pen. "So what happened?" he said.

"Have you heard anything about Marie?" Keller asked.

McCaskill shook his head. "Your friend Sanchez went to the hospital. He'll let Angela know as soon as there's news."

"Okay," Keller said. "This is what happened. Roy Randle shot Marie," Keller said. "And Shelby. Shelby got a last shot off and took Randle down."

McCaskill nodded. "Okay," he said. "And what about the girl? The one you were originally after?"

"She lied to us," Keller said. "She told us that both Randle and that kid they had picked up were dead. She set us up for Randle to ambush us."

"And do you have any problem telling this to the feds?"

Keller shook his head. "Later," he said. "Right now I just want to get out of here."

"Well," McCaskill said, "That's what I want to talk to you about."

"What do you mean?"

"Dr. Berry's out front. He seems a little worried about you."

Keller looked back down at the table. "About what?"

"He seems to think that if you get out, you might do something . . . rash."

Keller didn't answer.

McCaskill sighed. "Jack," he said. "I'm about to do something that I never do. I'm about to ask a question I never ask, because if the answer is 'yes,' then under the law, I have to do something about it. Up to and including breaking confidentiality and ratting out my own client." He leaned forward. "Look at me," he ordered. Keller looked up. "If I get you out of here," McCaskill said, "are you going to try to kill somebody? Somebody like Laurel Marks?"

"You're right," Keller said. "It's better that you don't ask."

McCaskill leaned back. "Jack—," he said.

Keller broke in. "Relax," he said. "I don't even know where to find her."

"I'm not sure I believe that, Jack. And it's not an answer, in any case."

"Am I being charged with anything?"

"Doesn't look like it," McCaskill said glumly. "They could charge you with interfering with an investigation, but this whole thing's got everyone in such an uproar, everyone seems to be waiting for someone else to do it."

"Then get me out of here," Keller said, "or I'll find a lawyer who will."

McCaskill stood up. His face was grim. "Fine," he said. "Wait here. This shouldn't take long."

Keller raised his cuffed hands. "I'm not going anywhere," he said.

After a few minutes, the door opened again. A middle-aged man in a deputy's uniform stepped in. He was carrying a hand-cuff key. He stepped over to Keller and began unlocking the handcuffs. "Looks like you're gettin' out," he said. The cuffs fell away from Keller's wrists. He began rubbing the marks the cuffs had made. The deputy looked at the red marks and scowled in disapproval. "That wasn't one of my people put those cuffs on too tight, was it?" he said.

Keller shook his head. "I think it was one of the FBI guys."

The deputy nodded grimly. "Figures. They come down here, play games in our jail, an' we get blamed."

He looked Keller in the eye for the first time. "You were with Jones when she got shot?"

"Yeah," Keller said warily. He wondered if this guy was a plant, a trick by the FBI to get him to open up and volunteer information. But the deputy didn't demand information; he gave it. "She's in surgery now," he told Keller. The next sentence seemed to load years onto the man's face. "It don't look good. I heard she lost a lot of blood. An' the bullet was close to her spine. She might not walk again."

Keller, still wary, asked, "You work with Marie . . . Deputy Jones?"

The man nodded. "She was . . . I mean she is . . . good people. And Shelby . . ." He shook his head. "God, I hate to think of what his wife and them two girls are goin' through." Then he looked up and extended a hand. "I'm Tom Wardell."

Keller shook it. "Jack Keller." He started to draw the hand back, but Wardell held on. He looked Keller in the eye. "Mister Keller," he said in a low voice. "Talk around here is that when you get out, you're goin' after the people that killed Shelby and shot up Jones." He held up a hand. "I don't want you to answer that," he said.

"I wasn't going to," Keller said.

Wardell grimaced. "Fair enough. But if you get 'em . . . well, a lot of people wouldn't be real unhappy." He released Keller's hand.

"I'll keep that in mind," Keller said.

The door opened behind Wardell. Scott McCaskill was standing there. "Time to go," he said.

Angela was waiting in the lobby. Lucas Berry was standing behind her. Angela ran to him and threw her arms around him. He hugged her back gently. "Jack," she said, her voice muffled by his chest. "Oh, God, Jack, I'm so sorry."

"I know," Keller said. He kissed her on the top of the head, hugging her tighter. Then he broke the hug and stepped back. He nodded to Berry. "Major," he said formally. "Thanks for coming down."

"Thought it might be an emergency, Jack," Berry said. He looked at Keller, shrewd appraisal in his dark eyes. "You want to talk?"

"Thanks again, Major," Keller said, "but I'm fine." He looked at Clevenger, the deputy behind the desk. "Where's my car?" he said.

She took a manila folder from behind the counter and handed it to him. "It's in the parking lot," she said. "You've got to sign for the keys and other property." McCaskill walked up and joined them as Keller fished in the envelope and pulled out the keys. He signed the property receipt without looking at the other contents of the envelope. He began walking toward the door.

"Jack?" Angela called out. "Where are you . . . *Jack!*" He walked out without looking behind him. She tried to follow, but by the time she reached the parking lot, he was gone.

233

nineteen

The sun was just rising as Laurel pulled the stolen car up to the gate. The dozing guard jerked to life as he saw the vehicle. He leaned out of his little window and regarded her suspiciously. She smiled at him. "Laurel Marks," she said. "My folks live at 100 Sandpiper Court."

The guard scowled. He obviously didn't know her. "I been away for a while," she explained.

He scratched his chin, still stupid from sleep. He muttered something under his breath, then picked up a loose-leaf notebook and began turning pages. He turned to her. "I don't see you on the list," he said.

She opened the door and slid out of the car. "Let me see," she said, standing by the window. He picked up the notebook and leaned partway out. When he did, she pulled the tire iron she had taken from the trunk out from behind the front seat and smashed it as hard as she could into the side of his head. The guard cried out in pain and she hit him again. He slumped over, then slid back inside the window. The notebook fluttered to the ground. She picked it up and tossed it back into the tiny guard shack. She opened the door and stepped inside. The guard was lying in the corner, moaning and dazed. Laurel hit him again. And again. And again until he stopped moving. She closed the door and got back in the car.

As she pulled into her parent's driveway, she saw Curt's Jeep parked out front. Her father's Cadillac was gone. The house was silent. As she got out, Laurel could vaguely hear the sounds of the mowers on the golf course. She caught a whiff of freshly cut grass. She stopped and took a deep breath, savoring the smell.

She found the spare key in its usual place, under the fake rock that sat in the bushes by the side of the door. She let herself in silently, slipping though the opened door like a wraith and closing it quietly. The caution was probably unnecessary; her mother was undoubtedly in her usual near-coma from the booze and sleeping pills that she used to hammer herself down into sleep every night. And Curt . . . it looked like that apple was falling close to the tree as well. But sneaking in had become an ingrained habit. She had tried as hard as she could not to be noticed in the house, not to attract her father's attention.

She padded silently down the hall and turned left past the living room. Her father's office was as she remembered it, and the key she was searching for was in its usual place in the top right desk drawer. The gun cabinet swung open with a slight creak and she surveyed the contents inside. She made her choices. She stopped by the kitchen for a few more supplies before heading up the stairs. She swung the door of her brother's room open. He lay sprawled on his back, his mouth gaping. He was dressed only in a pair of boxer shorts. An empty bottle of Jack

Daniel's lay on its side by the bed. Curt stirred slightly when Laurel put the barrel of the shotgun beneath his chin.

"Time to get up, big brother," she said.

Keller stood in the dim hospital lobby, studying the directory. The visitor's desk was closed at this late hour and the lobby was mostly deserted. He had located the ICU and was turning to head for the elevators when he saw Frank Jones standing at the bank of pay phones in a hallway off the lobby. He saw the older man slam the phone down in frustration. He walked down the hall. Jones's face turned to stone as he spotted Keller.

"Get out of here," he said in a low, dangerous voice.

"Frank," Keller said, "Frank, I'm sorry."

"Fuck you, Keller," Jones replied, "and fuck your *I'm sorrys*. You brought my girl nothing but trouble since the day you walked into her life. And now look what you've done."

"I need to see her, Frank," Keller said.

"You can't," he said.

"Frank—"

"*No*, Keller," he said. "You're . . . she's dead, Keller."

Keller felt his knees sag beneath him. He leaned against the wall to steady himself. His voice came out as a croak. "What?" he said.

"She died on the operating table. You got her killed, you son of a bitch. Now get out of my sight before I kill you." Keller watched him dumbly as he turned and walked away. His chest constricted as if he were being crushed by an iron band wrapped around it. He saw a chair nearby and staggered toward it like a drunkard. He fell into the chair, his body wracked with a fit of trembling. He huddled there for a good five minutes as the spasm passed. When he got up, the trembling had stopped. He walked slowly at first, like a sleepwalker, but by the time he reached the visitor's parking lot, his gait was normal. No one would think there was anything wrong with him unless they looked in his eyes. The parking lot was nearly empty at this hour, and he spotted Angela's Dodge pickup truck parked a few rows away from Keller's Crown Victoria. He stood staring at it for a few moments, then unlocked his vehicle and got in. He took a notepad from the backseat and a pen from the glove compartment. He wrote a short note, then walked across to Angela's vehicle and put the note under her wiper blade. Then he got back in his car and drove away.

Oscar awoke to Angela's hand on his shoulder. He blinked up at her for a moment, then started to get up from the chair where he had been dozing. She pushed him back down and gave him a kiss on top of the head. "How's she doing?" she asked softly.

Oscar looked at the draped figure in the hospital bed. Marie's face was almost as pale as the pillow on which she lay. Her eyes were closed. A small oxygen mask covered her nose. Other tubes and cables disappeared under the sheet.

"The doctors say it is too early to tell," Oscar said. "She lost a great deal of blood."

"How's her dad?"

Oscar grimaced. "Not well," he said. "He is trying to reach Marie's husband."

"Ex-husband," Angela corrected automatically.

"Yes," Oscar said. "He is angry. Her father, I mean. Angry that the husband is not here. He is also very angry at Jack."

Angela nodded. "I'll bet."

237

"Where is Jack?" Oscar said. "Is he out of the jail?"

Angela closed her eyes. "Yeah," she said. "But he left."

"Did Dr. Berry . . . ?"

Angela shook her head. "He wouldn't talk to Lucas. He wouldn't talk to anybody. He just . . . left." She smiled weakly at Oscar. "It was a good idea you had to call Lucas, though."

Frank Jones came in, his face set. "You people," he said, "need to get out of here." Angela stood up. "Mr. Jones," she said. "I'm sorry . . ."

Jones's face seemed to collapse. "Sorry," he said, his voice hollow. "My baby girl's lying there half-dead and you're sorry." He turned to them. "Now get the hell out." They looked at each other helplessly, then picked up their coats.

"Mister Jones," Angela said, "If Jack Keller comes by . . ."

"He's gone," he said. "And he won't be coming back."

Angela and Oscar looked at each other. "Why?" Angela said. "What did you say to him?"

"I told him she was dead," Jones said.

"*Madre de Díos,*" Oscar breathed.

"Why?" Angela whispered. "Why would you do that?"

He turned to them, his face bleak. "I wanted him gone," he said simply. "For good."

"You stupid bastard," Angela said. "Do you have any idea what you've done?"

"Get out," was all he said.

They rode the elevator down and walked to the parking lot in silence. "He is in pain," was all Oscar said as they approached her truck. She didn't answer, just shook her head. She noticed the paper folded under her wiper. She took it out and unfolded it. Her normally pale face became ashen as he read it. "Oh, my God," she whispered.

"What?" Oscar said. Angela handed the paper to him. "It's

238

from Jack," she said. "It's his resignation. He's quit his job with H & H Bail Bonds."

Oscar's brow furrowed. "I do not understand."

"It means," she said grimly, "that no one can say that anything he does now is done as my employee. So I can't be held responsible."

"He is going after the girl," Oscar said. "And when he finds her . . . I do not think he will be trying to bring her back alive. And if he kills her . . . if he crosses that line . . ."

"I know," Angela said again.

The streets of Fayetteville were mostly deserted this time of the morning. Even the most dedicated bar crawlers had finished the last-call drinks, satisfied their late-night munchies in the few all-night diners and the Krispy Kreme donut shops, and shambled off to bed. Only a few cars cruised slowly on Bragg Boulevard, their headlights adding little to the white-orange glow of the halogen street lamps, the hard white of lights in front of the empty businesses, and the brief splashes of neon color.

Keller took an exit off Bragg Boulevard, then a turn, then another turn, driving mechanically, as if on autopilot. He knew exactly where he was going. Laurel only had one place left to go, and therefore, so did he.

His cell phone buzzed. He looked at the caller ID. It was Angela. He hit the "Ignore" button.

The lights became fewer and farther between, until he was rolling through a darkened countryside. Since he had been cut loose from the police station, he had felt a sound at the edge of hearing, oscillating between the drumbeat of his blood and the remembered pounding of chopper blades. From time to time, he looked out the windows and saw the desert, the dirt and gravel wasteland blasted and crushed by the pitiless eternal hammer of the sun. He knew it was a hallucination, that beyond the darkness was the lush green landscape he knew so well. He knew it was a hallucination and he didn't care. He knew he should care, that not caring was a sign of something seriously wrong with him, but that was just another layer of things he didn't care about.

For the years since the war, his life had been like the desert, a desiccated wasteland devoid of human life. Angela had showed him that maybe, just maybe, there was a way out. Marie had been that way. For the short time he had known her, Keller had been fully human again. And now she was gone. He had been cast back into the outer darkness. This hunt, and his quarry, had taken everything from him, but the hunt was all he had left. After that, there'd be nothing.

Grace Tranh was brushing her teeth when her cell phone rang. She was inwardly raging about missing the story about the shoot-out at the farm. Someone else had gotten the call on that one. *I'm going to cut Howard Reed's balls off for this,* she fumed, *and have a goddamn necklace made out of them.* The sound of the running water almost made her miss the ring. She shut the tap off in time to hear it. She fairly flew to the bedside table and scooped up the phone. She saw the number on the caller ID and her heart began pounding. She flipped the phone open. "Hello?" she said.

"The story's almost over," a female voice said. "You wanna be there for the end?"

"What are you going to do?" Grace said.

"I'm going to make sure everybody knows the truth," the voice said. "About a lot of things. You care about the truth?"

"I'm a reporter," Grace said.

There was a mirthless chuckle on the other end. "That ain't no answer," the voice said. "Get a pencil. You got some people you need to talk to."

twenty

Keller slowed as he approached the gate. It was wide open. The guardhouse looked deserted. He looked it over warily. It was a moment before he saw the smear of blood on the lower sill of the window. Keller stopped the car and got out, pulling the shotgun from the rack by the driver's seat. He left the engine running.

The guard was lying on the floor of the guardhouse. One side of his head was oddly misshapen and his face was covered in gore. Keller bent down and felt for the pulse in the neck. There was none.

Keller stood up. He felt the throbbing of blood in his temples again, like the distant thrumming of helicopter rotors. He climbed back into the car and drove on.

As Keller pulled into the driveway of the Marks home, he saw a car parked there. The last time he had seen that car was in the driveway of Shelby's house. She was here. Keller stopped the car and got out. He stood for a moment and looked the place over. It was silent. There was no movement inside. He walked up to the front door and tried the knob. He was surprised to find it unlocked. Silently, he opened the door. It swung wide open, revealing the darkened, silent hallway beyond. Keller moved inside.

"Who's there?" The sound of Ellen Marks's voice startled Keller and his finger tightened on the trigger. He moved down the hallway, not answering. "Please," Ellen said. Her voice was ragged, as if she'd been weeping. "Don't come any closer. She'll kill him."

"I'll do it, too," Laurel called out. "'Less you tell me who the fuck you are."

Keller cursed to himself. "It's Jack Keller," he called out.

There was a brief murmur of conversation, then Laurel said, "Well come on in." Her voice sounded incongruously cheerful, almost playful. There wasn't a trace of fear. As Keller walked slowly into the living room, he saw why.

The curtains were drawn across the picture window, shutting out the morning light. In the gloom, Keller could barely make out the figure of Curt Marks kneeling on the floor in front of the couch. All Keller could see of his face were his terrified eyes and his mouth. The rest of his head was swathed in a cocoon of dull silver duct tape. The tape went from the back of his head to wrap around the double barrels of a 12-gauge shotgun, effectively fixing the weapon to the back of his head. Another clumsily applied lump of tape affixed Laurel's hand and wrist to the other end of the gun. Her finger was on the trigger.

"I ain't goin' nowhere," Laurel said. "So you better put that thing down or I'll splatter his head all over the fuckin' room."

Keller didn't move. He held his own shotgun trained on Laurel. "I didn't come to take you back, Laurel," he said.

243

They looked into each other's eyes for a moment as realization slowly dawned on her. Then Laurel smiled, a ghastly rictus without humor or joy. "Well," she said. "Guess Roy killed your sweetie back there. Looks like neither of us gives a shit anymore."

"Looks like it," Keller replied. He started to raise the shotgun. Ellen Marks's voice cut through the darkened room.

"Please," she sobbed. "Don't do it. Please. Please, don't."

Keller cut his eyes slightly to the side, keeping Laurel in his field of vision. He saw Ellen Marks in a chair to one side. Her wrists were bound to the arms of the chair with more duct tape. "Please," she said again, her voice a croak. "Don't."

"Ain't that sweet?" Laurel sneered. "She doesn't want anything bad to happen to her precious boy." She gave the gun barrel a little shove. Curt moaned in fear. "Too bad she didn't care so much about me."

"That's not true, Laurel," her mother said. "I don't—"

"Save it, Mama," Laurel snapped. "I didn't see you sayin' 'please don't' when Daddy was comin' in my room every night." Her voice broke. "Only one sayin' that was me. And no one was listenin'."

"I didn't know," Ellen whispered. "I didn't know . . ."

"BULLSHIT!" Laurel screamed. "You didn't WANT to fucking know! You drank yourself stupid every night so you wouldn't have to know! Because you didn't want to ever get your fucking HANDS DIRTY again!" She had risen to her feet, pushing Curt forward. He cried out, putting his hands out in front of him to keep from hitting his face on the carpet. He knelt there, sobbing, as Laurel stood over him. "And you," she spat down. "My big brother. You knew. You knew what he was doin' to me. But you made me lie. You told me to take it all back." She looked up at Keller. Her face was wet with tears. "You know why, Jack? You know why he made me lie? You know why he wanted to come back? Tell him, Curtis." Curtis's only response was a sob. Tears dripped onto the carpet. "What's a matter, big brother?" Laurel said. "Cat got your tongue? Well, I'll tell it then." She looked up at Keller. "Social Services took us out of the house. Out of this nice house. They put us in foster care. We were with some nice folks. They were . . . they were just nice. But Curt didn't like them, did you? *Did you?*" She gave the gun another shove. "AN-SWER ME!" she yelled.

"No," Curt blubbered. "It was horrible."

"It was just a trailer, Curtis," she whispered, "a little single-wide. But you liked the nice stuff too much. Just like Mama." She looked up at Keller again. "Plus, his friends made fun of him. Teased him about livin' in a trailer. He really hated that." She addressed the weeping boy again. "I would have done any-thing for you, Curtis," she said. "Anything. An' I did. I came back here. For you. So you could have the nice stuff." She looked up and wiped her eyes with the back of her free hand. "An' I was stupid," she said. "I figured Daddy would stop once he knew I'd tell. But he came back to me the first night we were back. He . . . he was laughing. He said he could do anything he wanted now because no one would ever believe a word I said again. And he was right. So take the shot, Jack. Kill me, I kill him. Everybody's happy."

"No," Ellen said. "Don't do it, Jack. Please. Put the gun down."

Keller looked at them both for a long moment. The only sound in the darkened room was Curt's sobbing. Then he slowly lowered the shotgun. Laurel's smile was like an open bloodless wound. "Put it on the floor. Kick it over here with your foot." Keller obeyed, his eyes fixed on Laurel. "You and I aren't done yet," he said.

245

"We'll see," she said.

The phone on the side table rang. "You better get that," Laurel told Keller. "I'm expectin' a call."

Keller picked up the receiver. "Hello?" he said.

"This is Special Agent Sanderson of the Federal Bureau of Investigation," a voice said. "We have the house surrounded. Who am I talking to?"

"Keller?" Sanderson said into the cell phone. He glanced up at the uniformed Wilmington PD officers taking up positions around the house. "Jack Keller? What the hell are you doing in there?"

"I came after Laurel Marks," Keller replied.

Sanderson tried to keep his voice from shaking. This was the first time he had been in a situation like this and he felt out of his depth. "Mister Keller," he said, "We got a phone call about a hostage situation in that house."

"I'd say your info was pretty accurate," Keller replied.

"Keller, if you're holding someone in there . . ."

"Not me," Keller said. "But Laurel Marks is holding a shotgun to her brother's head. Her mother's secured to a chair."

"Let me talk to her," Sanderson said.

There was a brief murmur of voices on the other end, as if Keller was having a conversation with someone in the room. "She says to tell you someone will be there soon to tell you what to do."

Sanderson took a handkerchief out of his suit jacket and wiped the sweat from his brow. "Okay, Keller," he said. "Is she holding a weapon on you?"

"No," Keller said. "I came in with a shotgun, but if I'd used it, her gun would probably have gone off. She has it secured to the back of his head with duct tape. The other end's taped to her hand."

"Okay, Keller," Sanderson said. "Just sit tight. Don't do anything stupid."

"You either, Sanderson," Keller said. He hung up.

Cassidey came jogging up. "HRT's been scrambled," she said. "They're on a plane out of Quantico. And I got hold of Clancy."

"What did he say?"

"He's on his way down from Fayetteville. He says he'll be here in about an hour and a half. He'll take over then. He said to just secure the perimeter and sit tight. Don't do anything."

Good, Sanderson thought. Clancy was the ranking agent. He'd know what to do. And HRT—the FBI's Hostage Rescue Team—was the best. All he had to do was maintain control for an hour and a half. That he knew he could do.

A uniformed officer walked up. "Agent Sanderson?" he said.

Sanderson nodded and put out his hand.

The uniformed officer shook it. "I'm Sergeant Dockery," he said.

"Thanks for your help, Sergeant," Sanderson said.

"Sir," Dockery said. "Our Emergency Response Team is already here. If we move fast . . ."

"No," Sanderson said. "HRT's on the way down from Quantico. We don't move 'til then."

"Sir," Dockery argued, "we have as much—"

"I already checked on what you have, Sergeant," Sanderson snapped. "You have a group of officers from other units pulled off other duties to train a few times a year. Your SOP manual's in the middle of being rewritten, so you don't really have an SOP. Thanks, Sergeant, but no thanks. Just hold the perimeter until our people get here."

Dockery clenched his jaw. He turned and walked off.

"You certainly do have a way with the locals, Mark," Cassidey said. "Calling in HRT for a single barricaded subject's kind of like swatting flies with a howitzer, isn't it?"

"Cassidey," Sanderson said, "If you don't have anything useful to offer . . ."

"I do, actually," she said. "I got one of the local uniforms to roust the head of the architectural committee out of bed."

"Architectural committee?"

Cassidey gestured at the house. "They're not going to let you build just anything in a place like this. They have a committee to make sure 'standards' are maintained. Anyone who wants to build a house here has to give the committee a copy of the blueprints. And they keep them on file." She looked smug. "You'll have a copy of the total layout of the place within the next half hour. Right down to the air-conditioning ducts."

"Good," Sanderson said. He turned his attention back to the house.

"Well, don't everyone thank me at once," Cassidey muttered.

The roar of helicopter rotors split the air. All around, officers glanced up. A white and red chopper flashed overhead, low enough that everyone instinctively flinched down, away from the noise. Sanderson saw the decal on the side reading NEWS 10 SKYWATCH.

"Damn it," Sanderson yelled. "Somebody get hold of that station! Tell them to get that fucking chopper out of here!"

One of the uniforms walked up. He was holding out a cell phone. "It's for you," he said. "Patched through from the station."

"Who is it?" Sanderson asked.

"Says her name is Tranh," the uniform said. He gestured toward the helicopter, which was making a lazy turn above the trees. "She says she's in that chopper."

"I haven't got time to make a statement to the fucking press," Sanderson snapped. He started to turn away.

The uniformed cop didn't lower the cell phone. "She said she's got info on the girl inside. Says she has a list of her demands."

Sanderson felt control slipping away.

twenty-one

"If we get permission," Grace yelled to the pilot over the rotor noise, "can you put us down on that golf course?"

"Are you out of your mind?" the pilot yelled back. "It's like a goddamn war zone down there!"

She looked down. He was right. Everywhere she looked she saw armed men. They surrounded the front door of the house in a semicircle, crouched behind their vehicles. She saw others positioned in a stand of trees across the golf course from the back of the house.

"The cops won't shoot if we get the okay," Grace said. "And I know the girl won't shoot. She needs us. Don't be such a damn pansy!"

"I'd have to put it down on the green," the pilot said. "Everything else is too uneven."

Grace slapped him on the shoulder. She looked over at Wayne. He was checking the battery pack on his camera. He gave her a quick thumbs-up. Grace raised the cell phone back to her ear. "Yes! I'm here!"

"This is Special Agent Sanderson, FBI," a voice said. "What the hell are you doing, lady?"

"Laurel Marks called me this morning," Grace said. "She gave me a list . . ."

"Wait a minute," Sanderson said. "You *knew* this was going to happen?"

"No," Grace said. "She didn't tell me exactly what she was going to do or when. She said I'd know where to go when the time came. But she said if I didn't follow her instructions exactly, people were going to die."

There was a brief pause. Then, "What are the demands?"

"That was one of her instructions," she said. "I have to deliver them in person. To whoever's in charge on the scene. Is that you?"

The reply sounded very tired. "Yeah," Sanderson said. "Yeah, that's me."

"I need to land the helicopter," she said. "Can we set down on the golf course behind the house?"

"I don't know," Sanderson said. "That'll tear up the course pretty bad. I don't know if I can authorize . . ."

"Agent Sanderson," Grace said. "If I don't get this list to you, in person, that girl in there's liable to kill someone. Are you *authorized* to let that happen?"

Another, longer pause. "Okay," Sanderson said. "But hang on. I have to let the people inside know what's going on."

"I'll wait," Grace said.

Laurel heard the throbbing pulse of the helicopter getting louder and louder. She smiled. *And there they are.* The sound kept increasing. *Jesus, they're low,* Laurel thought. She felt a moment of apprehension. *Maybe it's not the TV people,* she thought. *Maybe it's the cops, maybe they're getting ready to . . .* The noise filled the room, drowning out everything else, blotting out thought. She instinctively looked up. She noticed movement in her peripheral vision and snapped her eyes back down.

Keller was standing up. His eyes were fixed on the ceiling, on the source of the noise. Something was wrong with him. He was shaking all over. His hands were clenching and unclenching at his sides.

"SIT YOUR ASS DOWN!" she screamed at him. She snatched the shotgun she had taken from him up off the couch. She pointed it at him, clumsily holding the short weapon out in front of her with her left hand. "I'LL SHOOT YOU!" she yelled.

The sound of the rotors was diminishing. Keller looked away from the ceiling and down at Laurel. The look in his eyes made her flinch. They were totally flat, dead, like the eyes of a zombie. "I'll shoot you," she said again, "I will."

"Go ahead," Keller said, and started toward her. The phone started ringing. Keller ignored it.

Sanderson listened to the phone ringing. "Shit," he said out loud. "Shit. Shit. Shit. Answer the phone. Answer the phone."

Cassidey looked alarmed. "What's wrong?"

"They won't answer," Sanderson said. His voice was tight with panic. "Something's wrong. Get that guy Dockery back. Tell him to get ready to rush the house."

"But you said . . . there's no time to get organized . . ."

"Do it, Cassidey!" Sanderson yelled. She turned and ran toward one of the parked police cars.

. . .

Keller looked down the barrel of the shotgun. The sharp-edged thudding of the helicopter above had gone away, but the echoes were still beating inside his head. The room began to strobe wildly in his vision, images flashing like a television being channel-surfed at high speed by a madman, all the channels broadcasting from Hell.

Choppers over the desert, low and fast . . . squat, malevolent, ugly, weapons hanging off the sides like the stingers of giant insects . . . pointed at him . . .

Bodies tumbled like broken dolls, missing heads, limbs . . .

A flash of light out of the black desert sky, the Bradley exploding a few feet away . . .

Men screaming, burning . . . his own voice screaming, the taste of sand in his mouth . . .

There was screaming inside, too, Ellen Marks's voice pleading, the boy on the floor wailing in fear, drowning out the shrill ringing of the phone.

He saw the gun waver. *Do it,* he thought. *Pull the fucking trigger . . .*

The gun moved aside then. Keller stopped, feeling the disappointment go through him like a blade. Laurel pointed the shotgun at the bound figure of her mother in the chair. "Okay," she said shakily. "I get it. You want to die that bad." She laughed. "But you take one more step and they both die. And you don't. And probably all those cops come bustin' in when they hear the shot. So what does that get you, Mister Jack Keller?"

Keller's hands dropped to his sides. His shoulders slumped. Laurel audibly let out the breath she had been holding. "Get the phone," she said. Keller walked over and picked it up. "Yeah?" he whispered.

"Keller?" Sanderson said. "Keller, where the hell have you been? What's going on in there?"

"Nothing," Keller said. He sounded like he'd been drugged. "Everyone's still here."

"Look, tell the girl. The reporter she called is here. She's in that helicopter you've probably heard overhead."

"Yeah," Keller said. "I heard it." There was a pause, then Keller said something strange. "I don't like helicopters."

"What?" Sanderson said. "Look, Keller, I don't really give a shit if you don't like helicopters. Just tell the girl the chopper will be landing on the grass outside the house. The reporter will be coming to me. Tell her not to get too excited or upset. Everything's fine. Got that?"

"Yeah," Keller said. "Everything's fine."

"Keller, are you . . ."

The line went dead.

"Yes!" Grace yelled. She pumped her fist and grinned at the pilot. "Put it down."

He shook his head. "You people are not paying me enough for this shit," he muttered, but he turned the helicopter toward a landing.

"When Wayne and I get out, take off again. Give the station a high shot. Be ready to go live." The pilot nodded.

Luckily, someone had thought to pull the flag out of the hole. Fine white sand from the hazards around the green blew up in a cloud as the chopper settled onto the flat, bright green surface.

As Grace and Wayne exited the chopper, four black-uniformed cops trooped up. They were dressed in body armor and carried stubby automatic rifles across their shoulders. They wore bandoliers festooned with some kind of grenades across their chests. As the helicopter lifted off, they flanked Grace and Wayne, leading them around the building to the semicircle of police vehicles surrounding the house. A tall, dark-haired man in a suit was waiting.

"Miss Tranh?" he said. She nodded. "I'm Special Agent Sanderson." He looked at Wayne. "I'm sorry, but no cameras."

"Agent Sanderson," Grace said. "I'm afraid that one of the demands is that I be able to broadcast."

"Sanderson looked like he was grinding his teeth. "Are we on the air now?"

"Grace shook her head. "We'll let you know. And that red light on the end of the camera, over the lens," Wayne pointed to the tiny LED, "will go on."

"I knew that part," Sanderson said. "So what have you got?"

"Well, for starters," Grace said, "I'm supposed to give you this." She reached into the equipment bag and pulled out a folded sheet of paper. She handed it to Sanderson.

"What is it?" he said, beginning to unfold it.

"It was e-mailed to me this morning. You remember these people had gotten hold of one of those camera phones. This was apparently taken from inside the house."

A slender blonde female agent had come up and was looking over Sanderson's shoulder. "Whoa," she said.

Grace nodded. "Whoa is right." She didn't need to look at the photo again. She didn't think she would ever be able to forget it. The subject of the photograph, a boy of about nineteen or twenty, had apparently been made to hold the camera himself off to one side, so the picture clearly showed the shotgun taped to the back of his head. The picture was blurry, as if the boy's hands had been shaking.

"She wanted you to know," Grace said. "There's no way for her to miss."

"Yeah," the blonde said. "Even if a sniper gets a cortex shot, she could jerk the trigger as she falls."

"Yeah, okay," Sanderson said. "So we know she's serious. What does she want?"

Grace unfolded another sheet of paper. "The Cumberland County Sheriff's most likely took in a bunch of loose-leaf note-books from the scene where Roy Randle and those two cops were shot. There were fifteen notebooks in all. She wants you to give me number fifteen."

Sanderson stared at her. "I don't know anything about that," he said. "What's supposed to be in it?"

Grace shrugged. "I don't know. Something big, is all she'd say. Something about an old case."

Sanderson turned to the female agent. "Check it out," he said. "Call Cumberland County."

"On my way," she said and walked off.

Sanderson turned back to Grace. "That all?"

Grace took a deep breath. "No," she said. "There's one other thing."

"What's that?"

"She wants to talk to me. On camera. Live."

"Where?"

Grace looked at the house. "In there."

"No. No way." Sanderson said.

"Agent Sanderson . . ."

"We are not sending in another potential hostage." He looked at Wayne. "Or two. That's an absolute rule."

"I won't be a hostage," Grace said. "I'll be—"

"Lady, are you thinking at all?" Sanderson said. "You've got a dangerously unstable subject in there. This whole thing may be some weird way to get at you. Some sort of celebrity-stalker-type mania."

"Thanks for the promotion to celebrity," Grace said. "But I'm willing to take that chance."

"Mind if I ask why?"

Grace smiled. "You think Katie fucking Couric ever got to do a story like this?"

Sanderson gestured at Wayne. "And what about him?" he said.

"Me?" Wayne said. "I'm just nuts."

"You both are," Sanderson muttered. "But the answer's still no."

Grace thought for a moment. "You can't give her another hostage," she said. "But you can trade one, right?"

Sanderson rubbed his eyes wearily. "Miss Tranh," he said. "Do not—"

"No, think about it," Grace said. "I actually want to be in there. And I know she won't kill me. She wants to use me to tell the world something."

"And you want to use her to further your goddamn career!" Sanderson sneered.

Grace didn't flinch. "A fair trade, don't you think?"

Sanderson thought for a moment. Then he picked up the phone. "Go stand over there," he ordered, pointing a few feet away. "I'm going to talk to them inside." Grace hesitated, then nodded. She and Wayne walked off.

"He doesn't like you very much," Wayne observed.

"I know," Grace said. "So maybe he won't be so reluctant to let me go in."

Wayne grinned. "Grace," he said, "You are one crazy bitch. Will you marry me?"

Grace grinned back. It was an old joke between them. "You're gay, Wayne."

"Yeah," Wayne said. "But I'm not, like, fanatical about it."

Keller picked up the phone. "Yeah?" he said.

"This is Agent Sanderson," the voice said. "Put Laurel on the phone."

Keller held out the phone. "He wants to talk to you."

She hesitated. She still held Keller's shotgun in her left hand. Reluctantly, she put it down. "Slide the phone over here," she said.

"Don't worry," Keller said. "I'm better. I just got . . . a little shaken up by the helicopter."

"Yeah, I noticed," Laurel said. "You don't like 'em. Fine. Slide it over here."

"The phone's not going to slide too far on carpet," Keller observed.

"Okay," Laurel said. "But move slow. You make me nervous."

"Sorry," Keller said. He walked over slowly and handed the phone to her. She put it to her ear. "Yeah?" Keller could hear Sanderson on the other end. "Which one?" Laurel's eyes moved to her mother, then to Keller. "I've got a better idea," she said. "You can have 'em both. Just get the reporter in here." She pressed the button on the phone to break the connection and turned to Ellen. "Guess what, Mama?" she said. "You're gettin' out of here. You and Mister Keller."

"Okay," Sanderson said. "There's three hostages in there with her. Her mother and brother, and a guy named Keller."

"Who's he?" Grace asked.

Sanderson grimaced. "He's a bail bondsman. He came to pick Laurel up on a missed court date. Can you believe it?"

"Lucky he didn't get shot," Grace said.

"Yeah, lucky," Sanderson replied.

"Laurel," her mother said, "What are you planning? What are you going to do?"

Laurel smiled wearily. "Nothin', Mama. Me and Curt and that nice Chinese lady from the TV are goin' to have a little chat. Then I'm comin' out. And after that . . . well, Mama, I think you pretty much know what's going to happen after that."

"Please, honey," Ellen said, "Let Curtis go. He's sorry, aren't you, Curtis?"

"I'm sorry," Curtis said. "Oh, God, I'm sorry."

Laurel reached out with her free hand and gently ran it through the boy's thick brown hair. "I know you are, big brother," she said softly. "I know you are. It'll all be over soon. All you got to do is tell the truth." She looked at Keller. There were tears glistening in her eyes. "There's a pair of scissors in the drawer of that table," she said. "Cut her loose. Then you and her get out of here."

Keller retrieved the scissors. He cut away the duct tape binding Ellen Marks's hands and ankles to her chair. She stood up unsteadily, rubbing her wrists. "Just put the gun down, honey," she begged.

"Mama," Laurel said wearily. "I love you. After all the bullshit that's gone down, I still love you. But if you don't shut the fuck up, I'm going to shoot you."

Tears were running down Ellen's face as she moved toward the door. She shuffled her feet as if she was unwilling to go. "I can't," she said. "I can't leave my child." But she didn't stop moving.

259

"Sure you can, Mama," Laurel said. "To save yourself ? Sure you can. You done it before."

Ellen cried harder. "I'm sorry," she wailed. "I'm sorry. I failed. I failed you."

"Yeah," Laurel said. "You sure as shit did." She turned to Keller. "Get her out of here." Keller put his hand on Ellen's shoulder and pushed her in front of him. They walked out, down the long hallway to the front door. When they got there, Keller reached past Ellen and opened the door, slowly. He was looking at the barrels of at least fifty guns. He raised his hands high above his head. Ellen stood in front of him, as if paralyzed.

"Get your hands up," Keller hissed. Slowly, she raised her hands. Two people, a man and a woman, detached themselves from the crowd and came up the driveway. The man was carrying a portable TV camera. "Now walk," Keller said to Ellen as they reached the door, "Go towards the cops." She began walking, slowly at first, then faster. Keller stayed in the doorway. The female half of the team was a petite Asian woman who Keller vaguely recognized from the TV news. She started to say something, but Keller silenced her with a finger to his lips. As they went in, Keller slipped inside with them and closed the door.

twenty-two

"What?!" Sanderson said. "What the hell did he just do?"

"He went back inside," Cassidey said. Her face was slack with shock.

"I know that, God damn it!" Sanderson said. "What the hell for?"

"Maybe he changed sides," Cassidey said. "Stockholm Syndrome."

"No," Sanderson said, his lips drawn into a line. "Not Stockholm Syndrome. He's a cowboy. He thinks he's going to take her down himself. FUCK!" He slammed his hand down on the roof of the car he was standing behind. "All I need is some goddamn amateur in there." He turned to Cassidey. "How long till HRT gets here?"

She spread her hands. "I don't know. They're flying into the local airport. Another hour? Maybe?"

"Get Dockery. Tell him to get his local team, what did he call them, Emergency Response, online. We may have to force entry."

. . .

"What the—," Grace heard Wayne say. She dug an elbow into his ribs. The tall blond man who had slipped back in with them stood motionless in the shadowed hallway. He didn't speak, merely gestured with his head toward the end of the hallway. He put his finger back to his lips again. Grace turned and walked down, the hall, slowly.

"Laurel?" she called out. Her mind was racing. *That must be Keller,* she was thinking. *The other guy Sanderson was talking about. What the hell is he doing?* She had a good idea, however, that the girl with the shotgun wasn't going to approve of his presence. She decided not to mention him until she knew more.

"This way," Laurel called. They entered the living room. Laurel sat on the couch. The boy she had seen in the picture was kneeling in front of her, his face swathed in duct tape. Laurel was working with a pair of scissors at the back of his head, cutting away the tape there that held a shotgun pressed against his skull. It came away with a ripping sound. "There you go, big brother," she said. "We want you lookin' your best for your big debut." She turned to Grace. "Where you want to set up the camera?" she said.

"Dad?" The sound of his daughter's voice, weak as it was, snapped Frank Jones's head around. He'd been standing by the window, looking down unseeingly into the parking-lot traffic.

"Marie," he said. "Oh, God, baby girl . . ."

He walked over to the bed. He wanted to gather her up into his arms, but there were too many wires and tubes running out of her. He stood there, tears running down his face, and ran his hand gently through her hair instead. "Baby girl . . . ," he said again.

She looked up at him, her blue eyes cloudy. She licked her lips, which were dry and cracked. "Can I have some water?" she said, her voice a croak.

"I got you some ice chips," he said. He reached into the plastic tumbler by the bed and pulled one out. Gently he fed it to her.

She closed her eyes as if she were savoring a fine wine. "S'good," she murmured. "C'n I have another?" He gave her another. She opened her eyes. "I got shot, Dad," she said.

"I know, honey, I know."

"Did Shelby . . . did he . . ."

"Shhh . . . ," he said. "We'll talk about that—"

"No, Dad," she said, her voice stronger. Frank knew better than to argue with her when she used that tone of voice, weak as it was. "Tell me. I saw him get hit. What . . . what . . ."

"He's gone, Marie," Frank said. "But he got the bastard that shot him."

Marie closed her eyes. "What about Jack?" she said after a moment. "Where's Jack?"

"I don't know," Frank said. "He's not here. I . . . I sent him away."

"Angela," she said. "Where's Angela? She'll know where to find him."

"I sent her away, too," Frank said. "They're no good for you, honey. You've had nothing but . . ."

"Get them back, Dad," Marie said. "Get them back here. I need to talk to Jack." She reached out and gripped his wrist. "Please, Dad," she said. "Please."

"Okay, baby girl," he said, his voice choked. "Okay."

. . .

Keller couldn't see the living room, but he could hear the sounds of the camera guy setting up and the conversation between Laurel and the TV reporter. He used that clatter to mask the sound of his own movements as he crept down the hallway. Finally, he heard the camera guy speaking. "Okay, Grace, we're on live in five . . . four . . . ," he counted down until Grace began speaking. Keller stood in the shadows and listened.

"This is Grace Tranh bringing you exclusive live coverage from the inside of the Marks home in Wilmington, where a tense hostage drama is being played out. We're here with Laurel Marks, who has been holding her mother, her brother, and . . . ," there was a slight hesitation, ". . . one other hostage for several hours this morning. At the request of Ms. Marks, this reporter and my cameraman Wayne Lennox agreed to substitute ourselves for two of the hostages in order for Ms. Marks to make her statement. Ms. Marks?"

"My name is Laurel Marks," she began. Her voice was eerily calm, as if she were reading the words. "I and a man named Roy Randle was the people responsible for the killin's in the First Church o' God of Prophecy, The Sun-lyte Diner on Interstate 95, an' the Barnwell Foods plant. I confess to it all. I ain't sure who all I killed, but I pulled the trigger. Oh, and I also killed some motherfucker in a gas station outside o' Fayetteville, but that guy had it coming. I'm ready to take the punishment for that. But first people are gonna know the truth." There was a pause. "My father, Ted Marks, first raped me when I was twelve years old. He kept doin' it, at least once a week. When I tried to tell, Social Services took me." She looked at her brother and her voice cracked for the first time. "But my . . . my brother here, talked me into takin' it all back. So they sent me back here. But he knew. He knew it was true. Tell the truth, Curt. Tell the truth."

The boy was weeping openly. "It's true," he said. "All of it. All of it. Oh God, I'm so sorry, I thought he'd stop. He told me he'd stop . . . I'm sorry. I'm sorry."

"I know, big brother," Laurel said. "I know." Her voice grew stronger. "There's another story we need to tell. Roy wanted to tell you himself. But he's—" her voice broke again "—he's dead now. The police shot him. But there's a notebook that was delivered earlier to Miss Tranh here. It tells the true story of what happened August 10, 1990, at the studios here in Wilmington. You know the killin' I mean. Roy Randle got blamed for it, even though nobody ever went to jail. Roy wrote out the real story. We were going to tell everyone, once the time was right. And once we had ever'ones attention. Roy's dead now." She took a deep breath. "But I guess I got your attention, huh?" No one answered. "I guess we're done here," Laurel said.

There was another, longer pause, then Grace's voice, strangely subdued. "This is Grace Tranh, Channel Ten live."

"And, we're out," the camera guy said.

"Laurel," Grace said after a moment. "Are you ready to go?"

"I've got to break this stuff down," Wayne said.

"We'll come back for it," Keller heard Grace say. He heard them get up and come toward the hallway. Keller stepped into the room. "Hold on," he said. "we're not done yet."

Laurel was in front, with her brother right behind her. Grace and the cameraman were side by side behind them. Laurel had laid the shotgun down on the couch, next to Keller's. She was the one who reacted first. She turned around and tried to get back to the couch, back to the weapons. She ran into her brother, who fell back into Grace and the cameraman. Keller took advantage of the confusion to cross the room, passing them in a few long strides, and snatch his shotgun up off of the couch. He turned to look at the knot of people untangling themselves. He pointed the gun at Laurel. "You stay here, Laurel," he said evenly. He looked at the others. "You two better run," he said.

"Oh, my God," a voice said. "You're awake!" Angela was standing in the doorway. Oscar Sanchez stood behind her.

Marie turned toward her. "Hey," she whispered.

"Hey yourself," Angela replied as she came to the bedside. "You had us worried, girl."

"Where's Jack?" Marie said.

The artificial joviality vanished. Angela looked at Frank, who looked away.

"Where's *Jack?*" Marie insisted more loudly. The effort caused her to cough, and the cough caused her to groan in agony.

"Laurel Marks got away," Angela said. "Jack went after her." She swallowed nervously, unsure of whether to go on. "He was acting . . . he was acting strange. He didn't want to talk to anyone . . ."

"He thinks you're dead," Frank Jones said.

"Why?" Marie said. "Why would he . . ." Comprehension dawned in her eyes. "Oh, no. Dad, no. You didn't . . ."

"I'm sorry," Frank said. Tears were running down his cheeks. "I'm sorry."

"Oh, God," Marie said. She closed her eyes. "He's going to kill her."

Angela only nodded.

Marie shook her head. "No," she said. "He *can't.*" She tried to sit up, fell back weakly. She reached out and clutched Angela's arm. "You can't let him do that, Angela," she whispered desper-

266

ately. "If he murders her . . . in cold blood . . . Angela, he won't make it back from that. He *won't*."

Angela was crying too. "I know. I know. But he won't answer the phone when I call him."

Marie released her hold on Angela's arm. "Where's my cell phone?" she said. "He'll talk to me."

"I have it here," Oscar said, reaching into his jacket pocket. He smiled. "I thought you might need it when you woke up."

Sanderson and Cassidey had watched the interview on a portable battery-powered TV someone had brought up. When it was over, everyone turned their attention back to the house. All the guns came up as the door opened. Curt Marks came stumbling out, followed by Grace Tranh and her cameraman. No one else came through the door.

"What . . . ," Sanderson said. Officers grabbed the people fleeing the house and rushed them to the perimeter.

"Where's Sanderson?" he heard Grace yelling. "I have to talk to Sanderson!" A uniformed officer led her over. "That guy, that bondsman you told me about."

"Keller," Sanderson said. "Where is he?"

"What the fuck did you let him stay in there for?!" Grace yelled.

"I didn't!" Sanderson yelled back. He went in on his own!"

"Well," Grace said. "He's holding Laurel Marks at gunpoint."

"What the hell . . . she was giving herself up!" Sanderson said.

"Maybe he doesn't want her taken in," a voice said. Sanderson looked around. Clancy was walking toward them.

"What do you mean?" Sanderson said.

"One of the cops that got shot taking Laurel Marks's partner

267

down was this Keller guy's girlfriend," Clancy said. "The deputies she worked with are giving odds that Keller blows Laurel Marks away." He looked at Sanderson. "Sanderson, is there some aspect of this situation you *haven't* managed to fuck up?"

"You pull that trigger," Laurel said. "You're no better than me."

"Guess not," Keller said. "But you set us up, Laurel. You got Marie killed. And Shelby. You set us up for Randle to kill us all. And I have to do something about that."

The girl laughed bitterly. "Bullshit. You led 'em into it. It's as much your fuckup as anything. Only thing you're tryin' to do is make up for that."

The words staggered Keller. His vision blurred and he heard a voice in his head.

"Maybe, Sergeant, you fucked up, got out of your assigned area, and led your squad into an ambush."

"No," Keller said. "That's not it. It's not it." His head was vibrating now like an overloaded engine about to come apart. The dimness of the room felt like it was closing in, like Keller was entering a long dark tunnel. He heard a wailing voice echoing in his head. For a split second he was back in Kuwait, with the marines. He saw the kid from Jersey, rocking back and forth with his boom box in his lap, eyes closed, grinning like a death's head. *Goin' down,* the box howled, *Goin' down now. . . .*

Laurel's voice seemed to come from far away. "Well," she said, "you think shootin' me is goin' to make that better, go right the fuck ahead. It ain't like I was goin' to die of old age anyway."

"Okay," Keller said. He raised the gun.

•   •   •

"Ma'am," the nurse said, "You can't use a cell phone inside the hospital."

"I need to make this call," Marie muttered as she punched the buttons on the phone.

"Ma'am," the nurse said more insistently. She moved as if to take the phone away. Oscar stepped into her way, smiling apologetically.

"I am sorry, Señora," he said. "I do not wish to be discourteous. But she is right, it is an important call."

"I'm going to go get security," the nurse said.

"We will be here," Oscar replied. He turned to Marie in the bed. "You had better hurry," he said. "Try the speed-dial."

Marie hit the button.

Goin' down, Goin down now . . .

The voice taunted and pulled at him like a cold black undertow. The room seemed to be getting darker, as if the sun outside were growing old, dimming, dying. Keller felt his finger tightening on the trigger, waiting for the break and the explosion that would take them both into the final darkness.

The phone on his belt rang.

Keller took his finger from the trigger long enough to reach down and yank it from the holster. He drew his hand back as if to throw the phone across the room. Then he saw the number on the display. He raised the phone to his ear. "Hello?"

"Jack?" the voice was weak, but it was unmistakable. "Jack, where are you?"

"Marie," Keller whispered. "Marie."

"Where are you?" she said again.

"I'm . . ." He hesitated. "I'm at Laurel Marks's house."

"What are you doing there?" There was a cough, then a groan

269

of agony. The sound tore at Keller. He raised the gun again. Then Marie spoke again. "Jack. Please. Don't . . ."

"I'm settling some scores here," he said. "I thought you were dead."

"But I'm not," Marie said. "I'm here. I'm alive. And I'm telling you, I don't want any score settled. I want you, Jack."

Keller didn't speak. He couldn't, past the tightening in his throat. But Marie's next words hit him like the first shock of water in the throat of a man dying of thirst.

"Come see me, Jack," Marie said. "I need you."

"I need you, too," Keller said. "I'll be there as soon as I can."

"I love you," she said.

"I love you, too." Keller said. He broke the connection and put the phone back on his belt. "Get up," he said to Laurel.

She looked at him warily. "What?"

"Get up," he said. "I'm taking you out of here."

She stood up slowly. Keller walked behind her, out of the darkness of the living room, down the long hall, toward the door.

Toward the light.

twenty-three

"In sure and certain hope of the resurrection to eternal life through our Lord Jesus Christ," the preacher said, "we commend to Almighty God our brother Warren, and we commit his body to the ground, earth to earth, ashes to ashes, dust to dust. The Lord bless him and keep him, the Lord make his face to shine upon him and be gracious to him, the Lord lift up his countenance upon him and give him peace. Amen."

"Amen," the crowd intoned.

A few people jumped as the rifles of the honor guard cracked once, twice, three times, the sharp reports echoing in the crisp fall air. The flag on the coffin was folded and handed to the widow by Tom Wardell. Her two girls stood beside her, their faces streaked with tears. Barbara Shelby's face was composed. People gathered round, offering hugs and clichés. She smiled and acknowledged them.

Keller pushed Marie's wheelchair away from the graveside, moving with difficulty across the soft earth until they reached the brick walkway. She was still weak, and her doctors at first refused to release her from the hospital for Shelby's funeral. When she had told them that they could either let her out for that short time, in which case she'd come back, or she'd check herself out against medical advice, they relented, and only on the condition that she use the wheelchair and keep her nurses posted on where she was and when she was coming back. She had accepted the restrictions only after her first few tottering steps had left her panting and gasping for breath. It was going to be a long road back.

"If we hurry," Keller said, "We can have you back in time for lunch."

"Whee," Marie said. "More lime Jell-O. I can hardly wait." She turned to look at him. "Thanks for picking me up, by the way."

"No problem," he said.

"So does it look like Scott's going to be able to keep the FBI off your back?"

He shrugged. "That guy Clancy made a lot of noise about interference and obstruction of justice. But Scott thinks they're not really eager to make a big deal out of it, especially since they'd have to bring Sanderson back from his new assignment to testify."

"His new assignment?" Marie said. "Where?"

"Anchorage."

She laughed. "Damn," she said. "They must really think he fucked up."

"Letting a reporter into a hostage situation isn't exactly by the book."

"Not like she's complaining," she said. "You can't hardly turn on Fox these days without seeing 'a special report from Grace Tranh.'"

"Hey," a voice said from behind them. "Wait up."

Keller stopped. Tom Wardell came up, clad in his dress uniform. "Hey, Sergeant," Marie said.

"Hey," Wardell said. He gave a short, abrupt nod to Keller, who nodded back expressionlessly. Wardell turned to Marie. "What's this I hear about you quittin'?" he said.

Marie smiled. "Word travels fast."

He ignored the comment. "I hate to see you do it, girl," he said. "Sure," he looked pointedly at Keller, "you made some mistakes. But that's no reason . . ."

"I know, Sarge," Marie said. "And I may come back. But right now . . ." She shrugged. "Like I said, I love the job. But it doesn't seem to love me."

"Well . . . ," he said, then hesitated. "Well, keep in touch."

"Thanks," she said, "I will." They both knew it for a polite lie. Cops who left the job soon found themselves with nothing to talk about with other cops. They shook hands and Wardell walked away.

"He thinks I'm one of the mistakes you made," Keller said.

"Yeah," Marie said.

"What about you?"

She sighed. "I don't know, Jack. I love you. I think you love me. But the things we've been through . . . the things we've done . . . they've left scars. Inside and outside."

"I know," he said.

"But the difference between us, Jack," she said, "is that you love your scars. So much that you go out and look for new ones. You're like those people that take razor blades and cut themselves so they can feel something. I don't know if I can live with that."

He didn't say anything as they approached the parking lot. Marie's father was standing by her car, waiting. He started toward them. He stopped as Keller crouched down beside the wheelchair.

"It's not easy for me to trust people," he said, "or to let them in my life."

"I know," she replied.

"But I'll try," he said. He paused. "I'll work on it."

She sighed. "Yeah," she said. "You've said that. But I need more than trying, Jack. For me, and for my son." She motioned her father over. He didn't speak or look at Keller as he took the handles of the wheelchair.

"I meant what I said when I said I need you, Jack," Marie said. "So call me when you're sure. Call me when you know you can do it. Not just try." She didn't look back as her father wheeled her to the car.